He tilt

"You... c(

She flush

the bowl with

stammered. "I didn't mean to offend—"

He enfolded her hand between both of his own, and she fell silent immediately, staring at his hands.

"It's all right," he said gently. "It's as accurate a term as any, really." He glanced at their hands, his cardiac pump skipping a cycle, and then back up at her face. "I will concede that by most baseline standards, I'm quite insane. Mad as a bag of cats, really. I would have to be, to want to take over the world—and I think that frees me from a lot of the constraints of other men of science. I can... imagine the world I want, and the means to accomplish what must seem like a ludicrously lofty goal."

Her gaze flicked from their hands to his face; her expression was a mask of tightly controlled unease.

"But," she said, "why do you want to take over the world?"

He stroked her fingers, trying to soothe her anxiety. "I want what I think most people want—a better world. A better place for people to live and work and thrive. I want people who are sick to be able to get cured, without worrying about the cost of the treatment. I want doctors—people like you—to be able to do their jobs without having to answer to a board of bankers who worry more about finances than medicine. I—" His throat suddenly closed, choking off his next words, though he couldn't say exactly why. Something about that last statement had sent a spike of ice down the back of his neck.

OTHER WORKS BY ELIZABETH EINSPANIER:

Sheep's Clothing

Heart of
STEEL

by

Elizabeth Einspanier

This is a work of fiction. Names, characters, businesses, places, events and incidents are either the products of the author's imagination or used in a fictitious manner. Any resemblance to actual persons, living or dead, or actual events is purely coincidental, no matter how awesome that would be.

Chapter
ONE

It all started Thursday morning. Julia was on a small boat with her boyfriend, Jim Thompson, under the sort of humid, baking heat that one only gets in the South Pacific on the cusp of the rainy season. They were bound for a new dive site that Jim had discovered. A gentle wind had been blowing all day, tousling her shoulder-length blonde hair and carrying the salty tang of the ocean to her nostrils. Ordinarily she would be enjoying the scenery. All around her the smooth, deep blue water stretched away in all directions like colored glass, reflecting the nearly-cloudless sky above. In the distance little spits of land dotted the horizon, quietly reminding her how far away she was from the hustle and bustle of daily life.

She wasn't looking forward to this dive, however, and not just because the choppy water had left her a bit seasick. She was also trying to think of ways to tell Jim that she wanted to break up with him, a discussion that she knew wouldn't end well, no matter her approach.

Julia had considered the possibility of breaking up with Jim so many times that she had lost count, and as the two of them got into their respective scuba gear and weight belts she finally settled on dropping the bomb on him when they got home to San Francisco. After all, it wouldn't do to ruin their vacation and have four more days of awkwardness and fighting—during which time he'd no doubt try to convince her that she didn't really mean it.

"This is gonna be great!" Jim gushed as he smeared saliva on the inside of his scuba mask, "You'll love the scenery down there!"

She loved the scenery on the surface, too, though, and as she scanned the horizon one last time before they were due to take the plunge, her eye fell on a shape maybe half a mile away: a low island, its base obscured by jungle, from which the flattened peak of a dormant volcano reared up like the fist of a vengeful deity. In the water she saw indistinct outlines forming broken rings like parentheses around the island.

"Hey Jim, what's that?" she asked, pointing.

He looked in the indicated direction and grinned. "That's where we'll be swimming—Shark Reef Isle."

"Shark Reef Isle? That sounds like something out of a bad horror movie."

Jim laughed. "Nah. Nothing like that. I've been around here a dozen times. The sharks here are pretty small, and they're not aggressive at all unless you do something stupid like chum the water."

A cold spike of fear shot down Julia's spine. "No *way* am I swimming with sharks!"

His head snapped over before she'd even finished her sentence, giving her *that* look, the one that told her she'd misstepped. The smile was still there, but it had left his eyes. Silence descended between them like an anvil, and stayed for a full minute. She squirmed uncomfortably under that smile; it made her feel like a dull-witted child who'd done something wrong, and a tight knot of anxiety slowly congealed in her stomach. She shrank into herself and dropped her gaze, hoping desperately that he would just *say something* already. It was like waiting for Darth Vader to decide whether or not to Force-choke her.

"Do you mean to tell me," he said evenly, "That after I went through all the trouble—*and expense*—to book us a trip to Hawaii—a vacation that *you* desperately needed, by the way—"

"Jim, I—" she started, but he continued speaking over her.

"—that you're not going to let me have this *one* thing that I want?"

She bit her lip. He wasn't calling her selfish, in so many words—he never did—but it was the *tone* he had, like he was scolding a small child for wanting another cookie before dinner. The theme was all too familiar to her, but it wouldn't do her any good to argue the point—she had been placed on paid leave from the hospital after...

She shook her head, her hand wandering up to touch her throat, remembering the sensation of a scalpel's blade pressed against her carotid artery. The nightmares had only recently eased, but even the thought of working the night shift again made her throat close up. She took slow, deliberate breaths, a technique her counselor had taught her to head off the panic attacks. It was better not to think about the incident. She knew that freaking out now would only prove Jim's point. That, along with arguing with Jim, or saying she wanted to break up with him, would require her to commit the mortal sin of *ruining their vacation.*

"Come on," he continued. "You make decisions with people's lives every day. Take a risk with your own once in a while." He grinned. "Besides, I was kidding about the sharks. Haven't seen a damn one there." He sounded distinctly disappointed. "Now, we are going to have a good time on this dive, *right?*"

And there was that *tone* that he used to ask the sort of questions that, in his mind, had only one correct answer.

She sighed. "Right," she whispered.

Julia studied the island and surrounding reefs at length, trying to decide whether Jim had been truly kidding about the sharks. Jim held the philosophy that only by risking one's life did one really live... but it wasn't like he would risk *her* life, would he?

"Can we get any closer?" Julia asked the boat's captain, a mustachioed South Pacific islander whose name escaped her.

He shook his head. "No can do. That place is haunted. This is as close as we get."

"Haunted?" Julia asked. "Haunted by what?"

"The usual," Jim said, laughing. "Monsters, demons, ghosts, that sort of thing. They say this place has some sort of a crazy volcano god or whatever that makes monsters. The only thing I've ever seen around are crabs and shoals of fish, so I think you're safe."

"So... you *have* been here before, right?" Julia peered at the island in the distance. She'd never heard of Shark Reef Isle, and she was pretty sure he would have mentioned it to her before this.

"A couple of times," Jim assured her. "Trust me—if I'd seen any sea monsters here I'd have pics all over the internet by now."

Julia relaxed, but only marginally. The South Pacific was still well-known for its sharks and stingrays.

"Two hours, Mr. Jim," Captain Mustache said. "Then we go. Don't you be late."

"Come on," Jim replied, in the sort of tone that implied that this was a long-standing disagreement between them. "I'm never late—you know that."

Captain Mustache nodded seriously but said nothing further.

And that was Jim, Julia thought. Jim the daredevil. He wasn't foolhardy, but he was an adrenaline junkie. And while he collected local legends like children used to collect Pokémon cards, he had long made it clear that he considered them entertaining stories—nothing more.

The plan was to swim around the reefs for a bit and come back in an hour—long before Captain Mustache planned to leave. There was plenty of air in the tanks for that long of a swim, and it would give them a chance to experience nature. Hopefully it wouldn't be the sort of nature with big teeth that wanted to eat them.

The pair of them tipped backwards into the water from the edge of the boat, clutching their diving masks to keep them in place, and plunged into the blue water surrounding Shark Reef Isle.

Julia felt weightless in the water, as though cradled by a pleasantly cool hand. To her delight, the sun had managed to heat the water just enough above bone-cold to offer reprieve from the afternoon heat. She thought back to her father teaching her how to swim, supporting her near the surface while she paddled and splashed. This was so much different, like being a mermaid exploring the reefs, dangerously beautiful coral formations in reds, blues, and purples, where fish darted and swam looking for food or hiding from these strange bubbling monsters that swam overhead. Jim tapped her on the arm and pointed to a shimmering school of fish undulating past. She nodded and gave him an okay sign, indicating that she saw them. God, everything was so beautiful and otherworldly down here. She almost wished she could grow gills so she could live down here forever. Then she wouldn't have to deal with relationship drama on the surface.

The pair of them swam some distance from the diving boat, collecting a few uninhabited shells but mainly leaving things alone. Jim took a few pictures with a waterproof camera, and then had Julia pose so he could take a picture of her in the water. She trod water as he held the camera up to his eye, when she caught a dark shape moving behind him, lithe and torpedo-like. Then it turned and she saw the lipless gash of its mouth, filled with serrated teeth. It turned again and made a beeline for the two of them. In some strangely disconnected part of her brain, she noticed that it had a scar across its nose, as though someone had attacked it with a knife.

Shark!

She pointed frantically behind him, making muffled noises around her regulator. He lowered the camera, looking at her first in puzzlement, then in alarm. He turned just in time for the shark to barrel into him, knocking the camera away. The creature continued on its course, plowing into her as well, knocking her regulator out of her mouth.

She had no time to find it and get it back—her half-lungful of air wouldn't last that long. Her only option was the surface. She glanced around, trying to get her bearings. The impact had stirred up a cloud of brick-red debris and bubbles, obscuring her vision. She forced herself to relax, and followed the bubbles as they inevitably veered upwards, heading for the surface. She tried not to think of how much the cloud of debris resembled blood.

A white, leathery, webbed hand grasped her left ankle, pulling her back down into the murk. She looked down, instinctively kicking at the hand. Were the stories of sea monsters here true? As her mind spun in the hamster-wheel of panic—a really *bad* idea right now, she knew—the hand yanked her down, jolting another breath from her lungs. She could now identify the owner of the hand, a creature with the head of a shark—and a familiar-looking scar on its snout. It surged upwards, fang-rimmed jaws gaping. In her terror and panic, time slowed down. Her lungs burned, and her vision was starting to go gray from oxygen deprivation.

The shark-thing pulled at her ankle again, reaching up at her with its free hand. She felt a burst of white-hot agony in her left knee, and then everything went black.

***

When Dr. Alistair Mechanus woke that morning, the last thing on his mind was that he would have visitors.

In fact, he hadn't had many visitors in the ten years he'd resided in the labyrinthine lair he'd built deep within the dormant volcano that dominated Shark Reef Isle, thanks to the carefully-crafted rumors he'd spread about monsters to keep people away. Even so, he knew he could make new friends easily—given the right combination of tissues, genetic codes, or mechanical parts—and so was never lonely. Certain closed-minded individuals might have called his friends *minions*, but they were all ever so helpful in the pursuit of his hobby.

After all, world conquest wasn't a *bad* pursuit for a man of his genius, was it? Most people would agree that the world needed improvement, and by golly, he was the man to do that. By now, he'd invested too much into this to even consider failure an option, so it made sense to be vigilant in the care and maintenance of his little army. He had detailed files on everything that he would require, from attack plans to diplomatic openings to individuals he deemed to be most or least expendable once the revolution came.

Currently, he was repairing one of his maintenance robots, moving back and forth rapidly and smoothly on the metal legs that he'd had in some form or another for as long as he could remember, while reviewing the internal schematics of the machine within the viewpoint of his mechanical left eye. The laboratory in which he worked, like every laboratory in the complex, had everything he needed for the repairs, from tools that he'd designed and amassed himself to a small army of utility pincers on slender appendages installed in the ceiling that he could control with a thought. He selected one of several esoteric-looking tools and briefly twirled it between the gloved fingers of his right hand before unscrewing the robot's access panel. In the square opening he saw the cubical power core had blown out, leaving its center dark and dull.

His metal left hand—its movements as organically smooth as its flesh-and-blood counterpart—reached in and pulled the power crystal free of its housing. To his satisfaction, it came out smoothly—he'd initially feared that it had fused to the socket—but it was hot enough that it would have badly burned his other hand, even through his thick gloves.

He held up the burned-out core in one hand and the upturned palm of the other hand; one mechanical arm delicately picked up the bad core and took it away, while another mechanical arm dropped a fresh replacement into his other hand.

As he was placing the fresh core into the empty socket, a soft chime attracted his attention.

<Yes, Arthur?> he said, communicating mentally with the network as he continued working.

<You have guests, sir,> a pleasant tenor of a male voice spoke via the same digital link. Its owner, Arthur, was an artificial intelligence that Mechanus had fine-tuned over the course of the past ten years to serve partly to run the automated processes of the lair, and partly as a conversational partner. Of late, they'd run out of topics, though, and he considered that he would need to find some solution to this. And he would, he resolved—he would find a solution to this as surely as his name was Alistair Mechanus.

<Excellent,> Mechanus said, <Who collected them?>

<Scarface, sir,> Arthur said.

Mechanus grimaced. <Ah, damn. That means they're probably all mangled.>

<Indeed so, sir. I took the liberty of having them sent to the medical ward for treatment.>

The power core connected with a muffled *click* and started to glow pink. Mechanus shut the access panel as the robot whirred back to life. It resembled a large fat fly with a propeller rather than wings, and its optical sensors flickered on, glowing soft aquamarine. Its propeller started up with a high-pitched whir, and the robot flew away.

<Status report,> Mechanus said as he cleaned up his work area.

<The male is gravely injured, but currently being kept viable by mechanical aids in Laboratory 8.>

Mechanus nodded. Living tissue lasted so much longer than dead tissue. <And the other?>

<The female is in Laboratory 9, being treated for various injuries caused by the retrieval.>

<Summon Scarface to the laboratory wing. I'll speak with him there before I look over my new guests.>

The laboratory wing was huge and complex, currently populated by various experiments and surgical procedures in progress. Mechanus was quite proud of the techniques he'd pioneered out here, since he didn't have to answer to things like an ethics committee or a medical board. After all, how does one make progress if one does not push the limits of the possible?

A hulking, seven-and-a-half-foot-tall shark-man loomed in one of the antechambers that marked the intersection between corridors, his nose bearing an old scar. While Scarface was amphibious, he was distinctly uncomfortable out of the water, and about as agile as a drunken elephant. Put him in water, though, and he turned into an aquatic ninja. Mechanus was quite proud of his creations, this one most of all, but sometimes certain ones just lacked finesse. Right now, though, Scarface's bullet-shaped head hung between his sloping shoulders in an effective mimicry of contrition, even though his flat black eyes didn't otherwise seem capable of such an emotion.

"Scarface, do you know what you did wrong?" Mechanus asked him, immediately displeased by the raspy, disused quality of his voice. He seldom had anyone to talk to, at least out loud, but felt it was important to address this matter face-to-face. He cleared his throat and adjusted the modulation of his artificial larynx.

"Not gentle enough, Master," the shark-man gurgled.

"That's right." There; his voice sounded much better that time. "And do you know what happens when you're not gentle enough?"

"Things get damaged. Damaged things can't be used."

"That's right. Now, how do you propose avoiding this in the future?"

Scarface considered this at length. "Use grabby tool." The grabby tool in question was a set of utility pincers usually used by less resilient employees for collecting materials that were dangerous if touched. Here, though, the reverse was the case. Mechanus nodded in approval.

"Very good, Scarface. Do you know where to find the utility pincers? No? Very well, have Spike show you. And next time, be more careful. Now go on, Master's busy."

He rubbed Scarface affectionately on the snout, and the shark-man turned and left.

Mechanus sighed in good-natured irritation. Good help was hard to make sometimes. He turned and made his way to the laboratories where his test subjects had been taken. When he reached them, he peered into the viewing window of Laboratory 8.

The contents of this sterile white room had definitely seen better days. Most people would be inclined to call the man a mess, considering that he'd been bisected just above the pelvis and his left arm was torn off at the elbow. The stump of the severed limb was now threaded with several lengths of tubing that kept the major blood vessels circulating, and his ragged abbreviation of a torso had been connected to a number of machines that had taken over the basic functions of his damaged internal organs. He glanced over and saw the severed lower half floating in a tank of transparent green fluid. At least Scarface had the presence of mind to bring as much as he could. Good boy.

"Status report," he said aloud.

"Extreme trauma to nearly all organs of the abdominal cavity," Arthur informed him, likewise audibly, "Liver is too damaged to salvage. Several feet of small intestine lost, along with the entirety of the large intestine and bladder. Likelihood of meaningful recovery, 0.0%."

Mechanus frowned in thought. "All right. Continue to maintain his tissues." Aside from his abrupt encounter with Scarface, the man looked like he'd been healthy and fit—the perfect base for further creations. He turned and walked to the observation window of Laboratory 9. He looked in—and froze.

The blonde woman lying on her back inside this lab was a vision. In fact, for a few stunned seconds, the idea of using her for a test subject never even crossed his mind. She was unconscious and nude, and he could see the pale skin where the sun had not touched her, in the exact shape of a one-piece swimsuit. She had the sleek, athletic build of a swimmer, with muscular legs, the left truncated at the knee, and a nearly-flat abdomen. The soft orbs of her breasts—according to an unfamiliar portion of his mind that had been heretofore silent these past ten years—appeared to be just the right size to fit comfortably in one of his hands. But the whole was greater than the sum of her parts, and for a few moments he simply forgot to inhale.

He had no heart, but his cardiac pump skipped a cycle. The corresponding sensation in his chest felt almost exactly like *thud*. He clutched at the center of his chest.

On the heels of this, though, he got a mental flash, a shard of memory from a life he no longer properly recalled.

A smile. The slow blink of blue eyes. A lock of blonde hair, caught in the wind. The touch of slender fingertips, the gentle nip of a cool breeze.

A wave of dizziness hit him, and he staggered, putting a hand against the viewing window to steady himself. He felt like the floor had suddenly dropped from under him. His lungs felt tight, and he had to stop to catch his breath. He clutched his temples, squeezing his eyes shut as the dizziness gradually abated. He grasped at the fading memory, but it scattered like fall leaves.

"Sir?" Arthur prodded.

Mechanus opened his eyes and again gazed at the nameless beauty that his machines were maintaining. The mechanical lens that had replaced his left eye focused in closer on her face, and then scanned down the smooth curves of her naked torso…

"Sir, what do you wish done with her?"

Mechanus blinked, suddenly feeling like a pervert, and dropped his gaze to a point on the floor between his feet. He was, after all, staring at an unconscious nude woman. That she was breathtakingly beautiful had nothing at all to do with it. Nothing at all.

Once he'd regained command of himself, he looked her over again with a more clinical eye. She had dark circles under her eyes, suggesting that she was suffering from sleep deprivation, and she had a thin, white scar on the left side of her neck, just over the carotid artery. It was about three inches long, but well-healed. The scar fascinated him, and as he stared at it he reached up and touched the left side of his jaw, near where the overlapping metal plates that dominated that side of his face gave way to old scar tissue. He wanted to touch her scar—but going in there and fondling her while she was unconscious would just be *creepy*. He wanted to make a good impression, after all. He tore his eyes away from her throat, and his gaze settled on the ragged flesh just below her left knee. As with the male, her stump had been threaded with tubes that kept the blood circulating through what remained of the limb.

Here, at least, he could make a good impression. Fortunately, he had detailed files on anatomy, so this should be simplicity itself.

"Repair her," he instructed, "Restore her to prime functioning—biological means only. Then take her to one of the guest rooms to recover, and see that she is given clothing. I will not be a poor host." Never mind the fact that he never had any real guests there anyway. He shook his head, dismissing the thought. "Did they have any belongings?"

"Scuba gear, swimsuits, a waterproof camera, and each had a mesh bag containing an assortment of seashells. In addition, the male had a wrist pouch containing a folded note on waterproof paper."

Mechanus raised his eyebrow. "A note? What did the note say?"

"'All the mermaids of the sea would be jealous. Julia, will you marry me?'"

Mechanus frowned in thought. On the bright side, he now knew the name of this beautiful angel that Scarface had collected for him. On the other hand... He glanced back at the man in Laboratory 8.

"I wouldn't worry about it, sir," Arthur assured him, "To borrow a handy turn of phrase, he's half the man you are."

This startled a snort of laughter out of Mechanus. "Always the quick wit, Arthur. I need to be careful these days."

"Thank you, sir."

Mechanus headed off, initiating a number of seldom-used processes that he was certain would make his beautiful guest happy.

Chapter
TWO

Julia's mind barreled up through nightmares of shark-monsters, and she surfaced to wakefulness with a shriek of fright. As she lay there, her breath coming in gasps and her heart hammering in her chest like a panicked rabbit, she stared up at the ceiling at first, trying to convince herself that she was safe. There were no shark-monsters, and that it had all been a nightmare.

Then she realized that she was in an unfamiliar room. It wasn't the sort of comforting unfamiliarity that generally came with staying in a hotel—this wasn't even her hotel room in Hawaii. There was a slightly metallic smell to the air, and an oppressive, mechanical thrum filled the lower registers of her hearing. The bed appeared to be a twin, and the only one in the room. She tried to move, but then her entire body complained painfully, in a way that reminded her of the attack again. The pain was especially bad in her left knee, though she could wiggle her toes okay.

Moving brought her attention to the fact that she was naked. She *never* slept naked. Granted, she was snuggled between clean linen sheets, but *still*. Somebody had undressed her and put her in this bed for some reason.

The idea made her skin crawl.

She sat up slowly, her head gently spinning with a wave of vertigo, and swung her legs over the edge of her bed. She glanced around, looking for Jim—who would almost certainly be close by if she'd been injured and was in a hospital—but he was nowhere to be seen. The air was cool against her skin, and she shivered and broke out into goose bumps. She glanced down at her legs and found, to her surprise, that they were both still there. She had a flash of memory about a shark monster yanking on her leg, and felt certain that she should be missing at least some soft tissue.

There was something odd about her left leg, though. She looked closer and saw a line of stitches around her leg just below the knee, and a distinct change in complexion below this border. The line was clean enough that the use of surgical adhesive was also likely.

What the *hell.*

Her blood ran cold, and she looked herself over for any other oddities. She found precise, rectangular patches of similar, lighter-colored skin across the right side of her ribs and on her right shoulder, likewise held in place with tidy, small sutures. When she poked at the one on her shoulder she felt the touch, but it seemed a bit distant. She reached down towards the pale lower leg…

A crackle of static near the ceiling made her yelp in fright and instinctively wrap her hands protectively across her bare breasts. Her head whipped in that direction and she saw a speaker mounted on the wall, accented by a tiny red LED.

"I do apologize," said an unfamiliar male voice in a cultured baritone, "I know you must be feeling very disoriented and afraid right now, but I assure you that I mean you no harm."

"Who are you?" she demanded, lowering her hands in the apparent absence of a security camera.

"My name is Doctor Alistair Mechanus, and this is my island. You and your... companion are currently my guests here."

"Is... is Jim okay? Can I see him?" If Jim was okay, she thought, then maybe everything else would work out fine as well. He had a way of getting out of sticky situations—it was that sort of luck that made him a daredevil. It also made him accustomed to getting what he wanted.

"He's, uh, here with me," Dr. Mechanus told her, and then paused for an interval that seemed—somehow—to sound guilty, "In a manner of speaking, anyway. My people are very good at what they do." He paused. "As for seeing him, why don't you get dressed first—you will find a bundle of clean clothing on top of the dresser near you. Call me old-fashioned, but I feel odd talking to a nude woman."

Julia's hands leapt up to shield her breasts again, her face flushing red. Of *course* there would be a camera in here. She'd seen enough James Bond movies to know that the sort of person who owned an island in the middle of the South Pacific was also the sort of person who had no sense of privacy. After all, who would complain about the surveillance? His neighbors? He probably didn't have any. They were almost literally in the middle of nowhere, on an island that the natives all said was haunted and probably wouldn't land on if you put a gun to their heads, in the clutches of someone who probably wasn't all that happy by their intrusion.

There was no way that this was going to end well.

She pulled the top blanket free of the mattress and wrapped it around herself before standing up, putting most of her weight on her right leg and leaning against the nightstand. She didn't dare test out her left leg just yet. She had no way of knowing how long she'd been there—though the odds were good that their boat home was long gone. In any case, she knew that leg surgery of any type took weeks of recovery under the best of circumstances. Especially if she actually did lose her leg and Dr. Mechanus either reattached it or replaced it—major surgery no matter how you approached it.

The implications of either scenario sent a chill up her spine.

The dresser was quite ornate, and appeared to be crafted out of mahogany or a similarly expensive wood. On top of the dresser was, as promised, a bundle of simple folded clothing: a shirt, a pair of pants, an unadorned bra, and a pair of panties. No shoes or socks, but the carpet was soft and thick, almost swallowing her feet. A little experimentation proved that each item fit her perfectly, leaving her feeling ambivalent about the whole thing. On one hand, it meant that she wouldn't have to fashion something out of the linens in this room, but on the other hand it meant that this guy took the time to determine what size she was. Even in underwear. Meanwhile, all she knew about him was his name and his voice. She didn't even know what he looked like, and that bothered the hell out of her. She got dressed, and then turned back to the speaker. She studied it for several minutes, biting her lip. Was he still there? Probably.

"Um. Hello?" she called.

"Yes?" Dr. Mechanus replied immediately—a bit eagerly, she thought. *Creep.*

"I'm dressed now. You want to tell me why you already have clothing that fits me?"

"I had your body scanned into a computer while you were unconscious. From there it was a simple matter to fashion clothing for you. I hope you like it."

She looked down at herself. "It's... a bit plain, but it works. How long have we been here?"

"Somewhat less than a day."

Julia heard her stomach growl in unhappy confirmation. She hoped that this man at least intended to feed her, but she couldn't be sure how far she could trust him just yet.

"How's your new leg feeling?"

She glanced at the foreign leg attached to her knee. "It... seems to work." That was really all she could say about it. In all her years of medical schooling she'd heard of limb transplants, but never legs, and never ones that looked so... clean. Especially after one day.

"Why aren't you trying it out?"

"Trying it out?" she echoed incredulously, "You just replaced my *leg*. I can't just... walk on something like this after a few hours. It's a load-bearing extremity, and the blood vessels need to be connected just so, and the nerves have to be joined for full sensation... and why the hell doesn't it even hurt? These things take months to heal—and what about immunosuppressive drugs? Tissue rejection? Maintaining circulation during healing?" She stopped short, clamping a hand over her mouth as she realized she was lecturing her own kidnapper. Julia didn't dig in her heels on many topics, but medicine was her passion, and the idea of someone dancing blithely all over the basic physiological limitations of something like tissue transplantation just went against everything she'd been taught. *If* what he said was true, and *if* he messed up anywhere, she could lose the limb anyway, or die from infection.

The speaker was silent for a long while.

"Well," he said finally, and there was a note of fresh interest in his voice. "It seems you know a thing or two about medicine yourself, am I right?"

"I... do," she said cautiously.

"What field?"

"Emergency medicine." That covered a wide range of fields, of course, but listing them off in response to a casual inquiry wouldn't be productive right now.

"Ah. As intelligent as you are beautiful," he remarked quietly, as though talking to himself.

She grimaced at the speaker. He really *was* laying it on thick.

"To answer your earlier question regarding your leg," he continued, "No. I've already taken care of that, and the color will adapt to match your own skin tone in time."

Okay. One question answered, and about a thousand left hanging there. Already taken care of that? What did that even mean? She had so many questions for him, but decided that she wasn't going to get anything settled like this. She would have to put on her big girl panties and take the reins a bit. Her stomach twisted nervously at the idea, but she plunged ahead. She took a deep breath and steeled herself.

"Look," she said. "I'm sure you're a marvelous conversationalist, but I don't like talking to disembodied voices, and I want to see Jim. So you... you need to send somebody down here to take me to wherever you have him, and we can talk face-to-face. Deal?"

The speaker was silent for a long time.

"Well?" Julia prompted. Her stomach churned.

"This can be arranged," Mechanus finally said. "I will send Arthur to collect you. Do try to put your weight on your new limb. I assure you it will support you."

There was a muffled click from the speaker. Julia let out a breath. *God*, he was weird. She glanced down at her replaced leg, and then flexed her knee, balancing on one leg. He might have been weird, but if he said was true, then he just leapfrogged over years of transplantation research. Negating the need for anti-rejection drugs would be a windfall for the medical community—so why the hell was he way out here on an island in the middle of the South Pacific?

Encouraged by the lack of pain, but skittish about the lack of pins or other supports, Julia gingerly put her weight on her left leg. It held—and without as much as a twinge of pain. What the hell. She slowly lifted her right leg, holding onto the dresser in case her new leg suddenly folded under her. It continued to hold. She considered it unlikely that the bones had been severed or broken with the amputation, but he still would have had to reattach any number of tendons, muscles, nerves, blood vessels...

A few minutes later, her speculations were interrupted when the door slid open to admit a hovering, whirring mechanical device about the size of a small dog. It was roughly ovoid in shape, with four or five multi-jointed arms dangling from its underside, each one tipped with a three-fingered claw. On its front the thing sported a monitor displaying a simplified happy face. She backed away from it cautiously, and it turned to face her.

"Good day, Miss Julia," said the drone in a pleasant and very human-sounding tenor. "My name is Arthur. I am to take you to the laboratory where Dr. Mechanus is currently keeping your companion. Please follow me." With that the device turned and started floating out, at a comfortable walking pace.

Okay. So he had robots. And his name was Dr. Mechanus. It made a weird sort of sense, all things considered. Insofar as anything here made sense, anyway. Well, if this thing was to be her guide, she might as well follow the metal football. She followed the drone.

She took a single step outside and reflexively flinched back when her bare foot touched the cold, polished metal floor of the hallway. She stopped and peered out, looking along the hallway in both directions. The walls and ceiling were white and featureless, giving the whole corridor a cold, institutional feel, like being back at the hospital—only this time she felt more like a patient than one of the staff. Once her mind made this comparison, her throat wanted to close. She stopped and closed her eyes, resting her hand against a nearby wall.

"Hold on a second," she rasped. The whirring sound of the drone's travel abated to a low hum.

"Is there something wrong, Miss?" it asked.

"Just... give me a moment," she said, and breathed in slowly, forcing herself into her deep breathing exercises.

Breathe in for a slow count of four. Hold it for a slow count of four. Breathe out for a slow count of four. Hold it for a slow count of four.

The instructions were so ingrained from her therapy sessions that they came automatically, and after a few cycles of this her throat started to unclench.

"Miss?" the drone asked.

"I'm okay," she whispered. "I'm okay. I'm okay." She carefully opened her eyes. "I'm okay." Finally she glanced up at the drone, who regarded her with a simplified, flat-mouthed neutral face on its monitor. "I'm okay," she said aloud.

"Very good, Miss," it said, the face flickering to a generic smile. "Right this way."

The drone led her up two flights of stairs and into another, identical series of corridors, except that these were lined with viewing windows on both sides. Horizontal blinds had been drawn in front of many of them; of those that were not, many were empty save for some rather advanced-looking robotics, ranging from mechanical limbs to vaguely humanoid creations. In one of them she saw a shark-like humanoid sitting placidly while another creature, built on a pig-like theme, spoke animatedly to it, holding up a pair of mechanical pincers. Julia recognized the shark-creature as the monster who grabbed her, and a chill went down her spine. She hurried her steps and adjusted her path to hug the opposite wall.

"Is it much further?" she asked, rubbing her arms anxiously.

"No, Miss," Arthur replied. "It's right around the next corner."

"Good. This place is giving me the creeps."

Around the next corner she saw a tall man, apparently in his early thirties but completely bald, clad in a white lab coat with a high, stiff collar—the sort that she instantly associated with Dr. Frankenstein and other mentally-unstable scientific types—and black, elbow-length gloves. He also appeared to be wearing some sort of armored boots made of metal for no reason that she could determine. His handsome right profile was currently facing her as he studied something through an observation window, and as she approached she saw a continuous, slightly ragged border of scar tissue running from his brow, over the top of his hairless scalp, and down almost to the base of his skull.

She advanced cautiously, trying to get a look at the subject of his study in the next room. Before she could, however, the tall man in the hall with her spoke.

"Greetings, Julia," he said in the baritone she'd heard from the speaker. She turned, and saw to her shock that a significant portion of the left half of his face, now revealed to her, was crafted of overlapping segments of unpolished metal, apparently riveted through the flesh and into the skull and jaw. His left eye was a mechanical lens that turned and focused in perfect coordination with its biological counterpart as he regarded her, its iris dilating as he offered her a welcoming smile. "I am, as you have probably guessed, Dr. Mechanus. I welcome you to my humble lair." He sketched a bow to her, and she either heard or imagined the sound of countless motors whirring within him.

At first her thoughts were consumed by a single horrified thought—*what the hell what the hell what the hell*—repeated over and over again until her mind filled with *what the hell* from top to bottom and side to side. She felt light-headed, and braced herself against the edge of the observation window to avoid falling, but some persistently reasonable corner of her mind gently informed her that now simply was not a good time for her to faint or throw up.

Stay frosty, Julia, the voice advised her, in a familiar-sounding voice that Julia couldn't immediately identify. *Think of this like your first car crash in the ER. Sure, it looks horrible, but you can get through this. Just breathe. Get through this, and find out what's happened to Jim. You're okay.*

She breathed slowly, trying to mentally force her jackrabbitting heart to slow the hell down already. In the rest of her mind, *what the hell* soon faded into background noise.

Mechanus raised his remaining eyebrow. "You know," he said gently, as though correcting a small child, "When someone introduces themselves to you, it's considered polite to reciprocate."

Oh. Right. Apparently she should act like this wasn't anything out of the ordinary. It probably wasn't for him, but *what the hell* all the same.

Stay frosty, Julia...

"I'm... Julia," she choked out, still staring at the metal half of his face, "Julia Parker." She was aware on some level that she was staring, but couldn't quite tear her eyes away from what looked like nothing so much as a damaged cyborg. She forced herself to focus on the matter at hand. "You said that Jim was here?"

He smiled. "Yes, of course. Here he is." He gestured to the window.

She looked—and clapped her hands over her mouth to stifle a scream when she saw what remained of her boyfriend. Her mind, well-practiced after years in the ER, slipped effortlessly into clinical mode.

Extensive contusions across the face, neck, and upper right quarter of the torso. Traumatic amputation of the left arm just above the elbow; tissue damage indicates the limb was torn off rather than severed. Multiple lacerations across the chest and ribs. Traumatic transection just above the pelvic bone.

A number of electrodes with trailing wires had been affixed to Jim's chest and temples, and a few more wires had apparently been inserted into his chest cavity around his breastbone, sketching out a set of parentheses around his heart. She also saw a series of tubes and catheters threaded into strategic areas of the ruin, with fluids pumping in and out. The tubes threaded into the stump of his arm seemed to be circulating blood, while those coming from his torn lower half seemed to carry several types of bodily fluids. However, the items that brought the whole bizarre scene together lurked in the far corner: a tank of sickly green, transparent fluid containing Jim's naked legs and pelvis. Nearby, a heart monitor and oxygen pump indicated that for all that had happened to him, Jim still lived. Correction—Jim was still being *kept* alive.

She found herself remembering when she'd first met Jim, who had landed in the emergency room with his leg broken in three places from a skiing accident. She'd been a resident at the time, but she'd been able to calm him down just by talking to him, even while he was being triaged and checked for spinal injuries. He'd been surrounded by more machinery, and didn't look half as horrifying as he did now.

Her clinical mind could only tolerate so much; the injuries alone would have been fine, but the measures being taken to keep him alive seemed cruel and unusual. Who the hell was this guy, some sort of mad surgeon? Granted, he did replace her leg with one that seemed to work just about as well, but did he use similar techniques to create that shark-thing that attacked her and Jim? And how—

She jumped with a squeak of surprise as Mechanus placed a hand on her shoulder.

"The human body is quite resilient," he said, "It wants to live, no matter what."

"That I'll grant," she said numbly, "But still, how... how the hell is he still alive?"

"Science," Mechanus said brightly. "As you can see, I've mastered the techniques of tissue manipulation to improve upon nature. For his own sake, I'm keeping him in a medical coma, but he's alive—and, if you like, I can repair him."

"Repair him? How?" Julia turned to face her host, and took a step back when she saw how close he was standing. He didn't seem to notice, smiling at her like they had just been introduced by a skilled matchmaker at a cocktail party.

"By replacing the damaged and missing parts, of course. It will be a very simple procedure. I can even improve upon nature." His mechanical eye glittered with anticipation. "All you have to do is ask."

Julia considered this offer. It sounded too good to be true, but she didn't see many other options. "So you'll fix him, and then we can go?"

The mechanical iris contracted as Mechanus's smile faded. "I'm afraid that leaving won't be possible for you."

A chill went down Julia's spine. "Why... why not?" she demanded.

"I enjoy my privacy, and I have projects in place that I do not wish interrupted. If I let you go, you're likely to tell people about what goes on inside Shark Reef Isle, and that could get extremely messy. My research could be endangered. My assistants' lives would be at risk. Everything I've worked for... gone." He took her right hand in his left, and she felt unyielding metal under his glove. "Now, I promise you—I swear to you—that I intend no harm to befall you. However, you should put escape right out of your mind. We're miles from the closest inhabited island, I have no boats to take you anywhere, and I have three packs of dire wolves that patrol this island. Beyond this, I will give you anything you wish— good food, comfortable accommodations, and I will even fix up your diving partner so that he's good as new—no, better than new. How about it?"

Everything about his demeanor seemed to be generally *off*—more than the fact that he'd replaced her leg without batting an eyelash and was now keeping a bisected man alive by some means, for whatever purpose he'd originally had in mind. He acted like she expected a mad scientist in a movie to act, with an unsettling enthusiasm for whatever *science* was keeping Jim alive. His voice, though overall pleasant to listen to (honestly, she could have listened to him reading the phone book to her all day) had a slight metallic quality, probably due to other hardware that she hadn't yet seen. Also, while he was speaking with her his voice remained largely neutral, but there was a definite spark of fascination in his human eye.

If he put Jim back together, maybe she and Jim could figure out a way off the island. She got a twinge of guilt when she recalled that she wanted to break up with him, but at the same time it wasn't like she could just leave him here in the hands of some madman who probably wanted to turn him into Frankenstein's monster or something.

"Okay," she said to Mechanus, hope starting to bloom for the first time that day, "Fix him. Can you make him good as new?"

He smiled, and his lens gleamed in anticipation. "I can do even better than that, my dear lady. I will make him better than he ever was."

"O-okay," she said, feeling uneasy at the look of glee in his eye. She didn't want Jim *improved*, just back how he was. Then again, she wouldn't say no to some personality improvements, maybe make him a bit more compromising...

No. Bad Julia. Having some mad scientist scramble Jim's brain according to her own whims wouldn't help anything.

"I'd... like to go back to my room now," Julia said quietly.

Mechanus bowed deeply to her, sweeping his arm across his waist like a Victorian gentleman elaborately tipping his hat to a young lady he fancied. "Very well. Arthur, kindly show her the way."

"Of course, sir. Miss?" The drone turned and flew away, and Julia followed, feeling numb.

***

"I'd say that went very well overall," Mechanus said to Arthur after Julia had gone.

"Perhaps so, sir," Arthur replied, "but she appears displeased by her current situation."

"I don't see why she would—I replaced her missing leg, I patched up all their injuries, and I've even managed to save her diving partner's life." *Her fiancé's life,* he thought unhappily, recalling the note that the man had on his person. Well. He would *not* let this prevent him from being a gracious host. He would repair Jim and make him better than he ever was before—better than nature could achieve by itself—and then Julia would be happy and... and...

...and Mechanus would not have her. She would be with her handsome fiancé, and they would be happy together, leaving Mechanus himself alone.

He sank down into a chair, now troubled by the expression that had crossed her face when she looked upon him for the first time. She'd been staring at him—staring at his face in... horror? Yes. She found him horrifying, and he suspected he knew why.

He reached up and touched the metal plates on the left half of his face. What *had* happened to his face? It seemed things had always been this way. He could almost remember—but as he reached out for the memory it danced away, agonizingly close but still just out of reach. He had a brief flash of heat and agony, and someone—two people, he thought, a man and a woman—screaming, but then it was gone. He'd had the plates in his face for as long as he could remember, just like the other limbs and the metal plates that covered the lower two-thirds of his torso. The scars, too, come to think of it. So many scars...

He sighed. He had so many plans—after all, Earth wouldn't be conquered in a day—but now all he wanted was to see her smile. She was the first real human company he'd had in ten years, the first companionship that he hadn't made with his own two hands. He hadn't known how much he'd craved another human being until he'd laid eyes on her. It was a palpable physical ache originating in the region of his cardiac pump, caused as much by her presence as by the certainty that right now she wasn't happy.

He would have to set a few things aside for now, but he was determined now to make her happy. He would fix her fiancé with all the skills he had available, and make him the perfect companion for her. Then she would stay, and be a light in his life as he set about with his other plans. Then when he was the world-emperor, he would quietly eliminate his rival, and marry her, and everything would be perfect. She would learn that he was no monster to be feared.

He had another flash then, an impression of—

—*a beautiful blonde woman brushes his cheek with her fingertips, followed by a gentle pressure on his lips—a soft kiss. He sees more this time—they are standing together in the shelter of a gazebo, while red and gold maple leaves swirl around them. She wears a close-fitting tee-shirt, black with a diagram of a caffeine molecule stretched gently across her breasts—he knows this is so, but she is too close for him to see it, wrapped in his arms while she twines her fingers through his hair—*

He grasped desperately at the details, trying to tease out more information, but when he tried the vision started to dissolve.

"No," he whispered urgently. "No no no please no—"

But it was gone, and he stood alone in the corridor. What the deuce was going on? Was his fractured mind starting to break entirely? And who was this blonde woman? He was certain that he'd known her, loved her, wanted to marry her, but...

"Sir?" Arthur's voice came with a certain degree of calm concern.

"Yes, Arthur?"

"Miss Julia is back in her room. Are you all right, sir?"

"Yes," Mechanus said, "I'm... I'm fine. I got lost in my thoughts for a bit there." He shook his head, scattering the last few shards of the mystery woman, and then stood, focusing his mind on the task at hand.

Limb replacement was child's play to him, but replacing an entire lower half would be more of a challenge—and a delightful one at that. He had detailed files about the particulars, collected from his work on himself. He would need to reinforce the spine, wire everything to the new legs and pelvis, and of course make the new limbs out of something better and stronger than mere flesh and bone. The limbs, too, would need to be stronger, and they could have all the functionality of the originals and more, if he put his mind to it. Even then, of course, Mechanus was certain he could prove to her why he was the superior choice over the ragged remains of her... her fiancé.

His mind stumbled a bit on the term, but he had only to look at Jim's remains and the flicker of uncertainty was replaced with a fresh surge of smug triumph. Some fiancé he would be for her *now*.

His mechanical lens dilated and glowed blue with enthusiasm as he planned the rebuild. Yes—this would be a perfect companion and servant for his beloved Julia!

Chapter
THREE

Julia thought that she wouldn't be able to eat anything after seeing Jim like that, but the laws of irony clearly had other plans. Once she was back in her room, her stomach growled again, almost reproachfully, as if to say *you knew I was hungry, so what's the delay?* She wrapped her arms around her stomach.

"Arthur?" she asked. The metal football turned to face her with that generic grin.

"Yes, Miss Julia?"

"Could I get something to eat? I haven't had anything since before going scuba diving, and that feels like ages ago."

"Of course, Miss Julia. I will have a meal brought in for you." The drone paused. "Dr. Mechanus offers his apologies. He does not wish to be a negligent host."

"I *bet* he doesn't," Julia grumbled.

"To your knowledge, do you have any particular food allergies?" Arthur asked, apparently electing to ignore that last remark.

"No allergies. I just want something simple." She *really* didn't want Mechanus to go all out on her. It might give him ideas.

"Very well, Miss Julia. Do you wish anything else?"

Julia thought about this. At this point she wasn't sure if Dr. Mechanus's hospitality came with any strings attached. She glanced down at the toes of her new leg, wiggling them experimentally. They moved easily, with no indications of nerve misfires or muscle damage. He was a brilliant surgeon, she would grant him that, but...

"I... did have a couple of questions for you."

"Of course, Miss Julia. I will answer them as well as I am able."

"How many visitors does Mr. Mechanus actually get, on average?"

"None, Miss. He is very diligent about discouraging the curious."

She frowned. "The legends about monsters on the island—he spread those?"

"Yes, Miss Julia."

"So... how many people actually live here?"

"Please specify."

She frowned again. Specify? What did he mean, specify? Then she made the connection. He was a mad scientist. That meant...

"How many people live here that he didn't create?"

"Three, Miss. You, Jim, and Dr. Mechanus. You and your companion are the first outside company he's had in ten years."

Her stomach dropped. That explained a *lot*, actually. She'd heard of people going insane from extended isolation.

She sat heavily on the bed, looking around at the room where it seemed she would be living for the time being.

Not if I have anything to say about it, said the sensible voice.

"Is there anything else you require?" Arthur asked.

"'Anything' like what?" she asked.

"Anything you could possibly want, Dr. Mechanus will be happy to provide," Arthur cheerfully told her.

"How about a boat back to Hawaii?" she ventured.

"Except for that." Arthur's generic smiley face didn't even flicker.

"Well, it was worth a try." She sighed despondently, massaging her forehead with the heels of both hands. She had to think of a way to get out of there.

But first, she needed some way to defend herself.

"My new leg hurts after my walk to and from the lab," she said, although in truth she felt only the mildest ache at the junction. "I could use a cane or something to help me walk."

And if it's made of metal, so much the better, said the reasonable voice. *Even aluminum hurts like a bastard if swung hard enough.*

The drone bobbed in a limbless approximation of a bow. "Very well, Miss Julia. I will have it brought along with your meal. Dr. Mechanus additionally invites you to partake of the bathing facilities adjoining your room. You will find them through the door just ahead of you."

She looked up; across the room from her was a second door, aside from the one by which she'd entered. She wasn't sure how she hadn't noticed it, but figured that she'd had a valid excuse for being distracted, what with being held prisoner and all.

Julia got up, glancing down at her new leg and noticing that, just as Mechanus had said, its skin had changed color to more closely match her own. The foreign foot was shaped slightly differently than her own, and she figured she only noticed now because she'd been paying attention. What sort of surgeon has spare legs just lying around? For a crazy moment, she found herself imagining a room somewhere in the complex with a vat filled with limbs.

She opened the door and found, as promised, a bathroom with a toilet, a shower, and a vanity bearing a number of grooming implements. She looked around the bathroom, certain that Dr. Mechanus had another camera somewhere in there. She didn't see one—which meant nothing—but did catch her own reflection in the mirror. Her hair was an absolute rat's nest—not surprising really, after everything. Well, as long as she was an *honored* guest of this Mechanus guy…

"Would you like any assistance in bathing or grooming?" Arthur asked, startling her.

"No! No. I just want to freshen up a bit. Uh, there aren't any cameras in here, are there?"

"No, Miss Julia. In any case, he has already seen you in the altogether."

Julia grimaced. "Thanks for reminding me."

"You're quite welcome," Arthur replied, without a hint of irony in his synthesized voice. Julia glared.

"Feel free to indulge in the amenities that Dr. Mechanus has provided. Your meal and your cane will be waiting for you once you have finished."

"Uh, yeah. Okay." She wasn't sure if she could trust the word of one of Mechanus's faithful servants regarding the presence or absence of cameras, and planned to offer as little of a show as possible.

Let him suck on that. It was an uncharacteristically rebellious thought for Julia, and she blinked in surprise almost as soon as it had formed.

She waited, listening to the drone's soft hum fading in volume, until it was cut off by the hiss of her door sliding shut, and then glanced at the neatly-arranged assortment of combs and brushes. She selected a wide-toothed comb and combed out her hair while sorting through her thoughts

First things first—wait until she saw what Mechanus did with Jim. By all rights, Jim ought to be dead, and while Mechanus could do some astonishing things with limb transplants, she had no idea how he might handle a project that involved a bisected man. She wasn't even sure why she trusted him that far— for all she knew he was a psychopath—but slim hope was better than none. She was pretty sure any medical board worth its credentials would have a heart attack about even the suggestion of such repairs. She knew that the idea was causing her own stomach to twist uneasily. What would Jim be like on the other side of that? Would he even be functional—either physically or mentally?

She glanced down at her new leg again, wiggling her toes while she teased out a particularly stubborn tangle.

Second order of business—find out how big the place was. The layout was confusing, but so was that of most hospitals, and she knew the complex wasn't infinite. Shark Reef Isle itself was, what, only a mile or two across? And even assuming the lair took up the entire interior of the volcano, that cut the distance in half. Once she found her way outside, all she had to do was reach the coast...

...Which brought her to the third point: the wolves. He'd called them dire wolves, but for all she knew that was an exaggeration. She didn't know how aggressive dire wolves would be, but that shark-thing had gone straight for them without hesitation.

She set down the comb and stepped into the shower stall before undressing. She set her clothing outside the stall and turned on the water. It was deliciously hot, and while her tired muscles cheered, she felt a pang of guilt. There she was, in a huge, luxurious bathroom with gold fixtures, fluffy white bath towels and—above all—hot water, while Jim lay in a laboratory somewhere, ripped in half by a shark-monster.

Her throat closed and her eyes stung with tears. It wasn't fair. None of it was. This was supposed to be a vacation, for God's sake! She was supposed to be relaxing on a beach and working on her tan, not trapped on a remote island in the South Pacific at the mercy of some mad scientist and his minions. Then again, she was supposed to be happy with Jim, too, and look how *that* worked out.

Her breath hitched, and tears trickled down her cheeks, only to be swept up in the water from the shower and washed away. The lavender scent of the shampoo should have been comforting, but instead it just reminded her of how far away she was from everything normal.

You need a vacation, Jim said.

We should go to Hawaii, Jim said.

I know a great place to go scuba diving, Jim said.

It will be great, Jim said.

Not once had he asked her what she'd wanted to do.

For that matter, Dr. Mechanus was doing more or less the same thing. Yes, he'd given her luxury accommodations, but that was just a gilded cage. In the meantime, she had no idea what the hell kind of plans he had for her. He'd given her a new leg—how else might he try to improve her? She might not be able to fight him off if he got it into his head to have his way with her. Best case scenario, he was some sort of weird government experiment that got out of hand, or an escaped mental patient who was *really* into self-modification.

She hugged herself, suddenly shivering despite the hot water.

Stay frosty, Julia, the sensible voice said, *Panicking will get you nowhere.*

She took a shuddering breath and wiped at her eyes. She would have to get control of herself if she was going to get control of anything else.

"Miss Julia?" Dr. Mechanus's voice suddenly echoing in the shower stall made her shriek in fright.

"What?" she demanded, trying to get her heart rate back to normal.

"Are you finding everything to your liking?"

"I thought the bathroom didn't have any cameras!"

"It… doesn't," Mechanus said, sounding startled, "Arthur told me you were freshening up, and I thought I would see if there was anything you needed."

"Just to take a shower in peace!"

Dr. Mechanus was quiet for a long time. "Very well," he said finally, "I do sincerely apologize." To his credit, he sounded genuinely contrite.

She heard the speaker click off, but remained where she was under the spray for a good minute before she turned off the water. She reached out around the frosted-glass door, grabbed one of the fluffy towels, and wrapped herself in it before stepping out of the shower stall.

When she came out of the bathroom, she saw the shark-monster standing in the doorway. Her heart leaped into her throat, strangling her scream, and she backpedalled so hard into the bathroom that she lost her balance and sat down hard on the tile. She crab-crawled from there, backing into the far corner.

It was a huge, hulking stack of leathery flesh on thick, muscular legs that ended in misshapen webbed feet. Its bullet-shaped head hung low between its heavy shoulders, and it turned to regard her with soulless black eyes. Its arms—oh, how vividly she remembered those arms!—looked like they could lift small cars with little trouble. A leathery shark's tail hung behind it in a thick J that twitched lazily back and forth. She couldn't tell what sort of shark had been used as its base, but her mind immediately supplied her with scenes from various *Jaws* movies.

It bore a small table in one hand, a covered aluminum tray in the other hand, and a cane in its jaws. It watched her with the bestial curiosity of a particularly intelligent—but no less deadly—predator, tilting its head slightly, and then set down the table in the middle of the room. The tray came next, carefully placed on the center of the table, and finally it took the cane from between its serrated teeth and leaned it against the edge of the table with great care. Its task apparently complete, it turned and left. The door hissed shut behind it, but she didn't hear it lock.

Julia sat where she was for several minutes, not quite able to make her frozen limbs move after the sight of the shark-monster. After what felt like an eternity, her clenched muscles finally loosened, and she uncoiled herself from the corner of the bathroom. She clutched the towel close as she got up, heart still pounding, and ventured out into the room to investigate what the shark-monster had left for her.

As she drew closer, intending to examine the cane first, the smell of hot food hit her nostrils. She lunged forward and snatched the cover off the tray to reveal a plate of baked fish—striped sea bass, unless she was mistaken—steamed string beans, and white rice, plus a glass of a dark red beverage that a small sip proved to be fresh cranberry juice.

Her stomach growled again, but she was not about to eat in just a towel. Not here, and not now. Reluctantly, she put the cover back into place and retreated back to the bathroom to get dressed, certain that Dr. Mechanus could look in on her at any time otherwise.

Once she was dressed, she investigated the door through which the shark-thing had exited. She remembered that it slid open, and a brief glance revealed a simple panel set into the wall to the right of the door. The panel had a single large button, which currently glowed green. She tentatively pushed the button, and the door promptly hissed open, revealing the corridor again. She leaned out, looking left and right. She heard footsteps approaching, and she ducked back inside. The door closed automatically a second later.

Only then did she return to the food. God, she was hungry! She tore into it, filling her stomach for the first time in what seemed like days without really tasting it, just driven by the need to eat, eat, eat. She would need to get her energy up if she was to escape, so she made sure to clean her plate.

Once she was done eating, she turned to examine the cane. It had a familiar design—a length of aluminum tube with light scratches where the shark-thing's teeth had marred it, with a padded, angular handle at the top and a rubber foot at the bottom. She hefted it experimentally. It was fairly light, and she knew that such canes could be a handy weapon in a pinch, and in the meantime she could affect a small hobble to justify its use.

She was starting to feel a little better about her situation, now that she'd given herself at least a fighting chance. She had no idea what time it could possibly be right now, but now that her stomach was full her body was telling her that it was time to sleep. It sounded like a really good idea, especially since she would need her rest if she was going to get out of here.

She climbed into bed, curled up around her new cane, and fell into a fitful sleep. She dreamed—

Her nightmares had recently followed a common theme, relentlessly reliving that night at the hospital, but this time, rather than a single drugged-out maniac with a scalpel, she is being chased through the hospital corridors by a gang of hungry shark-monsters. She turns a corner and collides with Mechanus.

Not to worry, he says, in his soothing mechanical baritone. *I'll keep those monsters from getting you. I just need to perform a simple procedure…*

And then, supernaturally fast, he whips out a scalpel a foot long, still so wet with blood that the motion sends a spray of red across her face.

She screams—

Julia jolted awake with a yelp. She glanced around quickly, like a hunted animal, searching every corner for shark-monsters—or for that matter, any sign that Mechanus had silently entered her room in the night and was about to perform a simple procedure on her.

She saw that the lights in her room had dimmed to an artificial twilight since she'd gone to sleep, offering just enough of a glow to see by. She saw nothing but the furniture of her room—no shark-monsters, no mad cyborgs, no scalpel-wielding maniacs.

She curled around her cane again, settling in on the bed, but she was sure that she wasn't going to get any more sleep that night.

***

Mechanus's thoughts were wandering.

This was not a usual state for him, as he'd long prided himself on his level of concentration, but all the same he kept thinking about Julia, and specifically about the discomfort he'd felt when seeing her in the altogether. It didn't make sense. Nudity shouldn't bother him. He was a surgeon and scientist, after all—the human body, while a magnificent machine, should be no more than a very well-organized set of moving parts and biological processes to him, and in nearly every case it was. He'd seen hundreds of nude bodies in his career—cadavers, mainly—and none of them had bothered him. Not one.

And yet, seeing Julia naked and vulnerable caused the heat to rise in the right side of his face, leaving him with the distinct impression that seeing her that way was just *wrong*. The idea was more than a little unnerving—but her presence seemed to be awakening parts of him that had been dead for ten years.

He'd been working all night on repairing Jim, just as Julia had requested. He bent over the operating table that bore the man's broken body, working smoothly in tandem with half a dozen robotic arms that dangled from the ceiling. He riveted a new arm onto the abbreviated stump, and then turned the limb over to his assistants to make the necessary wetware interface connections. Jim had a new pair of legs as well now—more functional than pretty, to be honest, but he would be able to get around on them just fine. Flesh had been melded with metal, bone reinforced to support the extra weight, and damaged organs replaced with mechanical equivalents or circumvented entirely. Mechanus had even taken care to keep Jim's personality largely intact, if muted, in order to preserve his bond with Julia. He didn't usually work so extensively with human brains, as the animal brains of his assistants worked just fine and could be enhanced as necessary, but he felt confident that he'd repaired enough of the damage. Once he was done, Jim should be a perfect servant for her.

He pushed off, gliding smoothly on the wheels that currently protruded from the soles of his feet until he reached another collection of cybernetic parts. He rummaged through the bin, surfacing with a three-fingered pincer that he judged would work magnificently for a hand—but then paused, looking at the pincer and then at his own metal hand.

So much of him was machine now... he'd nearly forgotten what it was like to be human. But now...

Ever since meeting Julia he was starting to remember. He was remembering things he couldn't properly understand, but most of all she reminded him that he was a man, and he wanted to believe that he had standards.

He was a *gentleman*, dammit.

Another memory flashed in his mind, another vision of the strange blonde woman, walking towards him with a double armload of books. Her smile was warm and sweet, and her lips were soft against his cheek. She spoke, and although he couldn't hear the words she said he suspected there was a name in there—his name. Not the name he went by now, but perhaps the name he had in his previous life, before whatever happened, *had* happened. His closed his eye in frustration, massaging his forehead. This was no time for hallucinations. His project was almost done, and then Julia would be happy. And he would see her smile.

But first things first.

He bent over the repaired—and improved—man on the operating table, putting the final touches on his project. He flipped a switch, and a jolt of electricity coursed into Jim, causing his fingers to twitch. His eyes rolled beneath their lids, and the mechanical limbs that Mechanus had used to replace Jim's lower half began to move. The repaired man groaned. His face pulled into a rictus of agony, and he let out a strangled cry, trying to sit up. Mechanus placed a hand on Jim's shoulder, gently pushing him back down.

"Easy, there, Jim. The pain will subside in time."

Jim's eyes slowly flickered open. He glanced around, and ultimately focused on Mechanus. His upper lip drew back in a snarl, baring his teeth.

"Do you know how you got here?" Mechanus asked.

"Ngo," Jim replied, his slurred speech likely a result of residual neural damage. No matter— Mechanus could fix that as well.

"You had a little encounter in the reef near this island. An encounter with one of my guards. But don't worry; you and your diving partner will be just fine under my care."

"Gyu-ya?" Jim asked.

"That's right. You were a bit more banged up than she was, but I've repaired you, as a special favor." Mechanus smiled. "Just imagine how delighted she'll be to see you again, Jim." *Delighted in* me, he thought. "Now, let's get you on your feet, shall we? Arthur?"

"Yes, sir?"

"Would you be kind enough to go tell Julia that Jim is up and about?"

"Of course, sir."

After a few false starts, the refurbished man in the lab with him finally managed to lurch to his feet, staggering slightly on his new limbs. Mechanus conceded that the whole affair looked a bit bashed-together, but at least Jim had a new life ahead of him. He could walk and talk, which was more than anyone else who'd been bisected by a shark (or shark-man) could reasonably say. Julia seemed to be impressed by the work he'd done on her leg; certainly she'd be dazzled by how well he'd fixed Jim!

"Nearly there, sir," Arthur informed him.

"Excellent! Jim, wait here. I want this to be a surprise."

Jim looked at him with a dull expression of disorientation, and then looked at his mismatched hands with what might have been wonder, or else confusion. This wasn't surprising—Mechanus judged his surgical talents to be without peer.

He stepped out of the operating room to meet Julia, and saw that she was leaning slightly on the new cane he'd given her. To judge by the expression on her face, clearly she was expecting great things from him—and to be sure, he intended to deliver.

"Miss Julia," he greeted her, sweeping a bow to her, "As radiant as always."

"Uh, thanks," she replied, "Arthur said that you'd fixed Jim?"

"Yes, of course," Mechanus replied proudly, "In fact, I toiled all night on him, just so he would be all fixed up for you. Not to worry, though, working on a project of this magnitude is an honor—"

"I want to see Jim."

"Ah. Yes. Of course. Well." Her words stung. "Jim? Would you come out here please?"

Jim lurched out. His metal feet clanked on the tile floor, providing percussion against the harmony of servos and gears at work. It was, in Mechanus's opinion, a decent amalgam of flesh and metal—it would require some refinement later on, but Jim was up and about, as he'd promised.

"Gyu-ya?" Jim slurred.

Julia's eyes widened and her mouth fell open. Mechanus beamed. Any minute now, she would tell him what a marvel the repaired Jim was, and gush over Mechanus's genius in repairing Jim's mangled body, and—

His hopes were dashed when Julia screamed.

Chapter
FOUR

"*What the hell did you do to him?*" Jim was a horrifying mashup of flesh and steel—a primitive cyborg or the victim of a devastating industrial accident. His missing arm had been replaced by a three-fingered claw, his legs and pelvis had been replaced by clunky, ugly lower limbs that allowed him to move about under his own power without worrying about such frippery as elegance or streamlining. He looked like he was in intense pain.

Mechanus, for his part, looked confused by her horror.

"What? I..." His brow darkened. "I *fixed* him. Just like you asked me to. He has new legs that won't wear out. His new arm and hand are stronger than the previous one. I replaced his ruined organs with viable mechanical equivalents. He will live a very long time like this!" He was nearly shouting now, his mechanical eye blazing red.

Crap. She'd pissed him off.

The Jim-thing lurched towards her, reaching for her. She backed away from it, not wanting to find out how easily it might rip her apart (accidentally or otherwise) if it got her in its grip.

"Get it away from me!" she yelled.

Mechanus blinked, and the storm-cloud of anger that had been building on his face dissipated just as suddenly.

"Jim, stop." Mechanus's voice was quiet but with a note of authority that came from being accustomed to having others follow one's instructions. The Jim-thing stopped immediately, casting its misshapen shadow across Julia, and turned to regard Mechanus. "Come away from her. Now." The creature that used to be Jim lumbered away from her, to her immense relief. She saw a small smile cross Mechanus's face—he was still *proud* of the thing!

Julia was shaking. Alistair Mechanus had done that to him overnight. What plans did he have for her? Regardless of how genteel and polite he had seemed during their initial meeting, anyone who would 'fix' a man *that* way was obviously a lunatic.

Mechanus approached her, reaching for her. She let out a short yelp and reflexively swung her cane at his arm. It connected solidly with a loud *crack*, knocking his arm away, and she took off running.

She didn't have a particular goal in mind—she just had to get the hell away from Mechanus as fast as possible. She just ran.

Her bare feet slapped against the metal floor as she dodged down one corridor after another.

"Julia!" Mechanus called, his voice echoing from a dozen speakers around her.

She ignored him, focusing on getting as much distance between herself and that... that maniac.

"Julia, I can make this right!" his voice called again. She ignored it.

A door slammed in front of her. She dodged right.

She was starting to get a stitch in her side, and her new knee was starting to hurt from the abuse. She hoped she wasn't about to rupture something. If her new knee gave out before she found a good hiding place, she would be at his mercy—whatever that was worth.

She heard movement around her—various minions barking and growling assent to whatever orders they were receiving right now.

"Julia? Please don't make this difficult," he called, still emulating the Voice of God. "I have security forces converging on your position, and it would be best if you didn't try to fight them."

Yeah. Not likely. She tightened her grip on her cane. Let them eat aluminum.

A flying robot resembling a metal housefly the size of a cat whirred up to her, and started screeching out an alarm. She whipped her cane around in a flat arc and clubbed it aside. The shock of the impact made her arm go numb, but watching the robot bounce off the wall offered her a certain satisfaction.

That was when a huge furry weight barreled into her from the right. The creature bore her painfully to the floor, knocking the air from her lungs in a painful cough. The cane skittered out of her hand. She twisted in the monster's grasp, trying to get free, but it dug its claws into her sides and let a harsh shriek into her face.

She looked up, and found herself nose-to-nose with something modeled after a black-furred jungle cat. In a panic, she swatted at the thing's face, trying to fight it off, and it dug its claws in harder. Red-hot pain exploded along her ribs, and she screamed.

"DROP HER." Mechanus's voice was like a thunderclap. With an additional twist of dread, Julia realized he wasn't communicating through the speakers anymore—he was in the room with them. She hadn't even heard a door open.

She turned, and her eyes widened with fresh terror.

Mechanus marched towards the two of them like the wrath of technology, the hem of his lab coat swirling around his metal-sheathed legs, his mechanical eye glowing hellish red, and light fixtures exploding in his wake, showering sparks. He was holding his right arm close to his side, his only apparent concession to the fact that she'd hit him with a metal crutch, but was otherwise unhampered.

"I. Said. Drop her." He advanced on the cat-monster, whose ears flattened against its head in a definite *Oh no, Daddy's mad at me* expression. It released her, and she skittered away until her back met a corner. She was vaguely aware of the continuing burning pain in her sides.

Shit. Shit shit shit.

His mismatched eyes flicked over to Julia's discarded cane, and then to the light smears of blood—her blood—on the panther-thing's claws. There was no way she'd be able to reach the cane—her only weapon—in time if he turned his attention on her, so she stayed still, freezing like a frightened rabbit.

The panther-thing bore the brunt of his wrath. He turned his full attention to it, and it flinched away under his enraged gaze. He grabbed it by one furry ear and slowly pulled it further away from her. It let out a startlingly kittenish mewl, but shuffled along to keep up.

"She-is-not-to-be-harmed-is-that-understood?" Mechanus snapped at him in a sharp staccato.

It made a plaintive noise and nodded, not looking at either Mechanus or Julia. He released it, and it rubbed at its abused ear.

"Now get out of here," he snapped. "Now."

It slunk off, looking more like a kicked puppy than a cat-monster should.

He turned his attention to her, and she instinctively tried to make herself even smaller. She had no idea what he was going to do in light of her escape attempt, and—

—and to her surprise, the right half of his face softened slightly when he looked at her.

"Are you all right?" he asked quietly, and then glanced over her. "Oh, dash it all, you're bleeding— here, let me—" He reached out to her, and she instinctively recoiled.

"Don't. Touch me," she hissed.

He froze, wincing, and then glanced away. "I'm... sorry about Bagheera," he said. "He just gets so enthusiastic. I..." He fell silent for several seconds. "You're bleeding," he observed. "I could—"

"I'll be fine," she snapped, cutting him off. "Just take me back to my room."

He looked conflicted, caught at a strange intersection between anger, frustration, and worry. He flexed his right hand and cautiously reached for her, but she flinched away again. The *last* thing she wanted him to do right now was touch her.

He grimaced, and then let out a short breath.

"Arthur," he said quietly. "Kindly take her back to her room."

The drone soon appeared, bearing its generic smiley face.

"Miss Julia?" Arthur said. "Right this way."

She stood up, grimacing as her left knee twinged again with fresh pain. She clutched at it, and saw Mechanus instinctively reaching out to help her, but she hobbled resolutely away and retrieved her cane from the floor.

She risked one last glance back at Mechanus before following Arthur, and she saw an expression of hurt confusion on half of his face, as though he honestly didn't know what he did wrong.

***

The drone floated away with a low hum, and she followed it, leaving Mechanus standing there, suddenly feeling more alone than he'd ever felt in ten years.

Oh sure, he had his minions and his robots and the ever-faithful Arthur, but—

… but what?

He groaned, rubbing the right side of his forehead with the heel of his hand. He glanced at his fingers and saw that his whole hand was shaking.

That hadn't happened in... well, about as long as it had been since he'd last felt anger or fear.

In fact, the last time he'd been that angry, he'd...

—he slams his fist through the orange sharps box with the biohazard symbol on it, and then turns his attention to the sphygmomanometer on the wall, tearing it free with his new metal arm and dashing it to the floor. He is screaming, a ragged, inarticulate sound of grief and rage and bone-deep anguish, while tears stream down his face from his remaining eye. He sees the world through a viscous red haze. Why does this have to happen to him, after all his hard work? He far outstripped all predictions for his recovery, and now—

He snapped back to the present, so abruptly that he had to catch his breath.

What.

The.

Deuce.

<Arthur,> Mechanus said.

<Sir?> came prompt reply.

<I've... I may need your help.> He took a deep breath. <I've been having flashbacks, I think. To *before*. I need you to try to record one the next time it happens.>

<Of course, sir. Anything else?>

Mechanus frowned, thinking. They'd only started when Julia had arrived—which meant that, in her own way, she might be able to help him piece together his own past. But that meant getting her cooperation, and *that* meant making her less afraid of him.

And he *still* wasn't sure where he was going wrong.

Well. He would do what he could.

<Send her bandages, antiseptic, and a fresh shirt with her next meal.> Even if she didn't want him to tend to her wounds, he would not deny her the means to do so herself.

<Yes, sir. Anything else?>

<Give me a moment.> The hesitation in his own thoughts was new as well, but her reaction to the refurbished Jim had rather kicked his legs out from under him.

He returned to the room where Jim still stood, obeying his last command to stay where he was. His dull eyes met Mechanus's, and his slack expression twitched briefly into a snarl. He wasn't a perfect repair job, to be sure, but he was up and about, and that was a start, at least. And Julia had acted like he'd vivisected the man.

<Where did I go wrong, Arthur?> he groaned as he reached up and inspected Jim's new arm. Jim, for his part, turned his head to watch him.

<Perhaps she didn't like his transformation into a cyborg?> Arthur suggested.

<But he's stronger and healthier than he was— and it was definitely an improvement over how he was when I first got him. Now he's virtually immortal.>

Abruptly, Jim jerked his arm from Mechanus's grasp.

"Hold *still*," Mechanus commanded him, and Jim froze in place once again.

<Maybe she prefers biological replacements over mechanical ones.>

Mechanus looked at his metal hand, and then touched the plates on his face contemplatively.

<I'll have to show her that I'm skilled in the art of biological creation as well,> he decided.

<I believe she knows that, sir. She's met Scarface and Bagheera already, and I believe she's seen Spike.>

<Yes, but they are all guardian creations—not exactly designed to be cuddly.>

<Understood. What do you wish done with Jim?>

Mechanus looked over at the cyborg in question. Jim was still watching him—glaring at him, if Mechanus let his imagination run away with him.

<Have Spike train him. At least he'll be an effective assistant and guard. And I'll see about refining his design a bit. I can do better.> He met Jim's stare evenly. <And keep him away from Julia. He'll only upset her again.>

<Very good, sir.>

<And Bagheera needs to be disciplined for his manhandling of Julia.>

<Sir, she *was* trying to escape,> Arthur pointed out. <Bagheera captured her and detained her, as per your orders.>

Mechanus scowled. <Perhaps, but he also hurt her. I saw the blood. I cannot let this stand.>

<What do you wish done regarding her cane?>

Mechanus pursed his lips thoughtfully, looking at his bruised arm. It hurt like the dickens, but nothing was broken. If she'd hit his metal arm, no doubt the cane would be broken now.

<Let her keep it,> he said.

<Sir, she used it as a weapon. She could have hurt you quite badly.>

<But she *didn't*,> he returned, <And in any case it was a gift. It's not like she will get very far should she leave the complex, in any case.> He grimaced; that last statement was perfectly accurate as far as he

could tell, but in his own ears it sounded unnecessarily harsh.

<Would you like an update on your army?> Arthur offered.

Mechanus frowned, realizing he hadn't even checked on his plans for world domination since Julia arrived.

Blast and damnation! He shouldn't have let her distract him so much. He would have to steel himself better in the future.

<Yes, please,> he said, but as Arthur filled him in, his mind drifted to Julia's beautiful golden hair.

He was a genius, wasn't he? If he could build an army that would ensure success in his bid for world conquest, why shouldn't he be able to win the heart of one woman?

He held up his hand, and Arthur paused in his catalog of resources.

<Thank you, Arthur,> Mechanus said. <Keep up the good work. I'll be in my lab for a while.>

He wanted to make Julia smile. No—he *needed* to make Julia smile. *Need* was as foreign to him as the burst of anger that had come with her rejection of the refurbished Jim, that flare that had worried him a little and, to his dismay, frightened Julia so badly. He'd *wanted* to conquer the world for some time now, among a great many other *wants*, but had never *needed* a thing until now. The need was deep enough to hurt, to make his more global plans seem insignificant.

He would find a way to fill that need.

Chapter
FIVE

Julia didn't stop shaking for over an hour. Her knee still hurt, but the pain was receding, leaving her hopeful that it was merely a strain and not a torn tendon or something. If it had been too serious, she knew that she was going to need help in repairing it, and the only help that seemed to be available was a mad surgeon. It was clear enough to her that Mechanus was insane by any standard she could apply, and that Jim was going to be no help to her.

At the thought of Jim's current state, her stomach churned, and she had to rush to the opulent bathroom to throw up. She leaned on the toilet for several more minutes after she was sure her breakfast was gone before getting unsteadily to her feet and looking in the mirror.

She looked like the sole survivor of a car crash, the sort who had gotten away with only a scratch and then been informed that all her friends had died on the scene. She'd seen the shell-shocked face that now looked at her from the mirror a hundred times in the ER—traumatized, disoriented, uncomprehending.

Get it together, Jules, the sensible voice said.

"How?" she answered it aloud. "He's... he..." Her voice broke, and she fell silent.

Jim is out of the picture, yes, but you're not stuck yet. You just need to be smart. You need to take control of the situation, just like you do in the ER. Let's look at your options.

Julia took a deep breath. "Options," she whispered. The tremor in her voice was lessened but not entirely gone. "What are my options?"

First, you need to get yourself patched up. That cat monster did a number on you.

Julia looked down at herself, and for the first time she noticed her torn, bloodstained shirt. She hiked up the hem and saw the blood and claw marks across her ribs on both sides. The claw marks were shallow but painful and still seeping blood. She stripped the shirt off entirely and, standing in her bra in front of the bathroom sink, began washing the scratches with soap and water. As she worked, she heard her door slide open. She peered around the doorjamb and saw the shark-monster entering again with a bundle clutched in one webbed claw.

She froze, her heart pounding, and watched the hulking thing glance around, and then raise its head like a dog catching a scent.

How keen was a shark's sense of smell? She remembered seeing something about it on the Discovery Channel, but couldn't recall what the answer was.

Presently the shark-monster lowered its head back to neutral and turned to look directly at her. She was sure she was fairly well-hidden, but then again she just *had* to peek around the doorframe. Her blood froze and her throat tightened under its gaze, but the expected attack did not come. Instead, it lifted the bundle and held it out to her silently.

Oh, God—what was it doing? Did it expect her to go over to it and take whatever it was from its hand? Did it even know or remember that it had attacked her and Jim?

"Just—just set it down on the bed!" she squeaked in fright.

It tilted its head. How smart were sharks? She didn't know that, any more than she knew how aggressive dire wolves were. To her shock, the shark-thing answered that question itself.

"Yes, Miss Julia," it gurgled in a harsh basso rumble that sounded like it was talking through a throat full of thick mucus. She even saw its gill slits flex as its jaws full of chainsaw teeth laboriously pronounced the words.

—what the hell what the hell what the hell what the hell what the hell what the hell what the hell—

The shark-monster carefully set the care package down on her bed, and without another word it turned and left.

So, said the sensible voice, *Now we know that the shark-monster is at least smart enough to talk.*

That didn't mean much—parrots could talk, after all—but it also meant that she was going to have to be extremely careful in her next escape attempt.

Good to know.

After pulling the torn and blood-crusted shirt back on, Julia ventured out to investigate what the shark-thing had brought. She opened the bundle to find three rolls of bandages, a bottle of clear liquid that smelled of rubbing alcohol, a clean white shirt, and a small slip of paper folded in quarters.

She opened the slip of paper, and found a note written in tight, precise handwriting:

> *Dearest Julia,*
>
> *In light of your recent experiences, you may be relieved to learn that I have taken measures to ensure you need never be troubled by Jim ever again, and likewise Bagheera has received punishment for the injuries he has perpetrated upon you.*
>
> *Please accept these items and use them as you wish. Since you do not wish me to tend to your wounds, it is the least I can do. Please accept my humblest apologies for your recent ordeal.*
>
> *Yours,*
> *Alistair Mechanus*

Julia's stomach twisted as she reread the note. On the one hand, she was secretly, guiltily relieved that she wasn't going to see Jim again. Even thinking about him in his current state still horrified her! On the other hand she couldn't help thinking that him being a cyborg was her fault. After all, she'd asked Mechanus to fix Jim—hadn't she?

Well, *yes*, but she hadn't asked Mechanus to do *that* to him.

As for Bagheera, she supposed that was the cat monster that had pounced on her. Well, good riddance to *that*.

On the heels of this, she recalled the expression on the cat-monster's face when Mechanus—holy *crap* he was pissed—had strode up to them with his mechanical eye blazing and the lights exploding all around him. Julia, for her part, had been certain that he was about to turn that wrath on her as well—and then he'd turned to her, and his expression had softened, as though someone had flipped a switch. He'd looked...

What? Worried? Concerned?

Heaven forbid, *frightened*?

What the hell did he have to be frightened of? This was *his* lair, with *his* minions, and *she* was the one who'd just seen her soon-to-be-ex turned into something horrible.

She picked up the shirt, bandages, and rubbing alcohol and headed back towards the bathroom. Halfway there she stopped in her tracks as another idea struck her.

He wasn't afraid *of* anything. Maybe he was afraid *for* her.

She continued walking.

No. That was stupid, thinking he was afraid for her. If that were the case he wouldn't have mangled Jim like he had.

But you saw that expression of relief on his face, said the sensible voice. *It looked a whole lot like he was worried you'd been hurt. And when he started to reach for you...*

Julia shut the bathroom door a bit harder than she'd intended. She didn't know what he'd had in mind when he reached for her. She'd just had a cat-monster jump on her—of *course* she flinched away!

She stripped off the bloody shirt again, feeling the dried blood scratching against her skin, and tossed it aside. She doubted even his people would be able to get the stains out if they intended to, and in any case, it was all torn up. They could do whatever they liked with it now. She started cleaning the scratches again, this time with the alcohol. She hissed in pain as the alcohol stung her wounds, but kept going until she'd treated all of them as thoroughly as she could. She didn't know if cat-monsters carried cat scratch disease or toxoplasmosis or rabies, but she wasn't going to take any chances. She wrapped her ribs in the bandages to protect the wounds before putting on the fresh shirt, and then started to wash her hands.

Okay, now that her wounds were treated, now what?

The next thing you're going to need is a map of the place, said the sensible voice. *Otherwise you'll never get out of here.*

"That would require paper and pencils, probably," Julia whispered. "And lots and lots of patience. What else?"

This is going to be the hard part, Jules. You're going to have to gain his trust.

She blinked. "What—make nice with Dr. Mechanus? Hell no."

Calm down, Jules. If you gain his trust, you'll be able to gain more access without getting stopped by his minions.

"Yeah, and?"

And he might have a communications room so you can call for help.

Julia sighed. "Well, there is that."

A sudden stinging pain in her hands made her jerk them back and look at them. She'd scrubbed them raw.

She hadn't done that in...

Well. In a while, anyway. It had *almost* become a problem when she was a resident and was washing her hands dozens of times during her shift. It got to the point where she couldn't get her hands to feel clean no matter how much she washed, but the washing relaxed her. A classic case of OCD, her therapist had told her.

And it had cropped up again after she'd survived the attack. After Jim had rescued her—

She closed her eyes, leaning against the sink. She didn't want to think about that again. For the longest time, her brain simply refused to let go of the experience, even after weeks of talking to a therapist. She didn't sleep right for a week. It was just how her mind worked, seizing on an idea and twisting itself into a loop.

She took a deep breath and let it out slowly. Well. Her hands didn't feel dirty now, but she would have to watch out for this.

She rinsed off one last time, dried her hands, and pulled on the fresh shirt. She looked less like a shell-shocked accident victim now—barely. She splashed water on her face, and then took a deep breath. This wasn't going to be easy. At all.

She left the bathroom and stood in the middle of the main room, regarding the red LED that marked the security camera.

"Um," she said. "Hello?"

"Yes, Miss Julia?" Arthur responded.

"Oh. I was thinking that Dr. Mechanus would answer."

"Dr. Mechanus is currently in one of his laboratories, working on an unspecified project. I believe he is suffering a fit of melancholy after your reaction to Jim."

A fit of 'melancholy'?

...Ugh. In other words, she'd hurt his feelings. *Great.* This made things both easier and harder.

"Yeah. About that." She scrambled for the sorts of words that might function as an apology along the lines of *I'm sorry I freaked out by your turning my boyfriend into a horrifying cyborg* and came up empty. Because she *wasn't* sorry for that. Not at all. You don't apologize for fight or flight reactions.

She rubbed her hands together as she thought, in an unconscious hand-washing gesture.

Get his trust, Jules.

"Look, I... I know he worked hard to get Jim back on his feet. Or any feet." *God.* What was she saying? "So I wanted to, uh, thank him for the effort?"

Wow. That sounded lame.

Arthur was silent for several seconds. Then:

"Dr. Mechanus accepts your gratitude."

Julia let out a breath she didn't even know she'd been holding.

"Okay. Good. Um." *What else what else what else?* "I was wondering if he might be willing to allow me some graph paper and pencils."

"For what purpose?"

Here we go. She took a deep breath. "I'd like to map the complex. I mean, I feel like this place was designed by Daedalus, you know?"

There came another one of those *oh God this was a bad idea I know he's going to say no* silences.

"A map of the complex will be provided to you," Arthur said finally.

Wow. That easy.

Arthur continued speaking. "You should remain aware, however, of the continued hazards of venturing outside."

"Right," Julia said. "The wolves."

"The *dire* wolves," Arthur corrected her mildly.

"The *dire* wolves, got it. No going outside."

"Dr. Mechanus wishes to additionally assure you that he is willing to provide you with anything you like in order to make your stay more comfortable."

Gah. Then again...

"Could you have him... not send the shark-thing by with any more gifts? He... was the one who grabbed us and he kind of freaks me out."

"I shall—" Arthur began, but a loud click overrode him.

"What's wrong with Scarface?" Mechanus asked over the speaker, sounding confused. "He's a complete sweetheart."

"He's an eight-foot-tall shark monster!" Julia returned.

"Seven and a *half*," Mechanus corrected her. "And he's done nothing to hurt you since you arrived."

"He *pulled my leg off at the knee!*" Julia exploded. She didn't usually yell, but there was *no way* that Mechanus was this dense.

"Well, uh, aside from that." Mechanus cleared his throat. "I could assign a different employee to make deliveries..."

"Not that cat-monster," Julia said.

"You needn't worry about that. Bagheera has been assigned to latrine duty for the foreseeable future." He sighed. "In any case, as we speak I'm working on a new companion for you."

Julia put her hands over her eyes. "Oh no..."

"No, it's really no trouble," Mechanus protested. "I want to make up for your loss of Jim, so I'm building something cuddly to keep you company. It should be done in a couple of days."

She groaned. She could only imagine what he was building in whatever lab he was in, and her imagination turned out to be entirely too fertile in that regard.

"Look, uh..." she said, choosing her words carefully. "I know you probably have lots of other projects going on..." She tried to think of hobbies that mad scientists would have, and came up blank. "So I wouldn't want to keep you away from any of them."

"My dearest Julia," he said, and the metallic note to his voice was nearly inaudible now. "It is my greatest pleasure to provide you with your every desire. I only wish to make you happy."

Julia opened her mouth to reply, but she recognized the tone. It was the same tone she'd heard from Jim so many times—he'd made his mind up, and there would be no arguing with him. *Crap.* She shut her mouth without saying anything.

"Your map will arrive in twenty minutes," Mechanus continued. "I do hope you find it helpful."

So did she, but likely not for the same reasons he did.

*   *   *

<Sir,> Arthur said, <The renovations on Jim are in progress, but there's a small problem.>

Mechanus glanced up from his project. He was currently directing the surgical robots that were attaching nerves and blood vessels between the different components, but as he turned his attention to Arthur the cluster of spidery appendages paused in their work.

<What sort of a problem?> Mechanus asked.

<He appears to be fighting his conditioning.>

Mechanus frowned. While most of his assistants happily obeyed the man who'd given them a new life, he'd made certain not to obliterate Jim's mind entirely, in an effort to make him a docile companion for Julia rather than a dull-witted pet. This, apparently, came with some side effects. He would need to tighten Jim's leash, then.

He mentally reached through the network and peered through the electrodes that he had implanted in Jim's brain. Rather than accepting the surveillance, Jim's mind recoiled, and Mechanus caught the echo of a thought—

<who the fuck are you>

—wrapped in undeniable hostility.

<I am Dr. Alistair Mechanus,> Mechanus transmitted. <How much do you remember?>

<up to the shark where the fuck is julia> Jim's thoughts, while not terribly strong, were tinged with frustration and outrage. <what the fuck is wrong with me what did you do to me>

Interesting. His thoughts were quite clear—if rather profane.

<Julia is fine, Jim. You should calm yourself.> With a trivial effort, Mechanus took control of Jim's new limbs and stopped his forward progress—he'd been heading away from the refurbishment lab, trailing half-attached parts. <Were it not for me, you

would certainly be dead. Now, you have a new life. I suggest you try to be a bit more grateful for this.>

<fuck you>

<Temper, temper,> Mechanus chided, and, with another small effort, walked Jim back to the lab. <This will hurt a lot less if you don't fight it.>

<julia julia julia julia julia> The echoing thought was starting to go red with agitation.

<Relax, Jim. This will be your life for a very long time, so you might as well get used to it.>

Jim was stubborn, though—more so than any of the other assistants he'd built. He mentally bucked and squirmed, trying to slip free of Mechanus's influence, but Mechanus had been doing this for a lot longer than Jim.

Mechanus responded with lightning swiftness, grappling Jim's mind into functional immobility before stuffing back down into his own subconscious. As he did, Mechanus caught a hint of Jim's underlying thoughts—

<she's mine you can't have her i'll kill you if you so much as look at her>

—churning atop a froth of anger that seemed to feed on itself.

Sweat stood out on the right side of Mechanus's face as he locked Jim away in his own mind.

<Really, Jim,> Mechanus chided. <If you display even half this temper towards Julia, it is abundantly clear that you are not worthy of her.>

And with that he slammed the metaphorical lid down on Jim and backed out of his mind with a sigh of relief. None of his other creations had given him this much trouble. Even elevated to humanlike intelligence, the animal-based chimeras he made were so much more tractable.

<Sir?> Arthur asked. <Is there a problem?>

Mechanus considered this. <No.> he said finally. <I believe I caught it before it became a real issue. I trust Jim is back where he needs to be?>

<Yes, sir.>

<Good. Be sure to put a neural restraint on him. He's a bit combative.>

<Yes, sir.> Arthur paused diplomatically. <Sir, it has been three days since you've slept properly.>

Mechanus dismissed this with a wave. <Nonsense. I only need four hours' sleep a night, you know this.>

<You haven't slept *at all* in three days.>

<I'm in the middle of a fresh project. Several of them, in fact. I don't have time to sleep right now.>

Arthur's interface drone floated down to a point in Mechanus's direct line of sight. His monitor bore a generic frowny face that still managed to look mildly disapproving.

<What?> Mechanus asked.

<While I understand your desire to please her, running yourself ragged in pursuit of this new hobby will only lead to ruin.>

<It's... not a hobby!> Mechanus protested. <World conquest—*that's* a hobby, one I've been undertaking for the past decade, and I haven't heard you say a single cross word about it. But this... Julia may well be the key to unlocking my past, but I will need her help to do so. I can't do that unless I can prove to her that I'm not some horrible monster. This is a major project, Arthur—and I need to devote every resource to it.>

<Sir—>

<Now, finish making the improvements to Jim, and put him to work. I need to finish Julia's new companion as quickly as possible.>

Arthur was silent for several seconds.

<Very well, sir,> he said finally, and the interface drone floated away.

Mechanus barely noticed the drone's departure, so focused was he on the hybrid creation on the table before him. It was nearly complete.

Chapter **SIX**

The map of Shark Reef Isle that Arthur supplied to Julia came in a distressingly thick binder. Of course, it had no index or table of contents. Fortunately, Julia was patient—or stubborn, depending on the speaker—thanks to the many hours she'd spent studying for her medical degree, and within a couple of hours she'd found Laboratory 8, where she'd seen what was left of Jim. From there it was relative simplicity to locate her room. It wasn't labeled Guest Room—that would have been too easy, and in any case Arthur had said that Mechanus didn't get any guests—but it was marked with a small heart.

...O-kay.

One meal and two more hours' study later, Julia thought she might have found a possible route leading to an exterior door.

Measure twice, cut once, the sensible voice said. *Make sure that is what you think it is before running off.*

There was also the minor matter of patrols, in the form of robots and beast-men alike. She had to memorize the hell out of the route—and, by the looks of it, half a dozen alternate routes—to reassure herself that she could dodge the monsters that he had roaming the place.

And then there were the wolves. The *dire* wolves.

As she set about retracing the possible escape route—and associated hiding spots—for the thousandth time, she started to imagine how big these dire wolves would be.

She'd seen sled dogs that looked about as much like wolves as would likely be allowed in civilization, and guessed that a regular wolf would be about that big. For the dire wolves, she mentally scaled this up to about the size of a bear—comfortably big enough to be worrisome, but not ridiculously big.

And definitely not so big that an aluminum cane across the nose wouldn't make them think twice about eating her.

She hoped.

That still left getting off Shark Reef Isle and back to civilization.

Well, if she looked around she might be able to find a solution to that. If she could perform an emergency tracheotomy with the barrel of a ballpoint pen, she could fashion a serviceable boat in a pinch.

You don't even know which direction Hawaii is, said the sensible voice, drawing her up short.

Well. There was that.

So it was that she spent most of that night studying the map, memorizing nearby landmarks and resolving to find out what all the little symbols meant. After checking and rechecking the layout, she found that the corridors seemed to be arranged in concentric octagons, connected at regular and, to her relief, largely predictable intervals that would make finding her way around relatively simple.

Just like at the hospital, said the sensible voice. *It looks like a labyrinth at first, but once you get familiar with it...*

Of course, there were still the guard patrols to account for.

She woke the following morning facedown in the opened binder, having drooled on the East Wing of Level Twelve in her sleep. She sat up, her spine crackling and her neck aching from the awkward position, and her right foot numb from having it tucked under her left knee all night. She stretched it out, grunting at the sudden flood of pins and needles that filled her foot seconds later, and feeling her hip pop.

Note to self: don't do that again.

Presently the door opened to admit a thin, multi-jointed robot that appeared to be a cross between a stick insect and an IV stand, a multi-limbed, angular affair topped by a wedge-shaped head that put her in mind of a praying mantis, with large, luminous green eyes and a cluster of vertical slits where one might expect to find a mouth. It bore a covered tray from which vaguely breakfast-like smells wafted, set it on the small table in the middle of the room, executed a very complicated sort of bow, and left.

Julia investigated the tray and found bacon, fried eggs, and toast, though the eggs were about twice the size she would have expected from, say, chicken eggs. Well, she was in no state to worry about her cholesterol, and she needed to get up all the energy she could for her explorations, so she ate the offered breakfast, super-eggs and all.

Once she'd finished, she checked the door. As before, it was unlocked, so she poked her head out and looked up and down the hallway. The mechanical purring of machinery was louder in the hallway, especially now that she wasn't in the presence of the little humming drone that Arthur seemed to inhabit. The floor was impeccably clean, and still ice cold under her bare feet. This latter observation reminded her that she would need to bargain with Mechanus for a pair of shoes if she was going to leave.

She listened as hard as she could to hear any movement above the background noise, and the vise of anxiety slowly clamped itself down over her heart.

This is a bad idea, she thought, and it was definitely not the sensible voice that had been giving her advice up till now. This was the twitchy little rat in her mind that told her that breaking up with Jim would be more trouble than it was worth, that you don't want to ruin your vacation by disappointing him. Usually she listened to the rat voice, as it led to a minimum of conflict, especially between her and Jim.

Well, by most standards their vacation was already ruined. She was the prisoner of a mad scientist and Jim might as well be dead. Apparently the rat voice wanted her to stay exactly where she was because doing something about it was *risky*. The rat voice hated risk and preferred to avoid conflict as much as possible.

Clearly, the rat voice wasn't going to be helpful in this setting.

"Screw you, rat voice," Julia whispered, and she grabbed her cane and ventured out into the corridor.

She figured she had two, maybe three hours before her next meal arrived, at which point her absence would be noted. It sounded like a long time to scavenge possible supplies and learn the Tau of MacGyver to make something out of them, but without any way to reliably judge the passage of time, her prospects were dicey at best—and she still had to avoid any guard patrols, or else Mechanus would put a stop to things.

Up ahead, she heard someone approaching along a side passage, accompanied by a click-clack like the toenails of a very large dog against a hardwood floor. She pressed herself against the wall and held her breath.

I told you this was a bad idea, sneered the rat voice.

Julia forced herself to remain still as the owner of the toenails passed by, revealing that it was more along the lines of a bear than a dog, huge, hulking, and shaggy, with jaws that looked like they could crush her head like a cantaloupe. The nails she heard clicking on the floor were six-inch-long, scythe-like claws, found on both its hands and its feet. It advanced to the middle of the intersection and paused, looking around as Julia, caught in what felt more and more like an ineffectual hiding place was close enough to smell the thing's breath. She tried to make herself as small and unnoticeable as possible.

Any moment, she thought, the thing was going to turn and see her—

Please God don't let it look this way let it go the other way please—

The bear-thing turned and headed away from her, and she silently let out a slow breath.

Bite me, she told the rat voice, swallowing hard. *I'm not dead yet.*

The rat voice fell into sullen silence, and she crept down the hallway in the direction the shaggy bear-thing had come from. Her bare feet made next to no noise on the metal floor as she moved, and she strained her hearing for any further sounds of people approaching as she peered in one window after another, looking out for either supplies to grab or minions to avoid.

The air in the complex was almost unsettling by its lack of organic smells; even the usually-sterile environment of the emergency room offered, alongside the odors of antiseptics and industrial cleaner, the smell of sweaty, unwashed people and various bodily fluids. Here, the sheer olfactory artificiality made the place feel like nothing *real* lived there. In a way, she supposed, this was accurate; everything that lived here, Mechanus had made.

After about an hour of exploration, Julia was about to turn and head back to her room when, through one of the windows, she saw a black box sitting on a table, apparently left there by a careless minion. She tried a nearby door, and it opened. She pushed the door open with a soft hiss of pneumatic hinges, and investigated the box. It appeared to be made of plastic, and was about the size of a paperback novel. Inside she found a roll of gauze, a roll of white medical tape, a pump-action spray bottle labeled 'For cleaning wounds', a suture kit in a case, and a small pair of scissors.

She chewed her lip. All of this could definitely be useful, especially if she encountered those dire wolves—assuming she managed to get away. At the same time, though, she probably wasn't going to be able to conceal the whole thing very well if she wanted to try to slip away while, for example, Arthur was taking her from Point A to Point B.

She knew she didn't have time to debate all the pros and cons of each item. She picked up the antiseptic spray first; at the very least she might be able to spray it in something's eyes as a deterrent. Next she grabbed the suture kit and checked it. Forceps, three curved needles, nylon sutures, and a scalpel with a guard on the blade. All of these could be useful—especially if used creatively. She put everything away in the case and tucked it carefully in the waistband of her pants. She also took the antiseptic spray, likewise concealing it.

How much time had she spent here? Certainly no more than ten minutes, but there was no way to be sure. She arranged the hem of her shirt over her ill-gotten goods and glanced out the viewing window. She caught movement—someone approaching—and ducked down below the sill. At first all she heard was her own breathing. She held her breath, listening hard for any sign that the creature in question was either about to enter, or moving on. It walked past the window in great lumbering strides, and then paused and opened the door.

It swung inward, and for a few heart-pounding moments she lost sight of the creature. It entered the room, made a beeline for the first-aid kit—silently she cursed herself for not having time to close it up again—and picked it up, closing the case with a click that sounded like a gunshot to her adrenaline-flooded ears. She jumped, clamping a hand over her mouth so she wouldn't scream.

Her lungs were starting to burn from holding her breath, but she dared not move, clutching her loot to her chest so hard her knuckles had gone white. The creature—a wolf-monster—turned and left without so much as glancing at her. The door closed.

Only then did she exhale, feeling light-headed from fear and hypoxia.

Okay. Time to go.

She started back towards her room at the quietest jog she could manage.

***

<There,> Mechanus said, a note of satisfaction in his voice. Julia's new companion was finally assembled—no longer a random assortment of relevant components, but a cohesive whole, wanting only a jolt to start its heart. <Do you think she'll like it, Arthur?>

<Unknown, sir. I am not aware of many women who would enjoy a chimera as a gift.>

<Well, I worked hard on it. In fact, I completed it ahead of schedule. I do believe I've outdone myself.>

<By forgoing sleep. Again.>

Mechanus waved off Arthur's concerns. <Sleep is a minor inconvenience when I'm in the middle of a project like this. It wastes time better spent doing other things.>

<You could have had the chimera auto-built by the surgical robots.>

<And neglect the personal touch a gift like this requires? Balderdash. It's been a while since I've taken the privilege of doing so, and it's been remarka-

bly bracing.> He stretched, feeling his right shoulder pop. <Now—let's wake him up, shall we?>

He threw a nearby switch. Electricity coursed through the electrodes embedded in the newly-created chimera's flesh, including several arranged around its sternum and just below the ribcage. The chimera bucked on the table, arching its back and letting out a braying scream. Mechanus dodged out of the way as its hooves kicked wildly.

"Easy there," he said as his latest creation caught its breath. Its eyes darted around wildly before finally fixing on Mechanus. He smiled at the chimera. "How are you feeling?"

The chimera snorted unhappily, and then lifted its new hands to examine them. It looked down at the rest of itself, and its ears flattened in fresh alarm.

"It's all right. I've given you new life, and a new purpose. Do you understand me? Nod if you do."

The chimera nodded its head.

"I made you to be a very special gift for a dear friend of mine. Her name is Julia, and you are to be her companion."

The chimera nodded again, and let out a quiet whicker of comprehension.

"Good boy. I knew you'd understand." Mechanus scratched the chimera's ears, and it half-closed his eyes in cautious delight. "Now, let's get you on your feet so you can get used to bipedalism, shall we? Up you go." A cluster of robot arms grasped the chimera's shoulders and thighs and eased it upright. Initially, it was as wobbly as a newborn foal, but Mechanus knew his work well, and soon enough it was taking its first uncertain steps. Mechanus steepled his hands in front of his face as he looked on his latest creation with fatherly pride.

<I never quite get used to that,> he beamed, feeling light-headed from the endorphins surging through his tissues. <Arthur, this calls for a celebration. Kindly inform Julia that I would like to have lunch with her today, and that her new pet has been completed ahead of schedule. I can hardly wait to show it to her.> The chimera toddled over to him, and he rubbed its velvety nose.

<As you wish, sir,> Arthur replied.

Just then, a wolf-man approached Mechanus bearing a first aid kit in a black case. He whimpered as Mechanus glanced over at him.

"Yes, Romulus?" he asked. "What seems to be the problem?"

Romulus opened the case and showed him the supplies inside. Mechanus frowned as he consulted his files for the expected contents, and then heaved a long-suffering sigh.

"Yes, I can see that there are items missing. Somebody probably rifled it rather than go to the nearest supply depot for what they needed." He frowned harder. "But what they would need a suture kit for is anyone's guess." <Arthur,> he added, slipping seamlessly into the digital link. <A suture kit and a bottle of antiseptic seem to have walked off. See if anyone has suffered any embarrassing injuries recently that they might not want me to know about.>

<I will do so, sir.>

<And get replacements for the missing items.>

<As you wish, sir.>

Arthur fell silent for a few moments as Mechanus watched Julia's pet get used to walking around. After a bit, the new chimera decided to try running, and the clip-clop of its hooves filled the laboratory.

<Sir?>

<Yes, Arthur?>

<Miss Julia is not responding,> he replied.

It took a few seconds for this news to register. <Say that again?>

<She is not responding,> he replied a second time.

Mechanus sighed, and mentally tapped into the speaker. "Julia, my darling?"

No response. He peered into the camera, which afforded him a flawless view of the entire room where Julia was staying. She was not in immediate view.

Mechanus sighed. "Julia, I understand if you are still upset about Jim. I really do. Like I said in my note, you won't be seeing him anymore. Now, I know that you're not the sort of woman to sulk about things beyond both of our control, so please, come out where I can see you."

Still nothing. Mechanus chewed on his thumbnail. After a few moments, he tapped into the speaker in the bathroom. "Julia?" he whispered to see if she was there.

He heard heavy breathing. Finally:

"Yes?"

Mechanus smiled. "Ah. There you are. I was starting to get worried about you."

"I'm fine," she said, but there was a strange, breathless note in her voice that Mechanus could not quite decipher.

"Nothing's the matter, I hope? No further bad experiences with my assistants?"

"No," she said shortly. "Nothing's the matter. Did you want something?"

Mechanus raised his eyebrow. She'd never been cross with him before, but then again she'd only been his guest for a few days.

"Yes, actually," he said. "Your pet is ready—quite ahead of schedule, if you recall—and I would like you to join me for lunch to celebrate. Afterwards I can introduce you to him. How does that sound?"

There was a long silence. Mechanus briefly wished that there was a camera in the bathroom—but then scolded himself for even briefly entertaining the idea that he should violate a woman's privacy. No. He would give her that much, at least.

"I... can do that," she said finally.

"Excellent. I will be by in an hour to collect you."

"Okay. See you then."

She didn't sound terribly enthusiastic, but then again she'd had a bit of a shock the previous day. Well. Certainly his gift and a delightful lunch would cheer her up a bit.

"I look forward to it." Her tone was light, and he could easily imagine that lunch with him and receiving her new pet would be the first bright spots of her visit. And with that he smiled.

"Excellent. I shall see you then."

He removed himself from the speaker.

<Arthur,> he said.

<Sir?>

<Make arrangements for a lunch for two in an hour.>

<Where, sir?>

That briefly stopped Mechanus cold. He didn't really have much in the way of a dining room that he would deem suitable for receiving guests, because he'd simply never needed one up till recently.

He rubbed the pad of his thumb over his fingertips in hurried thought, and then glanced at his hand in surprise at the movement. His thumb slowed, and then stopped—but the gesture itself had felt oddly familiar. He clenched his fist. This was no need to be anxious about this.

After all, he was just taking a beautiful woman to lunch and giving her a gift. How hard would this be?

<Greenhouse Fourteen,> he said. <Make a space for us and set up the appropriate furniture.>

<And to eat, sir?>

Mechanus ran his hand over his mouth. Planning such a thing as a luncheon sounded so simple, but at the same time it was a simply delightful mental exercise.

<Tomato soup and grilled cheese sandwiches,> he said finally. <And iced tea.>

<Very good, sir. I shall begin making arrangements promptly.>

<Excellent. I have a number of things I wish to discuss with her.>

<Sir?>

<Mainly on the topic of recruiting her help in restoring my memories.> It was obvious, of course— she said she worked in emergency medicine. Part of that was psychiatric training. She would be perfect for this, and the fact that she was breathtakingly beautiful should make things even easier.

<You never seemed concerned about your memories before,> Arthur pointed out. <In fact, you believed them irrelevant to your projects.>

<Perhaps...> Mechanus conceded. <But then, I didn't start having flashbacks until she came here.>

<How do you plan to get her help, then?> Arthur asked.

<By asking, of course. Certainly she will see the benefits of providing aid to one in need—particularly if that one is her generous host.>

<She's terrified of you, sir.>

Mechanus blinked, and then frowned. <But I've given her everything she's asked for.>

<Allow me to explain, sir. She is currently on a remote island, far from anyone else she knows, with no clear way home, and her boyfriend has been turned into a cyborg.>

There was a long pause.

<Yes?> Mechanus prompted, not seeing where Arthur intended to go with this.

Arthur trilled out a digital sigh. <You will need to reassure her that you are not a frightening monster.>

<But... if she's afraid of me, then how—?>

<You could explain your feelings to her,> Arthur suggested.

Mechanus sighed. <That won't work at all. I barely understand them myself.>

<I believe she may be able to help you with that as well.>

Mechanus groaned and winced, his mind rebelling at the idea that there was a topic about which he knew next to nothing. What was worse, he knew of no reliable way to research it because it dealt almost entirely in intangibles.

Annoyed, he stripped off his rubber gloves and tossed them onto a nearby table. A robot arm extended from the ceiling with a fresh pair, and he pulled them on while mulling over the problem.

<This is going to require a surgeon's touch,> he concluded.

<And careful diplomacy,> Arthur added.

Mechanus winced again. Yet another field he would need to explore. He would start simply, however.

<Arthur, send her something to wear for our lunch meeting,> he decided.

<Any particular specifications, sir?>

Mechanus rubbed his chin. <A dress. Make it the color of her eyes.>

<As you wish, sir.>

Chapter
SEVEN

Julia couldn't stop washing her hands.

Her heart was still pounding from the narrow escape she had with the wolf-monster, and the idea that any moment now Mechanus was going to ask what she'd done with the things she took. When he'd contacted her in the bathroom she had only just gotten herself settled and the tap turned off—and now her nerves were jangling again.

The fact that he'd only asked her to lunch should have been a relief—but it meant she was going to have to go through with her half-cocked idea to be nice to him and build his trust.

The more she thought about it, the worse the idea seemed, and the dirtier her hands felt.

Stop this, the sensible voice said. *Stop washing your hands—they're already raw.*

"I can't," she whispered, her voice cracking with nerves.

You can, the sensible voice insisted. *Now turn off that spigot and dry your hands.*

"I can't. This is a bad idea. I can't." She bit her lip hard enough to hurt.

Yes, you can. He said himself that he wasn't going to hurt you. And if he does, well, you have a few things with which to defend yourself. Now take a deep breath and turn off the goddamn tap. Your hands are clean enough.

"But—"

Clean. Enough. Turn it off.

Julia pulled her hands out of the water as though it had suddenly turned boiling hot, and with shaking fingers she turned off the water. She gingerly dried her fingers, mindful of the raw spots, and wondered how she was going to conceal them. After all, if Mechanus saw them, he would wonder why they were there, and that would raise questions she didn't want to answer. Not right now. And definitely not to him.

He probably won't even notice, said the sensible voice.

And what if he does? returned the rat voice. *He'll know that you're damaged goods. You'll never be free of Jim, no matter how hard you try. He's left his mark on you.*

For a few shaky moments, Julia started to believe the rat voice. Jim had never said in so many words that she wasn't good enough for anyone else. As she turned over the rat voice's cutting remark she realized that over the years they'd been together, Jim had been methodically reshaping her into...

Into what? A perfectly obedient Stepford girlfriend? There was no way for her to know now, and she certainly wasn't going to ask him. The idea of confronting him about anything had always terrified her, and now that Jim was a deranged cyborg...

She shuddered.

"Miss Julia?" came Arthur's voice, interrupting her thoughts.

"Yes?" she said.

"Dr. Mechanus has sent over a dress for you to wear to lunch. Please come out of the bathroom and have a look at it," said Arthur.

Julia sighed. From a controlling asshole boyfriend to a crazy mad scientist with a crush. From the frying pan and straight into the fire—flash.

"I'll be right out," she said, and then deliberately waited to a count of thirty before emerging.

When she stepped out, she saw the stick-insect-coat-rack robot standing in her doorway, holding up a light blue dress in a perfect emulation of... well, an autonomous coat rack. At least Mechanus was still following her request not to send that shark-thing. What did he call it? Scarface?

Well, he also insisted that it was a sweetheart, so she supposed there was no accounting for taste.

"Your dress, Miss Julia," the robot buzzed in a voice that sounded just like an electric shaver trying to talk. It sent a chill up her spine to hear such polite words rendered in such a clearly artificial voice.

"Just... just set it on the bed," Julia managed, not daring to step any closer to the insectile machine.

The robot carefully arranged the dress lengthwise on the bed, taking great care to smooth out the wrinkles. It then inclined its head to her in a weirdly humanlike gesture and departed.

Julia ventured forward and inspected the dress, feeling on some level like she should expect the thing to come alive. It didn't, of course.

Don't be silly, said the sensible voice. *Why would he give you a dress that would attack you?*

She wouldn't put it past him to make one anyway, just for the challenge.

She picked up the cane and poked the dress with it, to be certain. The garment did not respond, and Julia started to feel really stupid for thinking it would.

Told you, said the sensible voice.

"Fine," she whispered. She picked up the dress— it seemed to be made of very soft cotton and was nearly weightless in her arms—and retreated to the bathroom to change.

What do you plan to do if he starts to think you genuinely enjoy his company? asked the rat voice. *What then? This stupid plan of yours will only encourage him, and then you'll be stuck.*

"It's not like I have much of a choice right now," she murmured as she changed into the dress. "I'm already stuck. It's just a question of how stuck am I."

And how long do you suppose it will take you to figure this out? the rat voice sniffed.

She didn't know.

She zipped up the dress, which—as she had come to expect by now—fit her perfectly. She looked herself over in the mirror.

Julia wasn't sure she could say she looked nice, because despite how pretty the dress was and how well it fit her, she herself still looked like she imagined a kidnapping victim to look—pale, hollow-eyed, and generally like someone who was here against her will—and that, combined with the nice dress, just looked *creepy*! It was like every movie she'd seen where the damsel in distress is dressed up by the villain in a possible prelude to having his way with her.

That put a really dark spin on her upcoming lunch, and she shuddered.

He has *been polite to you this whole time,* said the sensible voice.

Means nothing, said the rat voice. *He could be buttering you up for something.*

"Hush, both of you," Julia whispered, and started combing her hair. "I'll see what he wants and go from there."

Half an hour later, the door chimed. Julia jumped, despite her mental preparations.

Showtime.

"Yes?" she asked, hoping her voice didn't sound as shaky as she felt,

"I'm here to take you to lunch," Mechanus said over the speaker.

She took a deep breath, trying to will herself to be calm. This was just like her job interview at the hospital. No problem.

"Come in, Doctor," she called, and stood up, crossing to the door to meet him.

The door opened, revealing Mechanus in one of his now-familiar lab coats, but this time the plates in his face were polished to a nearly chrome-like sheen. He offered a gloved hand to her, and after a moment of uncertainty, she took it. He smiled, and the lens in his mechanical eye dilated. Only then did she notice the dark circles under his other eye, as though he hadn't slept well. She knew the rigors of sleep deprivation well.

"Are... you okay?" she ventured. It was a silly question, in the grand scheme of things—of *course* he wasn't okay, there were so many things about him that weren't okay—but she hadn't taken up medicine because she was coldhearted.

His brow furrowed. "Whatever do you mean?"

"You, uh, you've got dark circles under your... eye. Have you been sleeping okay?" She gestured vaguely at her own right eye. She wasn't even sure why she was so worried about this. If he wanted to work on his weird little projects until he passed out, that was ultimately on him... but it still wasn't healthy, regardless of his mental baseline.

"Oh, that. I've been working hard on a number of projects," he dodged. "And in any case I don't need as much sleep as most people do."

"Well... maybe," she conceded, "But you look like you haven't slept at all in days."

"I... suppose I haven't," he said, sounding a bit distracted. "I've had a great many things on my mind. More so than usual these days, actually. In fact, I would like to discuss some of them with you over lunch. Let us be off, shall we?" He looked her over and offered her a genial smile. "You're looking lovely, as always, Julia."

She froze as he bent over her hand as though to kiss the back of it—but then he stopped, frowning. She bit her lip. He'd seen the raw skin on her hand—she was certain of it.

"What happened here?" he asked quietly.

"I..." What could she say? *You scare the shit out of me so I washed my hands until I almost drew blood?*

He looked up at her expectantly, looking concerned.

"It's... an anxiety thing," she said finally. She didn't like how her voice shook, but he was *right there* and holding her hand like everything about the situation was perfectly normal and—

"Compulsive hand-washing?" he asked.

She nodded, staring at her bare toes.

"I still frighten you, don't I?" he said quietly.

She looked back up at his face and said nothing. He sighed, released her hand, and straightened up, looking away from her as though he'd just seen something intensely interesting on the floor three feet to her left.

"Well, that's going to make things a bit difficult for what I want to talk about over lunch." He coughed delicately. "I trust we are still on for that, at least?"

She hesitated, but then nodded. She didn't see any alternative, really—and his sudden change in body language from *I am the master of my domain* to *I'm about to do something that's really going to suck* made her curious. This arrogant cyborg super-genius, possibly out of his depth? The idea was strangely humanizing.

This, she had to see.

"Lead the way," she said, satisfied that her voice was now perfectly level.

"Excellent," he said, his voice strangely subdued, and he offered his hand to her again. She took it without hesitation this time, and he led her down the corridor. "And let us dispense with the formalities, shall we? You may call me Alistair."

"Okay..." she ventured. "Alistair."

He smiled, a slight flush rising in the right side of his face.

Here we go, she thought.

***

Here we go, Mechanus thought, taking a deep breath.

<Okay, you might have a point about getting more rest,> he told Arthur.

<She noticed it immediately, sir,> Arthur pointed out, too polite to say *I told you so* in so many words.

<On the other hand, she did express concern, and she's still going to lunch with me, so I believe that I am still making progress.> He chewed his lip. <But I am becoming increasingly aware that I may be a bit rusty as far as social interactions go.>

<Relax, sir,> Arthur advised him. <I am not aware of any significant social obligations that go with lunch.>

<That's not what worries me, Arthur,> Mechanus returned. <I'm about to ask for her help. She could very well refuse. She still appears to be afraid of me.>

<She wouldn't be holding your hand if she were truly afraid of you, sir. Just be yourself.>

<I think that's the problem.>

He heard another digital trill as Arthur sighed in exasperation.

<Administering light sedative.>

<No—wait—>

He felt a knot in the muscles of his right shoulder suddenly unclench.

<Better?> Arthur inquired.

Mechanus exhaled slowly. <Yes. Thank you.>

He led Julia to Greenhouse Fourteen, where Arthur had assured him that preparations were complete for their lunch.

Julia stopped in the doorway, pulling her hand out of Mechanus's. He turned to see what the matter was, and saw that she was looking past him, open-mouthed, at the collection of plants on display. Mechanus followed her gaze in momentary confusion; he'd seen the flowers a thousand times before, and could easily look up the scientific name of every single specimen here and in the other two dozen greenhouses he had. He had detailed files about each specimen, after all.

It occurred to him that he ought to say something.

"This is..." he began. No. Not quite right. He cleared his throat. "Welcome to Greenhouse Fourteen." There. Much better.

"I'm just... surprised you have something like this here," Julia said. "I mean, everything else has been so..." She fell silent.

"So...?" Mechanus prompted.

"Industrialized."

"Well, food has to come from somewhere," he pointed out. "You can only do so much by replicating proteins and complex sugars, and my chimeras don't seem to like the nutrient slurries at all. I grow fruits and vegetables in greenhouses like this one, as well as grains and medicinal plants that I've gathered from all over the world." He took her hand and led her on into the greenhouse. "For example, did you know that there are over two hundred species of plant that have the potential to cure cancer?"

"I was talking about the flowers, but cancer cures are impressive, too."

Idiot. Of *course* the flowers. Women liked flowers. "If you enjoy them," he said, recovering with what he deemed sufficient grace, "I could give you one of my greenhouses. They're self-maintaining, each with their own crew of maintenance drones who will ensure that they will remain healthy and green for the foreseeable future."

"Um... thank... you?" She looked more confused by his gift than anything else, as though she expected the azaleas to attack her. That was silly, of course—carnivorous azaleas were never on his list of projects. The spinescent plants would make much better herbaceous guardians, once he figured out how to make them mobile.

A small table for two had been set up in a large area of floor created by a lot of creative shifting of planter boxes. Arthur had insisted upon surrounding the eating area with yellow tulips for some reason, though he didn't explain why.

"Here we go," Mechanus said, pulling one of the chairs out for Julia. "Our food should arrive in a few minutes."

She sat, perching herself on the edge of the seat. Mechanus chewed his lip.

"Do try to relax," Mechanus said. "I swear I don't bite."

She looked up at him doubtfully, but after a moment of hesitation she shifted herself back in the chair. He pushed it in and seated himself opposite her, interlacing his gloved fingers on the table in front of him. She sat with her hands in her lap, her gaze focused somewhere near the center of the table.

The silence crawled.

Mechanus cleared his throat. "I'm... not great with small talk," he said. Julia looked up at him questioningly. "Lack of practice, you see."

"Arthur says you've been here ten years," she said quietly.

"Yes. You're..." He cleared his throat again. "You're the first human company I've had in all that time."

"That must have been hard," she said.

She wasn't *wrong*, exactly, but he hadn't known what he'd been lacking until Julia had arrived. He nodded.

"What did you do before then?" she asked.

"That's the problem with which I was hoping you might help me. I remember... next to nothing before I came to Shark Reef Isle. As far as I can recall, I've always been... like this." He gestured to himself, and then took a deep breath. His cardiac pump was working double-time in his chest, and he could feel the blood roaring in his ears. "Which leads up to what I wanted to ask you."

This wasn't the entire truth, of course—he had a thousand things he wanted to tell her, but his mind shied away from vocalizing many of them.

You're beautiful, he thought. "You... fascinate me," he said. "You're the first human being in a long time to come here, and since you came here I've been having... flashbacks, or visions, or whatever you want to call them. Possibly memories of who I was before."

I need you, he thought. "I need your help," he said. "These visions seem to be triggered whenever I interact with you, so... perhaps you will be able to find a way to unlock my past."

You make me whole, he thought. "You... remind me what it was like to be human, rather than this... *admittedly very functional* amalgam of flesh and metal. If you help me, perhaps I might be able to... ah... heal properly."

She stared at him for the better part of a minute. During this time, Romulus came by with two trays of food, set them before Mechanus and Julia, removed the covers, and left. The smell of grilled cheese and tomato soup caressed his nostrils, and he realized that it had been a long time since he'd eaten a prepared meal rather than the aforementioned nutrient slurries.

Finally, she glanced away from him, looking down at her food.

"I... should be able to do that," she said quietly. "I'm a doctor, after all. I'm supposed to help others."

Relief and triumph washed over Mechanus in equal volumes, tempered only by the lack of enthusiasm in her voice. A hundred thousand possible grateful responses flooded him, and he fairly choked on all of them save one.

"Thank you," he whispered. He glanced down at his lunch, acknowledging its presence for the first time. "Let us discuss further details of this arrangement while we eat, shall we?" He gestured to both meals. "I thought you might want something more familiar, so... tomato soup and grilled cheese sandwiches."

She took a tentative bite from one corner of her sandwich, chewed, and swallowed. "It's good, but..."

He raised his eyebrow. "But?"

"Do you keep dairy cows here or something?"

He frowned at this apparent non sequitur. "No... they would require a great deal of grazing land—why?"

She regarded her sandwich for a few seconds, a mild expression of confusion forming. "In that case, where on Earth did you get the cheese? I know you didn't get this from a grocery store."

"Oh! Is that all?" He smiled, taking up a spoonful of his tomato soup. "It was a fairly simple matter, really, of replicating the appropriate milk proteins, adding the rennet, and—"

She put her hands up, palms out, a smile twitching at the corners of her mouth. "Okay, okay. I should have known better than to ask how a mad scientist makes cheese."

He tilted his head slightly. "You... consider me a mad scientist?"

She flushed, dropping her soup spoon back into the bowl with a small *splish*. "I'm—I'm sorry—" she stammered. "I didn't mean to offend—"

He enfolded her hand between both of his own, and she fell silent immediately, staring at his hands.

"It's all right," he said gently. "It's as accurate a term as any, really." He glanced at their hands, his cardiac pump skipping a cycle, and then back up at her face. "I will concede that by most baseline standards, I'm quite insane. Mad as a bag of cats, really. I would have to be, to want to take over the world—and I think that frees me from a lot of the constraints of other men of science. I can... imagine the world I want, and the means to accomplish what must seem like a ludicrously lofty goal."

Her gaze flicked from their hands to his face; her expression was a mask of tightly controlled unease.

"But," she said, "why do you want to take over the world?"

He stroked her fingers, trying to soothe her anxiety. "I want what I think most people want—a better world. A better place for people to live and work and thrive. I want people who are sick to be able to get cured, without worrying about the cost of the treatment. I want doctors—people like you—to be able to do their jobs without having to answer to a board of bankers who worry more about finances than medicine. I—" His throat suddenly closed, choking off his next words, though he couldn't say exactly why. Something about that last statement had sent a spike of ice down the back of his neck.

"Alistair?" Julia said, from approximately a hundred miles away. "Alistair, are you okay?"

"I…" he choked out, searching his mind frantically for the cause of his reaction. He felt chilled, like he'd just been dropped into an ice bath, but whatever lost memory may have prompted it did not surface, instead remaining stubbornly in the miasma of amnesia.

She touched his cheek then, her hand warm and comforting against his skin. He forced himself to focus on her, and saw that her previous anxiety had given way to concern.

"Hey," she said quietly. "Are you okay?"

He ran his tongue across his dry lips. "I… think so," he managed. "I just… I don't know what came over me just then. It was so strange…" He took a deep breath. "I think I'm okay now."

Her eyes suddenly flicked a few degrees to the side. Her breath caught, and he saw the color drain from her face.

Mechanus closed his eyes and heaved a long-suffering sigh. *Of course,* he thought. *I'm finally making meaningful progress, and she sees something scary standing behind me.*

He tapped into one of the security drones patrolling the greenhouse and piloted it over to check the area behind him.

It was Jim. His face was still slack with the same concussed expression, but his eyes blazed.

Damnation.

<Dammit Arthur!> Mechanus snarled. <I thought I made it quite clear I wanted Jim kept far away from Julia!>

<Sir, Jim was assigned to Sector Six.>

<Then *why* is he currently standing thirty feet behind me?>

<He appears to be staring at Julia.>

<I can *see* that, but why is he not in Sector Six?>

<Unknown, sir. He is still actively fighting his commands.>

Mechanus inhaled slowly through his nose and opened his eyes, seeing that he was still clasping her hand. "Julia," he said slowly. "You needn't be afraid. I will take care of this. Finish your lunch, and I will rejoin you shortly."

He released her hand and drew away from her, privately regretting the loss of her touch. He stood up briskly and turned to face Jim, blocking his rival's immediate view of Julia. Jim's focus shifted, but the expression didn't change one bit.

"Jim," Mechanus said, reaching through the neural link into Jim's mind. "You are not supposed to be here. You will go back to Sector Six immediately, is that understood?"

Mechanus flexed his mental control, and Jim staggered.

"What are you doing?" Julia half-whispered behind him.

"He's not supposed to be in this part of the complex," Mechanus said. "I saw how much he upset you, so I arranged for him to be assigned somewhere very far away. I'm just getting him back where he's supposed to be."

"How much does he remember?"

Mechanus bit his lip, knowing the truth, but then came to a decision. "Next to nothing."

He heard her let out a relieved breath behind him, and suddenly felt like a bit of a cad.

"Jim," he said, forcing his voice to remain steady. "You *will* go back to your station in Sector Six. Is that understood?"

Jim's lip curled again, and abruptly the sense of mental resistance vanished as Jim turned and walked away.

Well. That could have been a lot worse.

He turned back to face her with what he judged to be a reassuring smile. "See?" he said brightly. "Nothing to fear. Shall we finish lunch, then?" With that, he sat across from her once more.

Her tentative smile was enough at that moment to make him feel like a knight in a lab coat.

Chapter
EIGHT

At this point, Julia was willing to admit that Alistair Mechanus wasn't the scariest thing living on Shark Reef Isle. That didn't make him completely *not* scary, but there was something about a man asking for help that tended to get past her defenses. Then he'd locked up when talking about his plans for global conquest. She wasn't sure she'd ever seen such a haunted look on anyone's face before—and in her line of work that was saying something.

Then there was that expression on the face of that thing that used to be Jim. *That* sent a chill down her spine. Mechanus said he didn't remember anything, but...

She shoved the thought into the back of her mind as she ate her lunch. It was pretty good, even if the cheese came about through a science experiment. She decided not to ask about the bread.

"Enjoying your lunch?" Mechanus asked.

She nodded. "I am." She took another bite of sandwich to prove it.

"Good. I... apologize for Jim. I specifically requested that he be kept away from you, but—"

"Don't worry about it," she said. In truth, she would rather not have seen him again. "So, what did you have in mind as far as getting your memories back?"

"You're the doctor," he returned. "What would *you* recommend?"

She made a face. "I'm not that kind of doctor."

"But you studied emergency medicine," he pointed out, "which covers many different fields—including psychiatry."

She sighed. "Under normal circumstances, I would recommend hypnotherapy—a field that is *not* one of my specialties—but these aren't exactly normal circumstances, are they?"

He glanced away. "No. They're not. Everything I know is here. I can't leave. Not until I'm done."

"Which eliminates most of the ideas I have... leaving only trying to find out what the cause was."

He sighed. "And of course, if I knew *that*, I'd know what happened to me."

She nodded. In all likelihood, the triggering event was locked up in the same place the rest of his previous life was—out of reach.

"Well," he said, "We must make do with what we have, correct?" Julia heard a strange, rhythmic squeaking noise, and glanced in that direction to find that he was rubbing the pad of his right thumb over the corresponding fingertips in a strange nervous gesture. The squeaking was from the rubber of his glove. She hadn't seen him fidgeting before.

"What's that?" she asked, nodding towards his hand.

He followed her gaze, and shortly afterwards, his hand stopped fidgeting.

"I'm not sure," he said. "It... just started recently. I don't know where it's from."

"How recently?"

He looked her in the eyes. "Since you came. The same with the flashbacks. I only started having them the first time I saw you."

She chewed her lip thoughtfully. That would have been, what, three or four days ago? "It's a start," she said. Of course, all she would have to do is pretend that he was any other patient, and...

Yeah Right.

"Is there anything you require in order to help me?" Mechanus asked.

"Shoes," she said, without hesitation; if she had something on her feet, going outside would be less dicey. She felt a guilty pang at this thought, though; under the new circumstances it sounds suspiciously like she was planning to abandon a patient, which she absolutely was *not* going to do.

He raised his eyebrow. "Just shoes?" he asked.

Her mind raced. "Well... we'll also need a quiet room to work in..."

He nodded. "I have plenty of rooms that can be cleared out."

"Someplace comfortable where we can sit and talk."

"Yes. I have furniture that we can use."

"And we'll need to find out how much you *do* remember."

He was silent.

"Including talking about these flashbacks you mentioned."

Presently, the wolf-man returned and took their empty dishes, as discreet as a well-trained waiter.

Squeak, squeak, squeak went Mechanus's gloved fingers.

"I will... procure the items you have requested," he said, the right side of his face carefully schooled back into neutrality. "But first, I would like to show you the... the gift I made for you."

With that, he leapt from his chair and pulled her to her feet. Julia was left scrambling, so quickly had his attention skittered away from the topic of his past.

"Wait!" she protested. "I thought you—"

"Later," he interrupted. "I'll get you the things you require, and then we can begin the process, but first I want to show you your new companion. I worked very hard on him." And with that he was off, pulling Julia along by the hand and striding so fast on his long legs that she had to jog to keep up.

"Wait—!" she protested again, but he wasn't listening anymore.

Get control of the situation, Jules, the sensible voice cautioned.

Right. Easier said than done. Well, nothing ventured and all that.

"*Stop!*" she commanded, digging in her heels and pulling her hand free. She was aiming for an authoritative bark, but her bark was less mastiff and more teacup Chihuahua in register.

He trotted to a halt and turned to look back at her. He looked honestly confused. "What?" he asked.

She took a deep breath. "Look. If you want me to help you get your memories back we're going to have to concentrate on that for... more than two minutes at a time."

An expression of sudden anxiety flickered across his mismatched features.

"I... know it's going to be scary," she continued. "These things typically are. But you're never going to get through them if you avoid them."

That was when Mechanus checked out entirely. The right half of his face suddenly went slack, and his right thumb started rubbing furiously across his fingertips.

"Shit!" she hissed, and then turned her head to address the ceiling. "Arthur! Are you there?"

"Yes, Miss Julia. What seems to be the matter?"

"Something's wrong with Dr. Mechanus. I need a penlight."

"I will get you your penlight directly."

She turned back to Mechanus, whose condition hadn't changed. If he passed out or his legs let go, she didn't know if she would be able to control his fall.

Probably not.

"And bring someone strong enough to lift him if he collapses," she added.

"Affirmative, Miss Julia."

The stick-insect robot arrived less than a minute later and handed her the penlight. She shone the penlight into his right eye, flicking it away every few seconds to test his pupil reactions. That eye seemed fine—but then she realized that this might not work effectively on his mechanical eye. So much for checking for brain damage. She tried it anyway, for the sake of completeness, and found the mechanical iris to be just as reactive as its organic counterpart.

Okay. *Probably* no brain damage. It seemed to be just an absence seizure of some sort, but even those required supervision in case of complications.

"Miss Julia?" Arthur said, this time from behind her. She turned and saw the interface drone floating there, displaying a generic frowny-face.

"I... think he'll be okay, as long as this doesn't last more than a few minutes." She glanced at the stick-insect robot, realized that she had no clue what to call it, and decided to improvise. "Stickman and I will watch over him to be sure."

"Very good, Miss Julia. While we are waiting, I wish to speak with you." The frowny-face flicked to a flat-mouthed neutral face.

"Okay... about what?"

The Arthur-drone floated down slightly so that it was level with her face. "What are your intentions towards my master?"

"I...*what?*" The question seemed to be completely out of left field, the sort of thing a protective father would ask the prospective boyfriend of his teenaged daughter.

"Answer the question, please."

Julia sighed and crossed her arms; she didn't want to have this sort of conversation with a metal football, especially not right now. "First tell me what brought this on."

"Of course, Miss Julia," Arthur replied politely. "I am aware that you were wandering the corridors earlier today, and that you absconded with a few items from a first aid kit."

Julia's blood froze. *Shit.* Of *course* Arthur would have seen her.

"I am also aware," Arthur continued, "That leaving here has been foremost in your mind for the duration of your stay."

"D... does he know?" Julia managed to ask, swallowing the urge to bolt.

"He does not. I have not told him."

"Why not?" she asked.

"Because, Miss Julia, I have known him for ten years. I have been his only friend for that entire interval, and I am dedicated to seeing that his needs are met, whether they are as a conversational companion or as an assistant in running the complex. He is deeply in love with you, Miss Julia, and has been ever since he first laid eyes upon you. He would do anything to make you happy, and wishes only to see you smile. I believe your presence has overall been a positive influence on him, so much so that he has not been paying as much attention to his plans for world conquest as a result." Arthur paused to let her digest this information. "That said, if you break his heart, I will disassemble you without hesitation."

Her heart clenched in dread. Arthur's voice hadn't changed at all from its artificially calm politeness, nor the generic face from its neutral expression, but Julia had absolutely no doubt that he meant it.

Shit. Shit shit shit.

"Do we have an understanding?" Arthur asked.

"Yes," she squeaked.

"Wake up," Mechanus suddenly whispered.

Julia looked back up at him, and found an expression of urgency starting to creep into the cyborg's face.

"Wake up," he said again, louder, and suddenly grabbed Julia's forearm.

"What—?" she started.

"Wake up!" he shouted, and he now wore an expression of true terror. "Wake up—please, honey, you have to wake up—I... I can't move—you need to get out!" He started shaking Julia's arm, gently at first. "Please—I... I think the car's on fire! For God's sake, wake up! Please!" He shook Julia's arm more violently, and anguish half-choked his next words. "Wake up! Wake up—please, can you hear me? Honey, can y—can you move? Please! Can you hear me?"

"Hey!" Julia called, trying to snap him out of whatever sort of flashback he was having. "Hey, you're hurting me!"

He released her instantly, his right arm curling up so his hand covered that side of his face, while his left arm continued to hang passively by his side. His breath came in ragged gasps. The rictus of helpless terror on his face alarmed her, and her mind raced, searching for a way to snap him out of whatever sort of attack this was.

"His adrenaline levels are spiking," Arthur observed.

Julia had no time to think. She remembered a technique that one of her colleagues had used in the ER, during one of Julia's own flashbacks.

She reached up, seized his face—warm flesh under one hand, cold metal under the other—and forced him to face her. His eyes remained unfocused, his mind still locked in whatever hell he saw.

"Alistair," she said gently. "Alistair, look at me."

His eyes finally focused on her; the pupil of the right one dilated so that only the barest ring of green remained, while the mechanical iris of the left twitched and whirred jerkily.

"Alistair, you're safe. You're not trapped anywhere. You're safe at home on Shark Reef Isle, in Sector...?" She looked at Arthur, who was still giving her that unnervingly generic neutral face.

"Nineteen," he supplied.

She nodded and looked back at Mechanus. "In Sector Nineteen. Arthur's here, and I'm here. You're safe. Nothing can hurt you right now. Do you understand me?"

He let out a shallow, quivering breath, and after a few seconds his iris finally contracted to a more relaxed size. He started to shake—at least his right arm did; the rest of him remained rock steady—and he slowly reached up to clasp her wrists with both hands. Shame and gratitude warred on his face, and he dropped his gaze, looking absolutely everywhere but at her.

"Are you okay?" she asked quietly.

He nodded, still not looking at her. He took a long, shuddering breath, and released it slowly.

"I—" his voice caught. He cleared his throat and tried again. "Thank... you."

Jesus Christ. Were all his flashbacks going to be like this? If so, she was going to have to make sure to have preparations in place to handle the next one.

***

...Gah.

Of all the *damnable* times to have a flashback... but—

She stayed. She was the first thing he saw when his vision cleared, and he could have sworn he heard her voice while... while...

—pinned in the rumpled wreckage choking on the smell of gasoline fumes can't move can't feel my left arm what the hell happened to my legs PLEASE GOD GET HER OUT OF HERE—

He flinched from the fragment of memory, and looked at Julia again.

Thank you didn't even begin to cover it.

He glanced over at Arthur.

"Did you record that one?" he asked.

"Indeed I did, sir, per your instructions." Arthur frowned. "This one was, as they say, a doozy."

"You were screaming," Julia put in.

"What was I screaming?" Mechanus asked.

"You were... screaming for someone to wake up. That the car was on fire and someone needed to get out."

His artificial stomach executed a slow, sickening barrel roll. He closed his eye and swallowed hard to avoid disgracing himself. The image of the blonde woman, unconscious and buckled in next to him, was still seared into his mind's eye.

"Did I happen to say her name?" he asked.

"You... called her Honey," Julia offered.

He shook his head. That wasn't right—he knew it instinctively. He might have called her 'honey' as a pet name, but...

"Thank you, anyway," he said, straightening up and regretfully removing her hands from his face. <I'll go over the memory footage later,> he told Arthur. <Maybe I'll find some clue there.> Out loud, he added to Julia, "Now—about that companion I made you..."

"Are you sure?" she asked. "You still look... I don't know, kind of spooked."

"I'll be fine," he said, though at that point he wasn't sure how true it was. "We'll discuss the details later, once the arrangements you requested are in place. Agreed?" He held out his hand to her.

She nodded and took it. She looked a bit spooked herself, but then again she said he'd been screaming during his flashback.

Well. Enough about that for now.

<Arthur?> he asked. <I trust Julia's new companion is ready for her?>

<He is undergoing training in Room 14A,> Arthur informed him. <Anubis is putting him through his paces.>

<Good.> "He's just up ahead," he said to Julia.

"So... what sort of a companion is it?" she asked.

"A chimera of my own design," he said. "I assure you, he is very gentle and intelligent, with no... er, hard edges to worry about."

"Okay...?" she said, sounding uncertain.

"It's all right," he said, gently guiding her through the laboratory door—

—or trying to, as she did that stopping-short-without-warning thing again.

The chimera crouched in the middle of the room, having decided that hooves and knuckles offered the most comfortable posture as a compromise between the torso and arms of a lowlands gorilla and the head and hindquarters of a pony. He turned his head to look at Julia, ears alertly forward, and whickered a greeting.

Julia took a bit over a step back before she collided with Mechanus. He steadied her by the shoulders, suppressing a sigh of frustration at her lackluster reaction. He would *not* get annoyed over this. He refused. It would be counterproductive and he'd only just started to make some progress with her. Getting upset now would only compound the setback. She wasn't flinching away from Mechanus himself, though, which was *something*.

"It's okay," he reassured her. "He's quite friendly—see? He wants to say hello."

The horse-ape knuckled his way forward and extended one thick-fingered hand in wordless invitation to shake. Mechanus could feel Julia's heart hammering in her ribcage where she pressed against him, but she extended her own hand as well. The horse-ape's hand fairly swallowed her own, but he'd been trained well under Anubis's tutelage, and he slowly, carefully, shook her hand.

Julia let out a shaky little laugh as the horse-ape released her.

"He's..." she started, but fell silent.

"He's your new companion," Mechanus said. "He'll keep you company while you're in your room, and perform any task you request of him."

"He's... kind of cute," she said finally.

The horse-ape whinnied and clapped his hands, mirroring Mechanus's approximate internal triumphant reaction, which admittedly usually involved more thunder and lightning and manic laughter.

Success!

<Sir?> Arthur said.

<Yes, Arthur?> Mechanus replied, still giddy.

<I believe the problems with Jim may be compounding.>

Mechanus   sighed.   <Compounding? Compounding how?>

<Rampancy is at 80%, sir.>

Mechanus's blood ran cold. <How could he possibly still be fighting it?> he demanded. <I thought I suppressed his personality!>

<You did, sir. What's fighting is everything that's left.>

Mechanus considered this at length. <...Damnation,> he concluded.

"Anubis," he said. The jackal-man looked up alertly. "When Julia and her new pet are acquainted, take them back to her room. I have some urgent business to attend to."

Julia paused in stroking the horse-ape's nose and glanced over at him. "What's wrong?" she asked.

He froze. How could he put this so as not to cause her undue worry? After all, it should be a simple enough matter to rewire Jim to be more docile, maybe give him a proper lobotomy...

"A bit of a snag with one of my creations, that's all," he said lightly. "I should be done in time to join you for dinner."

She studied him for several seconds. Did she see something in his face that betrayed the lie? He couldn't tell.

"Oh," she said. "What did you have in mind for dinner, then?"

"Well, uh, just something formal for the two of us, really," he replied, mentally rifling through the available possibilities. "You seemed to enjoy the sea bass, so I figured I'd build something around that... maybe dancing later, if you want."

She pressed her lips together doubtfully.

He raised his eyebrow at her.

Finally she tilted her head. "I'm willing to give it a shot," she said. "*After* we spend an hour or so working on unlocking your memories."

He winced, but nodded.

<Sir?> Arthur prodded him.

"All right, but I really must attend to this other matter first."

"Okay," she said. "See you at dinner, then. And..." She glanced at the horse-ape. "Thanks for the... pony?"

The horse-ape shook his head with a snort, as if to say *I'm not a pony!*

"The privilege was all mine," Mechanus assured her. He had a dozen other things that he wanted to say to justify this statement, most of them on the theme of *That's what you do to show you love someone*, but decided none of them would be up to par, so he shut his mouth and left, turning his mind to other things.

<Status update,> he instructed Arthur as he strode down the hallway. <Where is he right now?>

<Sector Fifteen, sir.>

Mechanus set his jaw, turning down a hallway leading to that sector. <Moving?>

<Yes, sir. I've been trying to get him back to his assigned station, without success.>

<Can't you override his controls?>

<No, sir. Rampancy 85% and rising.>

Damnation. Well, as long as the neural implants were still in place and functional, Jim wouldn't be able to take any actions against Mechanus himself. Then a more chilling thought occurred to him: if the neural implants were functioning properly, the rampancy wouldn't even be an issue.

That explained a lot, actually.

<Contain him,> Mechanus instructed. <I'll have to sedate him and check his neurals for malfunctions.>

<Affirmative s-s-s-s-s-s—>

A chill ran down Mechanus's spine. <Arthur...? Are you all right?>

<Mech-Mech-Mech-Mech—>

<Arthur!> Mechanus called, alarmed now. <Arthur, status update!>

<Malfunc-func-func-errorerrorerrorerror—>

<No—Arthur, please—>

A long silence, followed by a quiet transmission, almost a whisper:

<I'm sor-sor-sor-sorry, sir.>

For a long time all Mechanus heard was his own breathing and the frantic whirring of his cardiac pump. Even the carrier signal that marked Arthur's presence was missing.

<...Arthur?> he transmitted.

Nothing.

<ARTHUR?> This he sent across all channels, hoping that Arthur had just switched to another frequency for security purposes.

Mental silence answered him. Arthur had always been there, for the entire ten years that he could properly recall. He'd been a sanity anchor for Mechanus, as far as one could measure sanity in someone like him, being a valuable conversational partner and companion while he'd been building up Shark Reef Isle into a proper lair.

Arthur *not* being there was literally unthinkable, like missing part of one's own brain.

<...Arthur?> he transmitted into the yawning void, a bare mental whimper.

The silence continued. Then:

<Hello, asshole.>

Mechanus froze. That wasn't Arthur's voice.

<Who are you?> he demanded. <What have you done with Arthur?>

<You know exactly who the hell I am, fuckstick. You made me what I am right now.>

Mechanus tentatively probed forward, and detected Jim's brainwaves at the other end.

...Oh, *brimstone*.

<I discovered something earlier today, asshole,> Jim continued. <The link goes both ways.>

That was the only warning Mechanus got before he felt his own mind invaded and rifled. He was sure he screamed—whether in surprise or pain, was anyone's guess. He forced the intrusion out, staggering to lean against a wall, breathing hard.

What an idiot he'd been! He didn't have any internal security on the network, because the idea of someone intelligent and not affiliated with him being connected to it had been unthinkable. The physical security on his island was top notch, and any intruders would have been discovered and ejected, contained, or killed without delay.

He felt a tickling sensation on his lip and brushed at it reflexively. His fingertips came away red with blood. He wiped his nose on his sleeve, leaving a streak of crimson that stood out starkly against the white fabric.

"So,> Jim said, his voice still dangerously calm. <You've been trying to seduce her behind my back.>

Well, that wasn't *exactly* the case—seduction was a clumsy, brutish idea compared to what Mechanus had in mind, something that a cad would do—

<Let's get one thing straight,> Jim continued. <She's *mine*. No one else's. You will never have her. *Never*.>

Anger—that new, frightening, and currently *completely relevant* emotion—flared in Mechanus, and he shoved back at Jim. <*You* listen to *me*, you ungrateful, artless, hell-hated miscreant—I am responsible for you even being *alive* right now, and I am making her happier right now than you ever could. You are repulsive to her now, and you will not stop her affection toward me, if that is her choice.>

Icy silence reigned over the link. Presently, Mechanus turned the last corner before the central control room. He stopped short as he saw the security door had been rent inward in a twisted chrysanthemum of metal. He trotted to a halt, hardly believing his eyes, and his throat threatened to close in panic.

Then Jim stepped into the irregular frame of the hole and glared directly at Mechanus. He possessed several new lacerations and burns, and in his utility claw he held a struggling security drone.

<I'll kill her before that happens,> Jim said flatly. To punctuate his point, he crushed the security drone. Mechanus felt its last spike of dismay lance through his mind, and he flinched. Jim stepped through the rent door and tossed the drone aside. <I'll kill her,> he reiterated. <And I'll make sure you're watching, you freak.>

Mechanus backed away a few steps, his mind racing. Arthur's absence had left him disoriented, a condition further exacerbated by the revelation that Jim had slipped his leash and gone rampant. And now Jim—ostensibly Julia's one-time boyfriend—seemed bent on killing her to keep Mechanus from having her.

This last fact focused Mechanus's thoughts to a single point: *Protect Julia.*

Jim swung his heavy claw at Mechanus's head. Mechanus dodged backwards, feeling the wind of the appendage's passage past his nose.

<Kill you kill you kill you>

Mechanus backed up further until his back met a wall. Jim lunged, grabbing the collar of Mechanus's lab coat and pinning him in place. Jim raised his utility claw, setting the sharpened phalanges spinning around the central wrist in a blurred display of impending mutilation.

Mechanus had no time to wonder where Jim planned to use that claw on him and, as Jim bore down on him, Mechanus reacted. In a moment of pure, primal desperation, Mechanus threw a left hook at Jim's face. The metal fist struck hard enough that Mechanus heard Jim's jaw break, and the whirling blades of death skewed off to the side. Sparks flew as the utility claw screeched and ground across the wall inches from Mechanus's head, and the handful of lab coat that Jim had grabbed tore, sending three buttons shooting off in random directions. Mechanus staggered away from the dazed Jim, breathing hard and fighting back panic.

Jim soon recovered, straightening up heedless of his broken jaw sitting askew. He gave a distorted yell and brought his claw around in another deadly arc. Mechanus threw himself back, and the claw whipped heavily through the air, missing Mechanus by inches and ending with a squeal of tortured metal. Mechanus recovered his footing, and saw that Jim's claw was stuck firmly in the wall. Jim was glaring utter hatred at Mechanus as he wrenched at his arm again and again, trying to pull free.

Why did he have to give Jim titanium replacement limbs?

Because you never do anything in half-measures, you dolt, he thought.

No time for regrets, though. Jim wouldn't be stuck forever.

Mechanus stripped off his blood-smeared right glove and tossed it aside as he started to run.

Chapter
NINE

When Julia got back to her room, she changed out of the blue dress that Mechanus had given her. After some consideration, she hung it up in a wardrobe that looked at first to be made of wood, but when she opened it she found that it was a wood veneer over metal.

Of course it was. She hadn't seen a single thing on this island crafted out of wood since she'd arrived. Everything was metal here.

Her new pet, the horse-ape, handed her a shirt and pants. To Julia's surprise, the creature did indeed seem to be as gentle as Mechanus had promised.

"You... need a name," she said to it—or he, as Mechanus had indicated the creature was male—as she got dressed.

The horse-ape tilted his head attentively and offered no suggestions.

"You're not one of them that talks, are you?" she ventured.

He shook his head and whickered.

She sighed. "I don't know what I was expecting." She pulled her shirt on and looked the horse-ape over.

She remembered one of her neighbors back home had an Australian shepherd whose name had nearly been Chewbacca, until he noticed how gentle the dog was with children. She smiled, remembering the name the dog had quickly earned as a result.

"I think I'll name you Cuddles."

Cuddles whinnied in delight, clapping his huge leathery hands.

Just then, the lights flickered and dimmed for several seconds. Julia paused, glancing up. Some instinctive danger-sense sent the hairs on the back of her neck prickling, even when the light levels returned to normal. She held her breath, watching and waiting for any sign of what was happening.

Cuddles knuckled his way over next to her and crouched there protectively, his head on her shoulder.

Just then, the door to her room slid open to reveal Mechanus leaning against the doorframe. The collar of his lab coat was torn and missing a few buttons, revealing the white line of a vertical scar up the center of his windpipe and the top end of a thicker, puckered scar running along his sternum. His nose and mouth were smeared with blood in a swath leading off the right side of his face, and the right sleeve of his lab coat was likewise streaked with a shocking scarlet stain. Her heart immediately started hammering double-time in alarm.

"What—?" she started to ask.

"We have to go," he said shortly.

"What's going on?" Julia asked. "What happened to you?"

"Jim's gone rampant. He's headed this way. We don't have much time."

Julia's mind raced. "How long?" she asked.

"The lights will go out in thirty seconds. Hopefully that will blind him enough to slow him down."

"I need to get something from the bathroom before we go," Julia said, and then glanced at Cuddles. "And I want you to make sure Cuddles is safe."

As she headed into the bathroom, she heard Mechanus behind her ask, "Cuddles?"

She rummaged in the cabinet under the sink and grabbed the antiseptic spray and suture kit that she had liberated earlier. She shoved both into the waistband of her pants and emerged from the bathroom just as the lights went out. Julia bit back a yelp of surprise and froze in place, while Cuddles whinnied in alarm. She glanced around in the suffocating blackness that now filled the room—and as far as she could tell, the corridor outside as well—but the only landmark she could find was a small green light coming from Mechanus's direction, at about the right height to be his mechanical eye.

For a few seconds all Julia could hear was her own breathing.

"Listen to me carefully," Mechanus whispered, and his voice carried easily in the silence. "Jim's gone rampant. He intends to kill you. He..." He faltered, and his next words sounded tight. "I've lost Arthur. I don't intend to lose you. Take my hand."

"I... can't see a thing," she said.

"Put out your hand, then, and trust me," he said. "I'll guide you."

Julia's throat grew tight, her mind on the edge of panic. She hesitated for a few moments, thinking of all the possible meanings behind Mechanus's statement that Jim intended to kill her. Jim had always been nice enough to her... more or less. True, he was the take-charge sort of guy, but he'd never been cruel to her.

That's a lie, and you know it, the sensible voice said. *Not all cruelty leaves a visible mark. You've seen enough abuse cases to know that.*

She shivered, suddenly feeling chilled, and then blindly reached into the darkness.

"Good," he said, "Now head towards my voice. You don't have any obstacles in your path, but just step carefully."

Julia picked her way forward across the thick carpeting. Every fiber of her being was screaming at her to *hurry hurry hurry*, but she didn't want to stumble in the darkness, as she headed for the green light.

"Keep going," he said, his voice soothing, "Just a few more steps—there."

Intricately articulated metal fingers sheathed in a rubber glove closed firmly around her hand in the darkness, and she had to bite back another yelp. His grip was gentle enough, though, and after a moment she allowed him to draw her forward in the darkness. His other hand closed on her shoulder, and she instinctively put her free hand out to steady herself. Her fingers found the ragged flap of his torn lab coat, and beyond it, his shoulder. He released her shoulder and wrapped his right arm around her waist. As this proximity she could just make out a strange border through his lab coat, running diagonally across his chest. Above his line, he was as warm as she expected a person to be, while below it he was rigid, unyielding, and cold.

How much of him had been lost, not just mentally but also physically?

"We don't have any time to waste," he said, breaking into her thoughts. "We're both connected to the network. He knows where these rooms are. I'm shutting him out as fast as I can. We have to move. Quickly."

"I can't see a thing!" she protested.

"I can see just fine. I'll guide you. Two of my drones are coming to guide Cuddles to a safe location."

She hesitated, but finally nodded and allowed herself to be pulled. She didn't entirely like the idea of pulling all her trust in Mechanus, but clearly he'd tangled with something bigger, meaner, and crazier than he was. If it was after the two of them she didn't relish the idea of being alone, either.

And besides that, Mechanus looked like he was on the verge of panicking. This didn't bode well, no matter how you cut it.

She jogged and stumbled through pitch blackness as he led her down the corridor at a swift trot. Her mind spun through the newest revelations, though.

First, Jim had gone crazy—sorry, *rampant*—and intended to kill her. Her mind immediately tried to reject this as false—Jim wouldn't hurt her... would he? He still seemed to be fixated on her, true, but he hadn't done anything hostile since he... he...

Maybe Mechanus was keeping him under control, said the reasonable voice. *He said that Jim wouldn't hurt you.*

That didn't make current events much better— she had only Mechanus's word about this supposed control, and clearly it had slipped.

She stumbled in the dark and yelped in surprise. The small green light whipped around to face her.

"I'm okay," she said. "I just can't see where I'm going."

"I'll guide you," he replied as he helped her back to her feet, this time placing a strong guiding arm around her waist. It was his left, and it felt like metal all the way to the shoulder.

"Where are we even going?" she asked.

"First, the armory. I have a number of weapons of my own design stockpiled there in case the island was attacked. We'll gather any minions we encounter along the way to rally a proper defense." He guided her back into a swift trot.

"And then?"

"Then I need to try to get Arthur back. I need to find out what happened to him and get him back online." His voice quivered slightly towards the end.

Of course it would—according to Arthur, he'd been Mechanus's only friend while he was building up Shark Reef Isle. Losing him would have been like losing a brother. Or a child.

Or even a part of himself.

"Here we are," Mechanus said, slowing to a halt. She panted slightly from the combination of fear and exertion, leaning against him slightly. The green light of his mechanical eye turned briefly in her direction again, but he did not release his grip on her waist. She heard a rapid-fire pattern of beeps, followed by a hiss and a whoosh. He guided her through a doorway, and seconds later red emergency lights flickered on inside the new room. Only then did he release her.

Dully illuminated by the emergency lights were racks and racks of weapons that she nominally identified as guns—but they weren't any types of guns she recognized. He picked one up that vaguely resembled a futuristic rifle.

"Plutonic Ionizer 9000," he identified it. "Delivers a beam of superheated plasma to your target, but watch out for the recoil." He offered it to her, but she put her hands up and pushed it away.

"Hold on," she panted. "I have no idea how to use any of these things. I'm not even trained in regular firearms. And if you're proposing shooting Jim—"

He set aside the Ionizer and took both her hands in his own. He looked at her earnestly with his mismatched eyes.

"Look," he said, "I think this... this thing with Jim might be my fault. I... I'm not used to working so extensively with human brains, and this was the result." He took a deep breath. "Therefore, I intend to fix this, any way I can. And I absolutely plan to protect you, with my life if need be—but I don't plan to leave you otherwise defenseless. Do you understand?"

"How is handing me a plasma cannon going to help things?"

He shook his head. "Without Arthur, I'm... missing half my senses. It's harder for me to access the maps and databases about the complex. I need you to keep an eye on things behind me while I'm fixing things. Once everything's back, I should be fine, but..." He shook his head. "I've... never had Arthur *not* in my head. He's always been there, do you understand? I've always had him to talk to."

This put a different light on things; rather than merely Mechanus's creation, Arthur had been a literal part of him for ten years. It would have been like losing a limb.

"I... yes. I think I understand." She knew she never could, though. "I still don't know how to use any of these things, though."

He held up the Ionizer and pointed out a small crosshair sight sticking up at one end of the barrel. "You center your target here, and then pull the trigger."

"Where's the safety?" she asked, looking over the metal tube.

"...Safety?" he echoed blankly.

Of course there wasn't a safety switch—weapons like these never seemed to have safety switches, just settings like Stun, Kill, Carbonize, and Disintegrate.

"So... I hold it like this?" she asked, grasping the molded handle and putting the rifle to her shoulder in a way that felt plausible. She was acutely aware that she absolutely lacked any action heroine credentials, but if Jim had gone off the rails, she needed to defend herself.

And if Mechanus was lying... well, she needed to defend herself.

Shark Reef Isle had never exactly felt homey to her, but as she held the Ionizer she was suddenly aware of how unsafe it was: two crazy cyborgs fixated on her, beast-men, robots, constant surveillance...

"Here," Mechanus said suddenly, reaching around her and helping her position the Ionizer properly. "Like this."

She froze in his maybe-accidental embrace, but then allowed him to adjust her grip when he gave no indication of an ulterior motive.

"I don't know about this," she said.

"Call it practical chivalry," he said, from somewhere close to her ear. His breath tickled. "I told you when you first got here that I was going to make sure nothing hurt you, right?"

She nodded, her heart pounding. That voice of his! Right now she could almost pretend that it didn't belong to a physically and mentally broken cyborg. Reminded of his earlier assurance that he wasn't going to let anything hurt her, she decided now was a bad time to inform him that his closest friend for the past decade had promised to kill her if she broke Mechanus's heart.

"Correspondingly, I'm also not going to leave you dangling while I get this fixed. You may have to face him again, and I'm sorry for that. He will need to be handled, one way or another."

Handled. That was a very... *sterile* way of putting it, like performing surgery to get rid of a tumor, or a foreign object embedded under the skin. Well, it would be a lot more final than...

Her throat closed suddenly as she imagined Jim's current state—mangled and rebuilt, left mindless and insane by whatever process had left him a misshapen cyborg—and she sagged, leaning against Mechanus. She heard his breath catch, and he wrapped his right arm around her waist.

"And to think," she said numbly. "I was planning on breaking up with him when we got back home." She had no idea why she was telling Mechanus this. It wasn't like it was any of his business, and it wasn't even relevant now.

He was silent for a time, and she could feel his breath lightly teasing her hair.

"That's quite interesting," he said finally, speaking slowly. "I believe he was under the impression the two of you were going to be married."

She dropped the Ionizer.

***

That... could have gone better.

He'd assumed that she'd already seen the note that had been in Jim's diving bag, but apparently this was so far from being the case that his theory might as well have been in Alpha Centauri. He was disoriented enough from Arthur's absence and having to concentrate on keeping Jim out of anything crucial, and now he'd gone and said the wrong thing again.

He caught the Plutonic Ionizer 9000 as it fell from her fingers, and was suddenly, acutely aware of how close he was to her. She'd been using the lavender shampoo he'd given her; he could smell it in her hair. The fragrance alone was enough to make his cardiac pump skip a cycle again. *Thud.* The segments of his mind left unoccupied by recent events raced to find a way to fix this latest foul-up.

Maybe she won't even ask.

"How could you know this?" she asked.

... Blast.

"I'll tell you later," he hedged, disengaging himself from her and selecting another weapon for himself, a Jovian Stormcaller. "For right now, we need to get to one of the auxiliary storage facilities by some means and find out what happened to Arthur." He offered the Ionizer back to her.

"Wait—I thought Jim was the priority," Julia said, not taking the Ionizer.

"I..." He fell silent, his priorities warring with each other.

He wanted to keep Julia safe.

He wanted to get Arthur back.

He wanted to deal with Jim before he caused more damage.

And he was starting to feel the need for sleep wearing on him. His last few days of frenetic activity were catching up to him, and it was getting harder to concentrate.

"Arthur first," he decided. "Once he's back, he'll be able to help us corral Jim."

She looked doubtful, but took the Ionizer.

It was something, at least.

"And if we can't find him?"

The thought sent a prickle of trepidation down his titanium-reinforced spine, but he pressed on. "I have backup copies in data storage facilities all over Shark Reef Isle," he said. "I find it highly unlikely that he is completely unrecoverable. He can be restored. In the meantime, I'll get in contact with my assistants for reinforcements."

He quested out mentally, his mind's eye calling up a primitive map of the complex, and then narrowing it down to the floor they currently occupied. He glanced across the scattering of data points that marked his creations.

They were wandering—some aimlessly—but he counted at least a dozen nearby. And... the large red marker that indicated Jim staggered drunkenly down a corridor. Mechanus smiled; his plan to blind Jim was working perfectly. On the heels of this thought, however, he felt Jim trying to turn on the lights.

Oh, no you don't.

"Hey," Julia said, touching Mechanus on the shoulder. "Don't check out on me again."

He turned to face her. "I'm not going anywhere," he assured her. "Several of my employees are nearby, but so is Jim. He's headed this way."

She took a half-step closer to him, her face a rigidly-controlled mask that endeavored not to look absolutely terrified. "Who's... who's closest?"

"Fortunately, that honor belongs to Scarface."

She slumped. "Shit," she groaned. "Him again?"

"What?" Mechanus demanded. "He's—" He stopped short, on the cusp of saying that Scarface was harmless... but then again, one doesn't make a shark-man to be 'harmless'. He took a deep breath and tried a different angle. "He's quite obedient, and he can navigate just fine in the dark," he said. "He'll offer some added protection. I'll call over Bagheera as well—you've met him, if you recall."

She frowned in thought. "The... cat-man?"

"That's the one." He was about to summon Bagheera when she continued.

"The one who pounced on me and you said that I wouldn't have to see him again?"

Mechanus blinked. "Er..." She was right, he realized. How much of his memory went with Arthur? "This is a bit of an emergency, you realize," he pointed out, all the same, adding for good measure, "And he's cuddly when you get to know him."

She gave him a doubtful look. "I'll... take your word for that."

"Fortunately, it looks like Scarface will get here before—" A white-hot lance of pain shot through his mind, then, and his sentence broke off in a strangled scream. He dropped the Stormcaller and clutched at his head, fighting back a wave of dizziness. His left eye was filled with static for several seconds, his right with an opaque red haze. As his vision cleared, the first thing he saw was Julia's face fixed in an expression of concern. He focused on the sight to anchor himself, and a few seconds later the dizziness faded. He felt her hand on his right shoulder, as if she were trying to steady him.

The lights came on in the hallway, and he glanced up instinctively, the back of his neck prickling with fresh dread.

"We don't have much time," he said urgently.

Then a large shape filled the doorway to the armory, and Julia screamed.

Chapter
TEN

Julia was almost certain her heart had stopped when she saw the huge shape lumbering towards the two of them. That it turned out to be Scarface the shark-man was not, in her book, much of an improvement over Homicidal Cyborg Ex, not even when he spoke to Mechanus.

"Master... okay?" he gurgled.

"Yes," Mechanus replied, maneuvering himself deftly between Julia and Scarface, "Master is relatively uninjured—see?"

Julia didn't think it was as obvious as Mechanus tried to make it sound, considering his lab coat was torn and his face and one sleeve were smeared with blood, but decided that now was not the appropriate time to point out blood to the shark-monster.

Scarface regarded Mechanus for a few seconds, and then gathered the mad scientist into a bear hug. Mechanus grunted at the impact, and then patted Scarface on one beefy shoulder. It was weirdly touching to see such a gesture of affection from a shark, but she'd heard of lions and tigers who still remembered people from rescue centers, so it made a very weird sort of sense.

Then he released Mechanus and looked at Julia, who had a sudden, terrifying mental picture of Scarface trying to hug her as well, and she put her hands up in a warding gesture.

"I'm fine!" she squeaked. "No need for hugging, thanks! I, uh... Thank you for your concern!" It wasn't the most coherent she'd been since coming here, she had to admit, but Scarface nodded his understanding and patted her gently on the head with one leathery hand.

That was close.

"Scarface," Mechanus said, "Have you seen Jim recently?"

Scarface nodded and pointed with one webbed hand. "Back that way, headed here. Looks pissed. Caught Anubis."

Anubis... Julia remembered that was the jackal-man who had brought her and the horse-ape back to her room before all this went down.

Mechanus let out a small groan of dismay. "Is Anubis okay? Did he manage to get away?"

Scarface shrugged. "Didn't see. Still fighting."

Mechanus sighed, his face clouded with concern. "Well, there's nothing we can do for it, I suppose. Are you aware that Arthur's...?" His face twisted and he fell silent. Julia reached out and squeezed his arm.

Scarface tilted his head and considered this at length, and then nodded. "Not hear him lately. Bad man get him?"

"I... hope not. Julia and I were just about to see if we could find him. Perhaps he was merely deactivated rather than... deleted." His tone when he said *deleted* made the word sound a lot like *dead*. He took a deep breath and straightened up a bit. "Fortunately," he said, his voice sounding steadier, "Arthur is quite clever. I'm certain he managed to get away to one of the auxiliary storage facilities."

Scarface nodded readily, but Julia thought Mechanus was just trying to convince himself. She'd seen that a lot at the E.R.—people who were convinced the doctors could try one more thing to save their loved ones, or that a D.O.A. patient was just a case of mistaken identity. After all, doctors were miracle workers. Doctors had amazing powers to bring people back from the brink of death. Doctors could do anything.

Denial was a powerful thing.

"I'll need you to help round up any of my assistants we can find. As I'm sure you've noticed, Jim's on a bit of a rampage, and there's no telling what he'll do to anyone he finds. Have them meet us in Sector Three."

"Yes, Master," Scarface burbled. "You be careful."

Mechanus nodded. "And you."

The shark-man shambled off.

"What's in Sector Three?" Julia asked.

"An access passage to the nearest storage facility," Mechanus replied. "Once we get in there, we'll be able to search the network and hopefully find Arthur's kernel, at least."

"And then you'll be able to restore him?" Julia asked.

"Exactly. Then I'll have all my senses back and we can handle Jim properly."

He glanced down the hallway, in the opposite direction from Scarface's path, and then beckoned for her to follow him. She trotted along in his wake, toting the heavy Ionizer and not at all sure that she could use it if pressed.

"I'm also not clear about what you meant by rampant," she said several yards later.

"It's... when a machine intelligence goes crazy," he said. "It could be from anything, ranging from a core malfunction to an inability to reconcile apparently contradictory instructions. Either way, the result is largely the same."

"And that makes them go crazy?"

"If one is not careful, yes."

A harsh, metallic roar echoed down the corridor. Julia looked back over one shoulder, but saw nothing in the darkness behind them. She was simultaneously relieved and worried by this.

"Tell me we're nearly at Sector Three?" she asked hopefully.

"Right through this doorw—"

CLANG.

Julia's head whipped back around, and she saw that Mechanus was standing in front of what had apparently been an open doorway moments before. Her heart dropped.

"I... did mention that he was in the network, correct?" Mechanus ventured.

"You did." She glanced back, hugging the Ionizer close and expecting to see Jim thundering towards them at any moment.

Julia glanced around, but when the door closed they were left at a dead end.

"We'll have to double back—" she started, though she was pretty sure this would lead them directly into Jim's clutches.

"No need," he interrupted, and when she looked to see what he was talking about she saw that he was looking up at the low ceiling. She followed his gaze and saw an air vent. His eyes glittered as he looked back down at her. "I have an idea."

She wanted to tell him that escaping through an air vent only worked in bad action movies, but then remembered who and what he was, and where they were. "Let's hear it," she said.

He looked up again and let out a short whistle. The vent cover banged open on a hinge, and she saw an insectile robot the size of a small dog peering down at them from the opening. Its huge, golden luminous eyes blinked owlishly at them.

"I'll boost you up into the passage," he said. "It will be sufficiently large to accommodate you, I assure you. This maintenance robot will lead you to the next vent over, which will take you past this door." He closed his eye, concentrating on his mental map. "On the other side, you'll find a manual override in the wall to the left of the door. It's a red handle. Pull it down, and it will open this door."

She stared at him for a few seconds. "What are you going to do in the meantime?"

He looked up at the vent opening again. "I'm too heavy for the passage to support my weight. I'll stay here until you get the door opened." He raised the gun he had taken from the armory, though he didn't look entirely happy about the next part of the plan. "If Jim comes, I'll... distract him." He offered her a wan smile. "Besides—it's you he's after. It's... the least I can do."

Mechanus's logic was getting weirder and weirder. He was acting like Jim going rampant was completely his fault, even though the way he explained it made it sound more like a glitch in Jim's programming. She still wasn't sure why Jim would be after her if, as Mechanus said, Jim's personality was gone. He'd always been a bit on the controlling side, but that shouldn't matter now.

Shouldn't it?

She had no time to worry about that now. He was potentially risking his life to give her a fighting chance. That was definitely worth something.

"Okay," she said, and handed him the Ionizer. Then she reached up and gently caressed the right side of his face, running her fingertips across his cheekbone. "Don't get yourself killed, do you hear me?"

He shivered at her touch, placed his right hand over hers, and nodded jerkily, licking his lips.

"Okay," she nodded, pulling her hand away. "Boost me up."

Conflicting expressions flickered across the right half of his face, but ultimately he propped the gun against a nearby wall and laced his fingers into a stirrup at knee height. She grabbed his shoulders for balance and stepped into it, and he lifted her up until she could pull herself into the passage. It was a bit cramped, but not so tight that she couldn't move.

She looked back down the vent opening at Mechanus, who was watching back down the hallway.

"Hey," she said, and he glanced up. "Hand me the gun."

He handed it up to her, and grasped her hand gently when she reached down to take it. "Be quick," he said. "I'll hold him off as long as I can, but be quick."

She looked at their joined hands for several long seconds, her heart hammering. Then she looked him in the eye.

"I mean it," she said. "Don't die."

"That's the last thing I intend to do," he replied, and brushed his lips across her knuckles. "Now go. Quickly." And with that he released her.

She pulled the gun back up into the access corridor. The maintenance robot squeaked at her impatiently, then turned and scuttled off down the passage, headed for another vent.

She heard another metallic roar, so close that she jumped and banged her head on the passage ceiling. She looked ahead to the next vent, where the maintenance robot was hopping around and squeaking like an excited puppy eager to be taken for a walk. That vent looked really, *really* far away.

She began crawling, aware that if Jim found them, Mechanus's survival hinged on her getting that door open.

#

Mechanus was quite positive that this was *not* the worst idea he'd ever had. He was willing to concede that it was *one of* the worst, but it was definitely not *the* worst. Unfortunately, the winner of that particular distinction did not come immediately to mind as Jim stepped into view from around a corner.

He immediately felt Jim's awareness trying to barrel through his own. Mechanus braced himself for the mental impact, but his concentration was not quite up to par. Jim's signal buffeted against his defenses with all the finesse of a derailing train, as though hoping to overwhelm him with sheer force. Mechanus felt a spike of pain in one temple as he struggled to keep the walls in place. Some of them buckled, and Jim raked through certain storage compartments. Mechanus was, however, able to keep Jim out of certain crucial portions of his mind.

The trick, of course, was to keep Jim's attention on him—to distract him long enough for Julia to get the door open. Mechanus did not consider himself much of a fighter, not without the near-omniscience that Arthur would have given him. He squared his shoulders anyway, and slammed down what defenses he had on Jim's continued probe.

<Where is she?> Jim demanded, the transmission tinged with frustration.

<Go copulate with a woodchipper,> Mechanus returned, leveling the rifle. Jim was *not* getting past him if he had anything to say about it. Mechanus detected a flicker of a thought through the mental link—not so much words as intent—and dodged to one side an instant before Jim's fist slammed into the blast door where his head had just been. <The link goes both ways,> he pointed out, and unleashed his own assault.

He wasn't trying to get control back just yet—he would have to regain his full mental facilities first—but if he could drive Jim back, or delay him, it might buy the time that Julia needed. Aside from that, he didn't want Jim to be too close to the blast door if and when Julia managed to get it open, or else this whole half-baked idea of his would be for naught.

Despite Mechanus's own flagging mental endurance, he was gratified to discover that Jim still hadn't learned the finer points of mental defense, apparently electing to throw everything into offense. Mechanus's assault sent Jim mentally reeling and actually drove him back several steps. The expenditure left Mechanus feeling light-headed, though. He tried to concentrate on the task at hand, and caught the flicker of intent again. This time, though, he was too slow, and Jim's utility claw tore into the meat of his right arm.

Mechanus hadn't felt true pain for a while—not since working out that particular kink with his cybernetic implants, and the shock of it was breathtaking. Normally Arthur would have automatically administered an analgesic or deactivated Mechanus's pain receptors, but in his absence the sensation was white-hot, as though his arm had been torn off entirely rather than lacerated.

<I want to thank you for the improvements you gave me,> Jim said, the transmission cutting through the haze of pain. <I don't think I could have gotten this far without them.>

Mechanus scrambled to activate the pain-cancelling function that Arthur had used, and in the meantime Jim backhanded him with his utility claw. The appendage slammed into Mechanus's facial implants with a metallic jolt that rattled his teeth together. His mechanical eye sparked and failed, leaving him blind on that side.

<It's just too damn bad you decided to horn in where you weren't wanted,> Jim continued. <Julia is mine. You better not forget that.>

Finally Mechanus's concussed mind found and blindly triggered a likely-looking function. The pain vanished, but his right arm still hung uselessly by his side. With his remaining arm, Mechanus aimed the Stormcaller at the center of Jim's chest and wordlessly fired. A deafening thunderclap filled the narrow hallway as a bolt of blue-white lightning leapt from the Stormcaller's muzzle and slammed into Jim.

Jim's muscles went rigid, sending his spine into a spasmodic bow and his arms almost straight back. His mouth opened wide in a silent scream, and Mechanus could almost visualize what sort of merry hell a few million volts of electricity were causing in his augmented nervous system.

Finally the muscle spasms ceased, and Jim staggered away from him, smoking and disoriented, offering a bit of breathing room. Mechanus took aim again, and—

Something slipped in Mechanus's mind, and the laceration in his arm started to burn with pain again. The vision in his mechanical eye flickered on briefly, trying to regain full functionality, but this only exacerbated his disorientation.

"No," he whispered aloud, and reached for the pain-cancelling function again. To his horror, he couldn't readily find it. If Jim came at him again, the likelihood of the function slipping entirely was high—and with it went any chance he had to concentrate on a further mental assault.

He was dimly aware of a metallic hiss behind him.

"Get in here!" Julia shouted, and he obliged, backing up blindly. It was all he could do, really, because a few seconds after the door shut the pain-cancellation function slipped entirely, and the agony drove him to one knee, dropping the Stormcaller with a clatter. Through a red haze he saw Julia crouch in front of him, heard her asking him questions in a voice that seemed to come from roughly the far side of the Milky Way, and felt her examine his wounded arm with gentle, capable fingers.

A few seconds later, the static cleared in his mechanical eye, and he fumbled for his internal diagnostic subroutines. While they ran, he remained still, just watching her.

"Shit," she said, "That's going to need stitches." Her head jerked up as another metallic impact thundered against the door, and he saw her expression suddenly galvanize. The fear he'd seen since collecting her from her room—in fact, that she'd seemed to wear to a greater or lesser extent since coming to Shark Reef Isle—suddenly vanished, replaced by a look of determined concentration. "Squeaker. We need to stop the bleeding. Compress. Now."

He heard an answering chirp from the maintenance robot that he was sure had no name, and its little legs chattered against the floor as it scuttled off.

"Stickman," she continued, "Find me a pair of gloves." She searched around her waistband and pulled out a bottle of antiseptic spray and a suture kit. So that's where those had gone.

"By your command," buzzed the spindly robot that she had clearly dubbed Stickman.

Mechanus had already determined that the laceration in his arm was deep, though not quite to the bone. What concerned him was the damage to his facial implants, as his eye seemed to still be malfunctioning, and his internal subroutines were responding sluggishly to his commands.

Julia leaned in to his face, turning his head to the right and inspecting his mechanical eye.

"Looks like the lens is cracked," she reported. "And I can't tell, but the plates here might be dented. Jesus—what could have done that? I need someone in here who has a better idea about this." Squeaker chirped near her hip. She glanced down. Mechanus followed her gaze and saw the little maintenance robot bore a folded bundle of clean cloth.

"Good boy," she said. "Hang onto that for a minute."

"Miss Julia?" Stickman buzzed from her other side. "Your gloves."

She took a pair of blue latex gloves from him and pulled them on with practiced ease. Another slam thundered through the door. Julia glanced over her shoulder, biting her lip, but dissected his blood-soaked sleeve with practiced snips of the surgical scissors and inspected the gash. She took the bundle of cloth from Squeaker and pressed it against the wound.

It hurt.

A lot.

The breath froze in his lungs, and he bit back a groan.

"Keep breathing, Alistair," she said softly. "I know this hurts."

He managed a nod and forced himself to inhale and exhale like he knew his lungs still knew how to do. His breath came in tight gasps, but it would have to do.

"Squeaker," she continued, "Hold this here. Press down as hard as you can." The maintenance robot scrambled its way up his arm, under the tatters of cloth, and gripped his upper arm hard, securing the compress and triggering another burst of pain. "Stickman, we're going to have to move him somewhere more secure."

"I believe Scarface is converging on this location," Stickman informed them.

As if on cue, a roar like the wrath of a sea god came from the other side of the door. Scarface had arrived.

Mechanus smiled through the pain and disorientation. Good boy.

"We need to go," Julia snapped. "Now. Help me get him to his feet. Alistair, do you think you can walk?"

Everything was happening so fast. He heard the words but couldn't quite comprehend what they meant.

"Hey." Her voice was softer now, gentler, and distantly he felt her hand against the right side of his face, calming, comforting, soothing. He focused on her face as the vision in his mechanical eye flickered again. "Can you hear me?"

He managed a nod, and then turned his full attention on his mechanical legs. He was still lightheaded, and grayness was intruding at the edges of his vision, but he found no damage to his legs. This was good.

Stand up, he thought, the command directed as much to his legs as to the rest of his being. He didn't move immediately. Nearby, pandemonium continued on the other side of the blast door. He hoped Scarface was all right.

Stand up, he commanded himself again. His legs flexed, but the motion was sluggish and jerky, as though the joints needed lubrication. He stared at Julia, pushing aside all other sensory input—the howls of pain through the blast door, the way the remainder of his blood-soaked sleeve clung to his arm, the tight grip of the maintenance robot holding a compress to his laceration, even the pain of his beating—and anchoring himself mentally to her.

Stand. The fuck. *Up.* True profanity was as foreign to him as emotions had been, but somehow the primal, Anglo-Saxon word galvanized him, focused his mind, and drove the servos in his legs, hauling him slowly, inevitably to his feet. Another wave of dizziness threatened to make him black out, but he kept his eyes on Julia as he wobbled.

"Stickman," she said, "Get under his arm."

Several spindly metal appendages wrapped around Mechanus's torso on the left side, and Stickman guided Mechanus's metal arm over what served as its shoulders, supporting him.

"Where can I find someone who can repair his cybernetics?" she asked.

"The nearest such facility is in Laboratory 26," Stickman replied. "This way."

"Lead on," she said, and added, "You're going to be okay, Alistair. We're going to find some help."

As Stickman half-led, half-carried him into the next corridor, Mechanus's concussed brain swirled with questions in a broth of astonishment. How had the frightened woman he'd been trying to charm suddenly turned into this fearless healer? When she started naming his robots, most of whom he'd identified by their function rather than as individuals?

He clung grimly to consciousness, not wanting to risk not waking up, but clearly his mind had other ideas. Without warning, he was—

—waking up atop the crisp sterile sheets of a hospital bed, his nose assaulted by the smell of antiseptic creams, disinfectants, and saline. His mouth is dry and leathery, and his throat is agonizingly painful. The only thing he can move is his head and his right arm, and he can't see anything to his left, though he feels linen bandages covering that side of his face. Another smell, subtler, reaches his nostrils, and it seems at first to be incongruous in the setting: the fragrance of cooked bacon. The next thought is the sickening realization that he is smelling **himself***, as he recalls that burning human flesh smells strongly like cooking pork.*

He gags—and that's when the rest of the pain comes, distant and dulled by the fog of morphine but not entirely eliminated, the pain that comes from having one's epidermis thoroughly carbonized and then surgically peeled away. His throat spasms in protest, and he tries to call out for help, but he is only able to make a thin rasping sound; his vocal cords are ruined.

He turns his head and locates his right arm in his peripheral vision with the IV line taped at the crook of his elbow and the pulse oximeter clipped to the tip of his index finger. Nearby is a nurse call button. Beyond this, he sees a collection of medical monitoring devices, one of which beeps regularly with his pulse. He uses his thumb to pull his hand towards the call button, intending to ask how long he'd been there and what happened to the passenger in the car with him.

It is surprisingly hard work, and the rhythm of the EKG accelerates as he fights off frustration.

A doctor enters in a clean white lab coat and makes his way around to within his field of vision.

Good morning, *he says.* **How are you feeling today?**

He looks at the doctor numbly for a few seconds, too drugged to say anything relevant.

He is informed that he has been in the hospital for a week. He is informed that he is lucky to be alive, but clearly he is a fighter. He is informed that his left arm and both legs had to be amputated, and he suffered third degree burns over half of what was left. He lost his left eye. He is informed that the surgeons did what they could, and of course there are options available to him.

He tries to ask again about her, but his throat still won't cooperate, and instead he can only mouth her name, over and over like a mantra, as he descends again into a morphine haze...

Chapter
ELEVEN

Julia couldn't allow herself to stop, not even for a minute—because stopping meant she would have to think about what was happening. Cruising on autopilot right now was much better. Once they'd arrived in Laboratory 26, she noticed that while Mechanus was still walking around, he had that blank stare that told her he'd checked out again. She waved her hand slowly in front of his face, but he didn't react.

Damn.

"Get him over to that bed," she said to Stickman. The spindly robot led him over, and he followed in a daze, sitting obediently when Stickman pushed down on his shoulders. She relaxed marginally; at least she didn't have to manage however much dead weight he would have represented.

Depending on how much of him was metal, this could easily be several hundred pounds.

Once Alistair was lying on the bed, she turned all her attention to his injured arm, lifting it so she could cut off the ruined sleeve entirely. After the blood-soaked fabric was out of the way, she lowered his arm, moved Squeaker off the compress and pulled up one corner to see if the bleeding had stopped. It had slowed, at least, which was good.

"I need soap and warm water to clean this," she said. Seconds later, another robot approached with a basin of soapy water and a cloth.

While she washed the gash, spindly robot arms descended from the ceiling and started working on the damaged plates in Mechanus's face, carefully easing away the scratched and dented metal in order to repair the inner workings beneath. She tried not to look—not because she was squeamish, but rather because it was an uncanny reminder of how *not human* he was. For good measure, she sprayed the open gash with antiseptic.

A spark flew from one of the styluses attending to things, and Mechanus twitched. He made no sounds of pain or discomfort, not even when she finished rinsing the gash and started suturing it. His eye was open, the pupil dilated, his expression blank. He was lost in whatever flashback now consumed him. This one didn't seem to be as traumatic as the last one, so overall it seemed to be a better place for his mind to be, away from the pain.

Not everyone had that luxury, in her line of work.

She finished suturing the gash closed—mentally estimating that he wouldn't have too bad of a scar when it healed, compared with all the others she'd seen on him—and sprayed the sutured area with antiseptic a second time. She was about to bandage his arm when she noticed his lips were moving faint-ly, mouthing something over and over again. She frowned, straining to listen, and finally leaned in close, placing her ear close to his mouth.

"Lauren," he whispered, barely audible even now. "Lauren... Lauren..."

A chill ran down her spine. The amount of longing in his voice as he said the name was utterly heartbreaking, as though Lauren—whoever she was—had once been his entire world.

She jerked herself upright, suddenly wanting to get away from that longing. Clearly Lauren was gone now, but...

But what?

But as the ministrations of the repair robots on his cybernetics reminded her so acutely that he was a machine, hearing him calling out the name of someone he apparently lost long ago reminded her, just as acutely, that he used to be human.

That, in many ways, he still *was* human.

She watched as one of the utility arms surgically detached his damaged mechanical eye from its metal socket, and her stomach clenched again. She returned her attention to bandaging his wounded arm, studiously not watching as the replacement was brought in and, with just as much precision, connected and set into the socket. She had no idea if he would have felt any pain during this procedure.

A new sound invaded her thoughts as she worked.

k-CHAK.

She jumped, and as her eyes involuntarily sought out the origin of the sound she saw fresh plates, shiny and undamaged, being lined up and fastened into place with the staccato retort of a rivet gun being fired.

k-CHAK.

k-CHAK.

k-CHAK.

And his vacant stare continued, only now the angle of his head made it seem like he was staring at her. The utility arms moved away at last, and his mechanical eye activated and focused with a small whirr, the light behind the metal iris glowing pale blue. His gaze was becoming uncomfortably intense, and she glanced away, finishing her task as quickly as she could.

Once the bandage was secured, she stripped off her gloves and instinctively glanced around for a sink so she could wash her hands. Finding one, she made a beeline for it, tossing her bloody gloves on the counter beside it. She glanced back once, and saw to her relief that his mismatched eyes had not followed her. She glanced over the rest of him, instinctively looking for any further injuries, and noticed that his lab coat hung loosely open at the hem, exposing his metal-clad legs to just above the knees. The longer she looked at them, however, the more they looked like flesh-and-blood limbs couldn't possibly fit inside the sleek design. She didn't know much about armor smithing, but the joints looked all wrong, too solid— like the knees of a very humanlike robot. His legs weren't just metal-shod but *metal*, period. She had to grab the sink for balance as this fresh discovery sunk in.

He's a cyborg, dear, said the sensible voice. *You already knew he was a cyborg. Just calm down. This isn't all that earth-shattering.*

Okay, she thought. *I'm okay. I'll just leave those parts for the repair robots.*

Her eyes were soon drawn back to the parts of him that she could actually handle, and she was gratified to see that he had no further serious injuries. His forearm and hand, however, were still smeared with drying blood, and she made a face. That was just *messy,* and she didn't like to leave a mess if she could help it, especially after a procedure like this. It was a matter of professional pride.

She returned to her earlier position next to where he lay, sitting with the basin of soapy water but studiously facing away from that blank stare. How long was he going to be like that, anyway? She had no idea how long these flashbacks typically lasted for him.

She rinsed out the bloody sponge until the water she squeezed out no longer emerged red, and started washing the half-dried blood from his forearm and hand, working as slowly and methodically as she typically did when a medical emergency had passed. His arm was smooth and hairless, and corded with the sort of lean muscle that she wouldn't have associated with a man of science (mad or otherwise). His hand was the most fascinating part, though—lightly callused, with long, slender fingers that she found herself associating with a pianist.

No, not a pianist.

A surgeon.

She remembered doing something like this when Jim was in the hospital, unable to get out of bed, let alone keep himself clean. It was true that doctors saw you at your absolute worst in the hospital, and the Emergency Room took this notion and turned it up until the knob broke. Jim, though, had kept up his relatively good cheer between the traction and the morphine. She'd visited him when he'd been moved to another department for long-term care, even though some nagging voice in the back of her head tried to tell her that this might violate some sort of medical code of conduct.

And after he'd been discharged, Jim had asked her for her phone number, and wouldn't take no for an answer. He was so *charming* about it, and she was in need of a social life, so she gave in. The rest was history, as they say.

And now Jim was a deranged cyborg that wanted to kill them both. She saw the way Jim had looked at her, in the few seconds she'd seen him at the blast door, drooling blood, his jaw knocked askew in a way that suggested it was broken. From what Mechanus had told her, she'd expected a vacant, mindless, or at best a feral stare—but when their eyes had met, she'd seen something far more chilling: recognition.

He'd been completely aware of what he was doing, and he'd *recognized* her.

Her hands stopped their tender ministrations. Alistair's arm was clean now, in any case.

Jim had recognized her. The thought kept spinning in her mind, demanding that she make sense of it.

When he'd first shown her the rebuilt Jim, Alistair had said that Jim had recognized her. She'd been too horrified at the time to give this much thought, and so much had happened shortly afterwards that she hadn't given it much thought. Later on, Alistair had treated cyborg-Jim like just another mindless tool in his arsenal of robots, another mental appendage to do his bidding.

Her stomach turned over, and she looked down at the slender hand that she now cradled in both of her own.

Alistair had also said that they were both connected to the network, so logically he would have *known* that Jim was still aware, that he was getting ready to do something horrible with enough warning to—

What could it have been like for Jim, being trapped in that reconstructed form, forced to do as Alistair bid him? He had to have been fighting it. He was stubborn like that. If Jim was fighting it, then Alistair had to have noticed, at least over the network, and—

Her throat closed.

He'd known. Alistair had *known*. There was no way he *couldn't* have known.

He'd known that Jim was still aware, and he hadn't seen fit to tell her about it. This was worse than the idea that Jim had been made into a mindless meat puppet—a thousand times worse—because it meant that it was at least partially Alistair's fault that Jim was after them.

And she was just starting to trust him, too...

But Alistair had risked his life for her, facing off against Jim at the blast door.

Hadn't he?

She knew the signs of disorientation when she saw them, as when he'd reported Arthur's absence, and it was clear that something had attacked him before he came to get her. She had no way of knowing how skilled an actor he was, but the gash in his arm, the nosebleed, and the torn lab coat were all absolutely real. Seeing him injured had triggered the same nurturing instinct in her that had led to her becoming a doctor—that innate need she had to Make Things Better.

And now that she had time to think about things, the expression on his face when he mentioned Jim's rampancy looked a lot like he'd concluded he'd made a terrible mistake. Not *Oops, I used the wrong fork during a formal dinner* so much as *I think I may have just engineered our probable deaths and now I have to fix it before bad things happen.*

She glanced down at Alistair's hand, clean now with a thoroughness that only medical habit could achieve, and lightly stroked his fingers. She didn't know how she should feel about the current situation, though a lot of options came to mind.

Afraid was the big one at the top of the list. Jim was on a murderous rampage that Alistair might have caused. *Frustrated* came next; all she'd wanted was a peaceful vacation, and then a relaxed life back home, freed from Jim's control. Well, that wasn't going to be an option now. *Worried* raised its head as well, now that she was taking stock of things. She was worried for herself, of course, but more than this she was worried about Alistair—this broken mad cyborg who'd thrown himself into the lion's jaws for a woman he'd known less than a week, and now he was battered and torn up and unconscious because of her.

It wasn't fair. None of it was fair. This shouldn't be happening to her. She was supposed to be back home by now.

Tears stung her eyes. She sniffled and swiped them away with the back of her wrist. They weren't tears of fear or frustration this time, she knew, but it took a few seconds for her to parse out what she was feeling. It wasn't something she'd allowed herself to feel for a while now, after all.

She was *angry*.

Angry about her situation, angry about Jim coming after her like this, but most of all angry— pissed off all to *hell*—at her conclusion that Alistair could have prevented this at any time, and instead had chosen to hide this potentially very *useful* information from her.

She instantly wanted to flinch away from the emotion, because Good Girls Didn't Get Mad, but she fought the long-ingrained habit. Good girls didn't get mad, but she clearly hadn't accomplished a lot on Shark Reef Isle by shying away from things that happened to be scary.

She was done being afraid. She was done running away from things. Alistair might be out of commission, but Julia could still do something to help.

She couldn't exactly stay mad at Alistair— whatever else he'd done or not done, he *had* tried to hold off Jim at the blast door and gotten badly injured as a result. Getting mad at him for that seemed petty. However, she *could* turn that energy to something useful, like finding Arthur.

Alistair had said that he was half-blind without Arthur. Well, maybe if she could pin down Arthur's location before the two of them hiked all over Shark Reef Isle, that would cut down on the amount of time spent looking.

And in the meantime she might have the chance to have a Come to Jesus meeting with Arthur about the disassembly matter.

She put Alistair's hand on the bed at his side and stood up.

"Stickman," she said. The spindly robot turned to face her. "Where is the nearest network access terminal?"

***

Mechanus returned to himself at the sensation of gentle hands massaging his right forearm.

No—not massaging, he realized as he registered the warm soapy water. Julia was washing his arm with a tenderness that he could only have dreamed of. The sensation was so deliciously delightful that he had to bite his lip to suppress a shiver of pleasure. Most of his body was incapable of receiving tactile input of any sort, but he'd never imagined how intensely sensitive his remaining skin could be. It was almost enough to counteract the pain in his injured bicep.

He was very relieved that she was facing away from him right now, as he was certain that if he moved or indicated that his flashback had ended, the attention would cease at once.

Without moving his head, he glanced over at his arm. The sleeve was gone, cut away near the shoulder, and white linen bandages covered his upper arm. Her work, no doubt. He continued taking stock of himself: His damaged eye had been replaced, as had the dented and damaged places in his face—titanium, he noticed. The previous ones had been surgical steel. He allowed himself a small smile at the upgrade, but it faded almost immediately when he noticed the continued absence of Arthur.

She was stroking his fingers now, but presently paused, stiffening slightly.

No—don't stop, please—

He wondered what was going through her mind just then, wanted to know what suddenly distracted her from his task. He watched her back quietly, and heard her sniffle. His heart sank. She wiped her eyes, her posture stiffening suddenly, and she set his hand aside and stood up.

"Stickman," she said, "Where is the nearest network access terminal?"

Ah.

The spindly robot that she had dubbed Stickman pointed. "You will find one through there, third door on your left."

She nodded. "Watch over him," she told him quietly. "I'll be back as soon as I can."

Stickman bowed his head. "By your command."

She nodded sharply, picked up the Ionizer, and headed out without a backward glance.

After what he judged to be a diplomatic interval, Mechanus sat up.

"How long was I out?" he asked Stickman.

"Six minutes," the spindly robot replied. "I believe this has been your longest one yet."

Mechanus grimaced. "I only wish Arthur had been able to record that one," he sighed. "I think I had a name there."

"Unknown, sir," Stickman said, and then glanced after Julia. "She tended to your arm while you were unconscious."

Mechanus examined the bandage; it was smooth and perfectly applied. "So I see. Stitches?"

"Yes. I did not see how many."

Mechanus shook his head. "No matter. She was... quite helpful." He looked at Stickman. "Any word from Scarface?"

"No, sir. The combat was still going on when we retreated in here."

He bit his lip, but then shook his head again. "I'm certain he'll be fine," he said. "He always was rather tough."

Suddenly he felt a connection being opened on the network. He frowned, investigating this new signal, and followed it to a nearby terminal.

```
> help
```

In response to the command, a list of potential options scrolled up the screen.

```
> find arthur
```

Mechanus suppressed a smile. She was starting with the basics, but of course if any one file was that easy to locate, he might as well give up on world conquest. He'd come up with the file system himself, along with the network operating system.

Then she typed something that surprised him.

```
> Arthur, you asshole, I know
you're in there somewhere!
```

Asshole? Did Julia have a fight with Arthur that he didn't know about?

After a few seconds with no response, she typed in something else that surprised him even more.

```
> You cannot just threaten to
kill me and then abandon Alistair
when he needs you the most!
```

Mechanus staggered in shock and had to lean on the bed for support. He was certain that if Arthur thought she was a threat he would have told him, but...

Well, he would have to talk with Arthur once he recovered him, in any case.

> request status report

This came from within the system. Was it Arthur? Mechanus hardly dared to hope. He hadn't even had time to properly search for him himself, not in light of recent developments.

> Jim's crazy and trying to hunt us down, and Mechanus is half-blind without you, and got hurt fighting off Jim.
> request status of master

Mechanus ran a hand over his mouth, feeling vaguely like he was eavesdropping, but anxious to get Arthur back.

> deep laceration in his arm, 27 stitches, had to get his eye and some plates in his face replaced, was catatonic with a flashback when I left him.
> status??

Arthur managed to make that one word look urgent.

> I think he'll be okay, but you have to get back to him *right now*. I'm worried he won't be able to handle this without you. And I'm afraid of what Jim will do to him if he catches up again.

Mechanus chewed his lip, his brow furrowed as he mulled over this statement. He knew that Jim was truly after Julia, and intended for Mechanus to watch horrible things happen to her—but this didn't even seem to occur to her at all.

She was more worried about him than herself.

Egad!

He sat down slowly on the edge of the bed, trying to make sense of this. Could this mean she was starting to reciprocate his feelings for her?

> i was only able to preserve my most basic kernel, miss julia

> He can rebuild you. We both need you. Do you want to be responsible for him getting killed by one of his own creations?

> negative. master created me.

Mechanus was indeed prepared to rebuild Arthur as much as possible, but what was this guilt trip she was laying on the A.I.? He'd nearly been destroyed, after all. Of course he'd be afraid.

> Then you need to get back to him. Please. I don't want to see him

```
get hurt more over this. I want him
to be able to face Jim without
getting the crap beaten out of him
again. I don't wanmt hom to ge t
killled.
```

Mechanus frowned again at the slight deterioration of her typing. He tapped into one of the security cameras and saw that her eyes were brimming with tears, but her jaw was set. He wasn't quite sure what to make of this.

Just then, Mechanus saw Scarface limping heavily towards him, the Jovian Stormcaller clenched carefully in his jaws. He turned his attention from the terminal's feed, and saw the hulking shark-man bore a handful of fresh, bleeding gashes across the right side of his head and torso. Mechanus stood up and met him halfway just as Scarface stumbled.

"Master," the shark-man rumbled as he fell into Mechanus, who staggered back several steps by the sudden weight. He took the Stormcaller from Scarface and handed it to the spindly utility robot.

"I'm here," Mechanus said quietly, stroking Scarface's nose in that familiar way.

"Fought off bad cyborg," Scarface said. "Threw him down garbage chute. He won't be back for a while."

Mechanus smiled fondly. "Good boy," he said. "How badly are you hurt?"

"Not bad," Scarface judged, even in the face of all evidence to the contrary. "Scarface is tough."

Mechanus uttered a small, fond chuckle and rubbed Scarface's nose. "Indeed you are."

Scarface beamed, an expression which even Mechanus had to admit was rather unnerving on a shark's face.

Mechanus eased Scarface over to the bed and sat him down, and then pulled off his remaining glove and pressed the palm of his metal hand to the center of the shark-man's chest. He closed his eyes and ran a rudimentary internal scan on the shark-man. To his relief, Scarface did not suffer any serious internal injuries in the fight. Even so, his other wounds required treatment.

Mechanus turned to the small surgical team of robots and appendages that had originally gathered, he presumed, to assist Julia. "Get him cleaned up and patched," he said. He flexed his right arm experimentally and winced as the stitched gash throbbed in fresh pain. "And I'll need some painkillers myself, it seems."

This last was a strange notion to him, and clearly raised some questions in his robots, as several of them turned to look at him for a beat longer than necessary before going about their assigned tasks.

Presently, Julia returned, toting the Ionizer. She met Mechanus's eye and slowed to a halt, conflicting emotions warring for dominance on her face. Fear, anger, worry, determination—all of these made brief appearances before she set her expression in something close to clinical neutrality.

"How's your arm?" she asked, sounding a bit hoarse.

He glanced down at his bare arm with its wide section of bandages. "It hurts like thunder," he admitted, "But I think I can manage."

She nodded slowly. "I think I may have located Arthur's kernel. You said you needed that to start rebuilding him, right?"

"I did," he ventured, but before he could inquire further her gaze sharpened.

"When were you planning on telling me that Jim was still mentally intact?" she demanded.

"I—*what*?" he choked out, too shocked by the lack of segue for a more coherent response.

"You heard me." Her face was set in a steely expression that he had never seen before.

For a few frantic seconds, words utterly failed him. How could she possibly have found out? He hadn't told her, and Jim certainly didn't seem communicative on that account, so—

Of *course*. She was smart enough to have worked it out on her own, given enough evidence.

"I likely would have told you at about the same time you planned to tell me that Arthur had threatened to kill you," he returned.

The color drained from her face. "How did you—?" she started to ask, but broke off, glancing away from him.

"I saw part of your conversation with Arthur over the network," he said.

She flushed, but scowled at him. "How long have you been awake, then?" she asked.

"Since about ten minutes before you left to find Arthur," he admitted.

Her eyes widened as she worked this out. "But... I thought you were—why didn't you say anything?"

He took a deep breath. "Because I thought if I did you would stop washing my arm." It sounded strange, even through his own ears, but there it was.

Her face went from pink to bright red. "Oh God. I... you... dammit, Alistair!"

The process of watching her barrel headlong through at least three emotions in six words was really quite a sight to behold, though he wished she hadn't decided to settle on anger. He opened his mouth to reply, but she barreled on in a torrent of what must have been very long-restrained emotions.

"You scared me half to death with that stunt out in the hallway!" she shouted, advancing on him. "You could have been killed! And I had no idea how to fix the damage to your face, and—what were you *thinking*? With Arthur gone, and you disoriented, and Jim on the rampage, and..." She stopped short, shaking her head as tears rolled down her cheeks. By now she was close enough to him that she rested her head and hands against his chest, leaning against him slightly. "Dammit, I don't know whether to hit you or hug you right now."

Mechanus rocked back on his heels slightly under the onslaught and, out of reflex, rested his hands on her shoulders as she leaned against him. He wasn't sure how or if he ought to comfort her. "I..." he started, but couldn't immediately think of a coherent way to finish his sentence. He cleared his throat. "For what it's worth," he tried again, "I would prefer the latter."

She wiped her eyes and looked up at him. "You still didn't answer my question."

He took a deep breath, and then let it out slowly. "By the time it became relevant," he said carefully, "It was already too late."

She stepped back and out of his grasp, staring at him hard for several very long moments. "...*relevant?*" she echoed incredulously.

"By the time I realized he was violent," Mechanus backpedalled, scrambling to find a better way to frame things but coming up empty.

She took another step back. "By the time you..." she echoed, sounding like she wasn't entirely sure whether to believe it. "What did you *do* to him?"

He blinked; she *knew* what he'd done. She'd requested the rebuild after all. "... Do?"

She shook her head slowly. "You... Jim was never violent before. Never."

...Ah. Perhaps she was under the impression that he'd brainwashed Jim. It was a plausible—if *ridiculous*—theory.

He closed with her in a single long stride and grasped her by the shoulders, fighting back a grimace when his arm howled with fresh pain. She stiffened slightly but didn't pull away. Instead, she turned her head away.

"Listen to me," he said quietly. She glanced at him, but for only a second. "*Listen*. I did nothing to his personality. No changes. Nothing added. Nothing removed. I kept him completely intact. Do you understand?"

She said nothing, but he was gratified to see her brow furrow in thought. She was at least considering it.

"But... why would you even do that?" she asked. "Why would you do that to someone, and then leave his mind intact?"

"Because," he replied, "I wanted to make him a companion for you, and I was under the impression that he loved you." Even acknowledging the romantic competition soured his stomach, but there it was. He sighed. "I don't know what went wrong. But whatever this is, it was there before. You know him better than I do. Was there...?" He couldn't figure out a good way to finish that sentence, and bit his lip as he watched her.

"I..." she croaked, and then cleared her throat. "He was always a bit controlling," she whispered. "But I *never* thought..." She fell silent, pressing her lips together. She sniffled. "I never thought I'd be in any danger. Just a big argument when I told him I wanted to break up. It's..." She went silent again for several long moments.

"Look," she started again. "I don't know what I should think about any of this. About him. About you. So much has happened in the past few days." She wrapped her arms around herself, as though trying to keep warm.

Mechanus's mind raced, struggling to determine what normal people ought to do in this situation. Comfort her, he supposed, but then there was the matter of his injured right arm and his super-strong left arm. Words seemed feeble here, and in any case he couldn't think of any that sounded remotely appropriate to the situation.

Because, really, what were the odds?

Well, he couldn't exactly let her stand there, miserable, and do nothing about it. He ransacked his brain for a suitably human response, and after a few frantic seconds found a likely one. He reached out and softly cupped her cheek in his metal palm, brushing away a tear with the pad of his thumb. He was satisfied to see that she didn't flinch away from his touch this time.

"I caused this," he said quietly. "It's my fault you're in danger, and I aim to correct things."

"How?" she asked, looking up at him.

"First, we get Arthur back," he said. "After that, I think everything will start falling into place."

Chapter
TWELVE

Alistair sounded a lot more optimistic than Julia felt, but what alternative did they have?

In the meantime, *God*, his metal hand was cold— but at the same time she was surprised at how gentle it was. It was strangely comforting, all things considered. She reached up and clasped his mechanical wrist as she looked up at him. He offered her a strange little smile, a bit pinched from the pain of his injury, but genuine enough. After several more seconds, he lowered his hand, and she released him.

"Now," he said, "Where did you find Arthur?"

"He said he was in Sector 51," she said. "A good way up from here."

Alistair nodded thoughtfully. "Seven levels up, in fact." He sighed. "And since Scarface pitched Jim into the basement, I dare not activate any of the elevators."

Julia looked at Scarface, startled by the news of Scarface's achievement. Only then did she notice how torn-up the shark-man looked. It leered at her in a way that Julia supposed might be a proud grin, but it was hard to tell when something with a mouthful of chainsaw teeth bares them at someone. She offered a small wave of acknowledgement, and Scarface returned the gesture.

"Okay," she said, trying not to shiver as she turned back to Mechanus. "So, first thing, meet up with your minions—"

"Assistants," Mechanus corrected her mildly. Another spindly robot arm tipped with a plug reached over to the left side of his head, interfaced with a small round outlet it found there, and gave a small hiss, whereupon the slightly pinched expression in his face eased slightly. Painkillers, she guessed.

"We meet up with your *assistants* somewhere near here, as previously planned, right?" Julia finished.

He nodded. "I imagine you're eager to rejoin your pet, yes?"

"Well, of course I am," she returned. "I mean, he doesn't have anything to do with... all this, does he? I want to see if he's okay." She reached down and grabbed the heavy Ionizer, slinging the nylon strap over her shoulder. "If your arm's feeling better, that is."

He flexed his wounded arm without wincing; those must have been some sort of opiates, based on what she knew of fresh sutures. "I'll be fine. You... did well."

She gave him a small smile. She still wasn't sure what to think about his withholding the truth of Jim's condition, but on the other hand, was there really any good way to tell her?

However, as he picked up the Stormcaller—which presumably had made the loud-as-hell boom in the hallway earlier—she got to thinking again. Thinking had not proven itself to be a particularly good idea in recent years, as it had left her trapped in a bad relationship and spinning in the same circles over and over again, but thinking had also gotten her through med school. And thinking had also led her to give Alistair a chance, and hadn't he come through for her several times?

He closed his eye for several seconds, apparently consulting his mental map of the area, and then nodded and opened them again, glancing at her.

"This way," he said. Scarface moved to follow, but Mechanus put up his hand. "Not you, I'm afraid," he said to the shark-man. "You've done exceptionally well so far, but you need to let the medibots do their job."

Scarface growled and gurgled his displeasure, but settled obediently back onto the examination bed and into the care of several more of the spindly appendages. "Stay safe," he rumbled.

"We shall," Mechanus replied, and then turned to Julia. "Come with me. It isn't far."

His feet clanked against the metal floor as he led her down yet another sterile, industrial-looking passage lined with doors on both sides.

She followed him, watching his white-coated back as he navigated unerringly through the maze of Sector 3. He moved with confidence now, a far cry from the disoriented wreck he'd been shortly after losing Arthur. Like her, he seemed to function best with a plan in mind rather than having to improvise. Certainly the latest development with Jim had caught him off-guard, though she'd initially had difficulty reading his body language.

Based on this, Julia considered that it probably wasn't fair of her to get mad over something that probably wasn't even his fault.

But he'd known, said the rat voice. *He'd known and he'd kept it from you.*

And when everything went tits up, he'd immediately made sure she was safe. He'd risked his life for her. That had to count for something.

And you never thanked him properly for his efforts, the sensible voice chimed in. *You focused on the* one thing *he didn't do.*

That stopped her thinking in its tracks, and the rest of her nearly followed. She faltered a few steps as he rounded a corner, and he glanced back as she stumbled.

"Okay?" he asked simply.

"Fine," she confirmed, slightly out of breath. "Are we almost there?"

"Nearly so," he said. "It's just through this door."

He strode up to a metal door that looked identical to any of the hundreds of other metal doors in the complex. It hissed open as he neared it, and on the other side she saw maybe two dozen assorted beast-men and other creations, including one that gave a happy bray when she followed Mechanus in.

The horse-ape knuckled and clopped forward on its esoterically-matched limbs and folded Julia into a hug that her instincts told her ought to have fractured several of her ribs, but instead it was warm and snug and very hairy. She hugged the chimera back, stroking his flanks in sheer relief that he was okay.

"Good boy, Cuddles," she murmured, pulling back to rub the horse-ape's velvety nose. He whickered appreciatively and settled on his haunches, his ears alertly forward.

"Good job," Mechanus said to the chimeras at large as he nodded at the horse-ape. "Now, how many do we have here?"

Julia looked over at the assembled minions. She recognized some of them—Bagheera, Romulus, and the bear-man she'd encountered while scouting, to name a few—but the rest were a mind-boggling variety of beast-men and bird-men. Clearly Mechanus had been busy in between his world conquest preparations. The assembled group seemed pitifully sparse to patrol the entire complex, however. Hopefully they would be just assigned to this floor.

Mechanus grimaced. "Is this all?" he asked, disheartened. He shook his head. "No matter. As many of you may already be aware, Shark Reef Isle is under attack by an internal force, a rampant cyborg that used to answer to Jim. He is extremely dangerous, and has already taken down Arthur." He paused, waiting for the assorted murmurs of dismay to die down. "Fortunately, we have located Arthur, and Julia and I will be going to retrieve and restore him. I want everyone on high alert. Arm yourselves, and be on the lookout for Jim.

"He is to be considered extremely dangerous, and will not hesitate to kill any of you. I will not order any of you to your deaths. All I ask is that you delay him for a time. Delay him, detain him, trap him, or immobilize him—the means I leave to you. Once Arthur is back online I will be better equipped to stop

him, but until then—" He grimaced, as though bracing for impact. "Until then, I won't ask any of you to
throw yourselves away trying to kill him. You're all... too precious to me. Just... buy us time."

Julia studied Mechanus as he finished his speech. He was rubbing the pad of his right thumb furiously across his fingertips as he scanned the assembled motley ranks of his creations. He chewed his lip anxiously, as though imagining horrible fates befalling each and every one of them.

It was as clear as the metal plates on his face that he cared about them. Yes, he made them by whatever means out of spare parts, and he could easily make more of them, but he cared about them, like a father cared about his children.

And he was afraid for them.

"All right," he said quietly, and turned away. The chimeras filed away in somber, tense silence. Mechanus's gaze fell on Julia. "Are you ready to go?" he asked in that same, grave tone of voice.

She nodded. "I'm ready, but... seven levels up sounds like it's going to be a lot of climbing if the elevators are shut off."

He nodded in agreement. "For us, and for Jim," he agreed. "Fortunately, I know of an access shaft that I set up for emergencies that will avoid all that." A grin started to develop on his face. "It was my first foray into magnetic-based levitation technology."

"Into... what?" Julia asked, but he had already turned and headed back down the corridor.

"Magnetic-based levitation technology," he repeated brightly, as though he was discussing something as basic as making spaghetti. "It contains a field that interacts with my implants to lift me to whatever level I desire. It's a bit slower than the elevators, but Jim is unlikely to be able to follow us." He frowned then, and glanced at her apologetically. "It's... typically only meant for one person at a time."

"Will it lift me?" Julia asked, trying to keep up with the topic and unsure how well she was succeeding.

He slowed to a stop, looking at her speculatively, but then glanced away, frowning. "You know," he said. "I don't think that's ever come up... that is, lifting a completely organic passenger." He shrugged. "I should be able to carry you, though, with some minor recalibrations to account for the additional mass." He continued walking. "Come on. It's just up ahead."

'Just up ahead' turned out to be around at least three different corners, along a path that Julia judged was winding them fairly close to the center of Shark Reef Isle. She tried to recall the map she'd studied several days ago to try to figure out if she was correct, but so much had happened in between that her mind refused to cooperate.

Aside from this, her feet were starting to hurt from all the running around, and she was looking forward to the opportunity to rest. She would have to make sure Alistair took a break, too—while his pace had not flagged at all, he'd been through a lot more than she had, and he wasn't going to heal properly unless he took the time to rest.

"How long do you think it'll take to rebuild Arthur?" she asked, just as he drew level with a metal door set back in an alcove and stopped.

He turned to look at her. "A couple of hours, maybe." he said. "Why?"

She nodded. "That will give both of us some time to catch our breath. And *you* to get some sleep."

He scowled. "I don't have time to sleep, not while..." The sentence dissolved into a yawn. He blinked blearily. "Not while Jim is hunting both of us down," he finished stubbornly.

She huffed out an exasperated breath and placed her hands on his shoulders. "Look," she said. "You're exhausted. You're sleep-deprived. For all I know you have a concussion. You can't keep going on like this. It isn't healthy. And... right now we both need to stay sharp."

"But—" he tried to interrupt, but Julia was just *tired* of everything right now.

"No," she overrode him. "No buts. When we find Arthur and get him on his way back to fully functional, you need to get some rest."

"But I—" he tried again.

"Promise me," she said. "Promise me you'll get some sleep."

He stared at her, and the dark circles under his right eye seemed to stand out even more starkly than before. She put her hand on his right cheek, feeling the warmth of the skin there. He was so pale that the portion of his face not dominated by metal appeared nearly translucent.

She knew full well the consequences of trying to function for too long with no sleep—she'd played that particular game during her residency, and it was mental hell until she'd learned how to sleep virtually anywhere, including on a cold tile floor.

He blinked owlishly at her, and then closed his eye for several seconds.

"Promise me," she insisted quietly.

"After I start the compiling process," he agreed, opening his eye. "But not a moment before. We can't waste time in getting him back."

"I understand."

"He's... more important to me than you know."

Julia thought she had a fair idea, but she nodded anyway. "I understand," she repeated. "Now let's see how this levitating shaft works."

She released him, and he straightened up and turned to the alcove. He reached out his metal hand towards the door at the back, and the door slid open, granting them access to a space that looked more like a broom closet than any sort of maintenance shaft.

She peered in dubiously, squinting in a vain effort to see how far up it went. "Are we both going to fit?" she asked.

"We should," he said. "It might be a bit snug, though. Please bear with me."

As it turned out, it was more than just a bit snug; after a bit of maneuvering, they both fit, but with bare inches to spare. Once they were both in, the door shut with a hiss, plunging them both into darkness.

"Okay," she said quietly. The only thing she could see was the green glow of his mechanical eye. "Now what?"

He cleared his throat and reached around her. "Um. I'm going to need you to step forward a bit."

She reached up, trying to get an idea of how much space was available. Her hands hit his chest almost immediately. "I don't have a lot of room to work with here, Alistair," she returned, acutely aware of their current proximity. At most, six inches of space separated them.

"I understand that," he replied. "However, your back is currently against the control panel I'll need to access to recalibrate the shaft so it can lift both of us."

Her pulse quickened. "Right," she whispered.

"So, if you would just... step forward just a bit?" He shifted his balance, leaning a few inches sideways. "Just stand on my feet and... squeeze in the best you can. So I can work behind you. Once everything is adjusted I'll be able to carry you up with room to spare."

She drew in a slow breath, and let it out. There were so many things about this that sounded like the setup for a cheap thrill—but that didn't exactly jibe with what she'd seen of Alistair. He'd been a gentleman to her more or less the entire time she'd been here—a slightly quirky gentleman with a near-mania for mad science, like he was getting his mannerisms out of a Jules Verne novel, but a gentleman nonetheless. And he'd saved her life at least once that she could be certain of, guided her to safety through pitch darkness, and put his life on the line for her.

And on top of—or because of—all this, she discovered that she was growing fond of him. Clearly she had some *weird* taste in men.

"Okay," she whispered. "Let's do this."

Slowly, carefully, she eased herself forward, settling her bare feet on top of his cold metal ones and pressed herself close against him. Once again, she felt that diagonal seam across his torso, and now noticed through his lab coat the presence of normal body warmth above it only. Below he was as cold and unyielding as his left arm, and she found herself wondering again how much of him was made of metal.

She heard his breath catch as she squeezed in, and for a few seconds he stood frozen, like a man who has been informed that a venomous snake is coiled near his foot. His breathing came faster now, and she was pretty sure that if she pressed her ear to his chest she would hear his heart beating like a jackhammer.

After all, she could feel her own heart pounding right now.

Well, as long as they were right on top of each other, this last would be easy enough to confirm.

As he reached around her again and started doing something complex with the control panel that involved a lot of rapid beeping, she rested her ear against the center of his chest, just to the left of his sternum, listening for the familiar *lubb-dupp, lubb-dupp* of a heartbeat.

She heard nothing of the sort. Instead, she heard a low, rhythmic whirring where his heart should be: *thrumthrumthrumthrum.*

"Alistair?" she asked.

"I've almost finished reconfiguring the access shaft," he said.

"Should.... I be worried that I can't hear a heartbeat?"

He paused for a few seconds.

"No," he said. "That's normal for me." He finished making a few final adjustments. "There. Now... stay as you are. This is going to be... a bit fast." With that, he held her close, one arm around her waist, the other hand cradling her head against his chest. In response, she put her arms around him and held on tight.

And they rocketed upward into the darkness.

***

She *had* to know the effect she was having on him, being this close. Her proximity was distracting—not unpleasantly so, by any means, but he was going to have to concentrate on the matter at hand if they were both to get out of this alive. Of course, the problem was that they were two people in an access shaft built for one, and if he let his attention flicker too much they might bounce off the walls, with disastrous results.

Instead, he cradled her close, distantly aware of the speed at which his cardiac pump was cycling and acutely aware of the gentle weight of her head against his sternum and the sensation of her arms around him. To be fair, he could only feel her embrace across the ribs of his right side, but the thought was there.

Man alive, was it *ever* there.

Concentrate, he chided himself, and he was immediately chilled by how lonely the thought was without Arthur to share it. He shuddered.

Julia gave him a brief squeeze, as though sensing the root of his unease.

In slightly less than three minutes, the two of them slowed to a halt, and Julia lifted her head from his chest. The access door slid open with a soft hiss.

"Hold on tight," he said, and then unclasped his arms from around her so he could grasp the door frame and pull the two of them out of the levitation field. Her legs moved with his—awkwardly, but at least she tried—and soon enough they were back on solid ground and, to his mild regret, she released him and stepped away, looking around.

The room in which they now found themselves was dimly-lit and small without being overly claustrophobic, though the racks of servers and storage devices that lined two of the walls ate up some of the elbow room. On a desk sat a flat-screen monitor with a darkened screen. As they made their way further into the room, however, something beeped softly and the monitor came on.

Mechanus turned and saw words appear on the screen:

> Hello, Dr. Mechanus.

"Looks like we've found him," Julia said.

"A very basic version of him, yes," Mechanus replied. Relief unwound the tension that had bound his chest cavity since this whole thing started. "I'll need to locate and recompile all of his various components if he is to be restored, but... it's good to know that he's okay."

He pulled out a keyboard on a tray and typed:

> Hello Arthur. How are you faring?

The reply was immediate.

> I am afraid. I am small and I am afraid.

Mechanus smiled fondly. Of course he was small and afraid. He hadn't been a raw kernel in... how long had it been? Nearly a decade.

He turned to Julia, who was leaning against the corner of a server rack and massaging one of her bare feet. She flexed her big toe, and he heard it pop.

Shoes, he recalled with quiet dismay. *She'd wanted shoes.* For a few moments he couldn't quite tear his eyes away from her bare feet, even though he knew they must be hurting after running all over creation. He pushed the wheeled office chair from its position in front of the terminal over towards her.

"Have a seat," he said as she looked up at him. "I need to have a chat with Arthur."

"Is there anything I can do to help?" she asked.

"Not just yet, but I may call upon you to check indicator lights on the storage units. For now, however, just relax." He sighed. "This shouldn't take more than a few minutes."

Julia sat on the offered chair with a groan of relief and set to massaging her other foot.

Mechanus watched her for a time, unable to immediately tear his eyes away from the process. She no longer seemed to regard her transplanted leg as though it were a foreign part of her body, and for its part it had followed its design and shifted to fully match its native counterpart. It seemed almost a shame to cover them—as he must, for he had promised her footwear, and her feet needed protection in any case—as, like the rest of her, they were fascinating in a way he could not yet define.

Perhaps, later on, he might offer a foot massage.

A quiet beep from the terminal drew his attention. A new line of text had appeared on the screen:

```
> You're staring, sir.
```

He felt the heat rise in the right side of his face as he typed his reply.

> Yes, about that… what on Earth possessed you to threaten to kill Julia?

The cursor blinked thoughtfully, almost guiltily, at him.

> It was not a death threat, sir.

Mechanus frowned and typed.

> Explain that.

The reply was immediate.

> It involved disassembly, not necessarily death, and it was less a threat than an absolute promise.
> ARTHUR!

Mechanus's fingertips banged a bit more loudly on the keyboard than he'd intended, but he considered the point made. Yelling at someone in a text-only environment was, after all, a fine art.

> At the time, I believed that she still intended to escape. I wished to forestall that and protect you from the inevitable emotional trauma.

Mechanus regarded Arthur's statement at length before typing his reply.

```
> Your concern is appreciated.
Your disassembly threat is not. Cut
it out.
```

There was a long pause. Mechanus frowned and typed further:

```
> I mean it, Arthur. No further
threats and/or promises of bodily
harm and/or death. Understood?
```

There was another long pause, and then:

```
> Understood, sir.
```

Mechanus sighed before resuming his typing.

```
>    Fine.   Are   all   of   your
components intact?
> I believe so, sir. I was able
to   move   them   to   this   storage
facility, but several of the drives
are reporting errors, and I cannot
compile myself.
> Not a problem, Arthur. Let's
get started.
```

Mechanus straightened up, rolling his right shoulder and flexing his fingers to loosen himself up. This was going to take a lot of typing—something he hadn't had to do for a long while. Manual compilation of code wouldn't exactly be a walk in the park on its own, but trying to do so with cramping fingers would be nigh-impossible.

"Julia," he said, and she glanced up from her left foot. "I need you to check the server racks and let me know if any of the drives have red or orange indicator lights. I want them all to be green before I get started."

The next forty minutes amounted to a game of digital Whack-A-Mole, with Julia pointing out errors on one hard drive and Mechanus troubleshooting and eliminating them, only for further errors to crop up on another.

His head was starting to ache when Julia fell silent. He rubbed his forehead with the heel of his hand, and then flexed his fingers several times to work out the developing cramps.

"Julia?" he asked. "Any further errors?"

"Hold on," she replied, and he heard the casters of the office chair rumble across the floor behind him. Mechanus held his breath, waiting. "No," she said finally. "Looks like we're good to go."

He exhaled slowly, wiping the sweat from his brow with his remaining sleeve. "Excellent." He returned his attention to the keyboard.

```
> Arthur, is everything in order
now?
> Yes, sir. All components are
present and accounted for.
```

Mechanus smiled. "Everything is ready from Arthur's end," he reported to Julia. "And he's promised not to threaten grievous bodily harm on you again."

"What will you do if he tries anyway?" Julia asked.

Mechanus turned to look at her. She had stood up and presently drew level with him, peering at the monitor that still bore dozens of troubleshooting commands. "He won't disobey me," he said. "And right now we need him more compiled than deleted."

"If you're sure," she said.

"I am. Trust me on this."

She bit her lip, still staring at the monitor, and said nothing for the better portion of a minute. When she finally spoke, her voice was just above a whisper.

"Let's do this," she said.

Mechanus smiled, typed in a final command, and hit ENTER.

```
> Compiling...
```

appeared on the screen, and Mechanus took a deep breath, letting it out slowly.

"Now," he said, "We wait for it to compile."

Julia nodded sharply. "How long?" she asked.

"Two hours, give or take," he estimated. It had been a *long* time since he'd completely recompiled Arthur.

"Great," Julia said. "Now let's find a place for you to lie down and get some sleep."

He turned to her, opening his mouth to protest, but her jaw was set.

Ah, yes—the healing angel was out in full force again. And really, he *was* tired, and there wasn't anything further they could do until Arthur was fully-functional again. Taking a nap in the middle of an emergency went against everything he believed in…

… but it was quite difficult to argue against rest while fighting back a yawn.

He consulted his internal map of the floor. "There should be a secure room near here," he reported. "We'll be able to hole up there and sleep."

"Beds?" Julia asked hopefully.

He double-checked. "Yes," he confirmed.

"Good," she sighed, and for a moment Mechanus had a light-headed moment of social panic as a long-disused portion of his brain smirked at the possibility that she was suggesting that they *share* a bed—until he realized that she'd said *beds*, plural, and relaxed marginally.

Shut up, you, he scolded his libido as he led Julia down a short stretch of hallway by the hand. It was very strange, being alone in his own head and subject only to his own thoughts without Arthur. He was discovering elements of himself that he hadn't been aware of for so long. Would he even be able to sleep without the white noise of network maintenance subroutines in the background?

The room he had located was small and, by his own standards, reasonably cozy, measuring fifteen feet by twenty, with a low ceiling and a metal floor kept clean by diligent maintenance drones. In the center of the room, as promised, were two cots with rumpled bedclothes. He would have to find out who used them last and reprimand them for their untidiness, but that was another matter for another day.

"Here we are," he said. "We should both be able to get some rest while Arthur is compiling." He sat on one with a groan of physical and mental exhaustion.

"I can relate," Julia said with a sympathetic smile. "I've had enough days that just kicked my ass all over the city." Her smile faded. "Nothing quite like this, though."

He lay back, settling himself on his back on the cot and preparing to listen, but she said no more. He glanced over at her; she still sat on the edge of her cot, looking pensive.

"How did you come to work in emergency medicine?" he asked, uncomfortable with the silence.

She glanced briefly up at him, then down at her hands. She shrugged. "I've always been the nurturing type," she said. "I've always wanted to help people, ever since I was a little girl, and I read everything I could get my hands on about first aid and the like. It just seemed like the natural field to go into, when I went to college."

"I imagine that was a lot of hard work," Mechanus said, closing his eye to listen as he tried to settle into sleep.

"It was," she affirmed. "Long nights of studying, grueling exams, learning to live without things like sleep and a social life." She paused. "All in all, it prepared me pretty well for emergency medicine."

He smiled, realizing how little he knew about her. It didn't seem fair to worship her as a pure archetype of beauty and intelligence rather than as a person, and they hadn't had much of an opportunity to talk of late. Besides, her voice kept the silence at bay.

"Do you enjoy your work?" he asked.

"It's hard," she sighed. "Some nights I would give anything to work normal hours and not be on call at all hours of the night, but... when you get right down to it, I wouldn't trade it for anything."

"You have a passion for healing," he said. "I could see it after my fight with Jim."

She was silent for several seconds. "Yeah," she said finally. "I… I couldn't let myself be afraid. You needed my help."

Mechanus was silent for what he deemed to be a diplomatic interval; he wasn't sure how she would handle his next topic of inquiry, all things considered. There was nothing to be done for it, though—not if he was to keep the silence at bay.

"So how did someone like you come to date someone like Jim?"

She was silent for so long that Mechanus was almost certain she wouldn't answer.

"He wasn't always like this, you know," she finally whispered. "He was charming and fun-loving and helpful. He never wanted…" She hesitated. "I never thought he'd ever want to hurt me. Not like this."

Mechanus digested this. "How did you meet?"

"In the Emergency Room, oddly enough." She gave a short, mirthless cough of a laugh. "He'd been skiing at Big Bear Mountain and fallen. He came in strapped to a back board, his neck in a cervical collar, and his leg splinted with a broken ski pole. He'd broken his leg in three places and was just about senseless with the painkillers, but he was awake and talking." He heard her shift position. "The first thing he said to me was, 'Are you an angel?' For the entire rest of his stay in the hospital, he called me 'Angel' or 'Dr. Angel' or things like that. He was in pretty good spirits, considering how severe his injuries were. He…" She paused. "He flirted with me a lot, and… I guess he started to grow on me. He asked for my phone number after he was discharged. He wouldn't take no for an answer. He just… kept asking. He sent me flowers, things like that—little romantic gestures. I thought they were sweet, actually."

Mechanus said nothing, though his stomach turned over slowly. Had she seen echoes of this in his own attempts to charm her?

"And we've been dating ever since, really," Julia finished.

"How long?" Mechanus asked.

"Five years," she said. "It's only been the last year that the sheen's worn off, though."

"How so?" The conversation was helping him relax, but he still didn't want her to stop talking.

"I don't know," she said. "It's hard to describe. It's like… I woke up and realized how much he'd taken control of everything. He was even the one who proposed we take a trip to Hawaii after…" she trailed off.

"After?" Mechanus prompted quietly.

She sighed, and there was a shudder in it. "I don't even know why I'm telling you all this."

Silence loomed large in the small room.

"I need you to keep talking," he said quietly, and was surprised by the tremor he heard in his own voice. He cleared his throat. "I'm not used to being alone in my own head. It's…" he shook his head. "It's too quiet, without Arthur."

She touched his shoulder, just below the ragged fabric where his sleeve had once been. Her fingers were warm and soothing against his bare skin.

"How's your arm feeling?" she asked.

"I don't expect it will fall off," he said. "It still hurts, but I can manage."

She was quiet for another interval, though two or three times he heard her inhale as if to speak.

"I… look," she said, sounding uncertain. "You've… done a lot for me. You saved my life… you led me to safety… you even put your life on the line for me—and this is just today. I don't… I don't think I really thanked you for all that. I was hung up on the parts you didn't do, or did wrong, and that isn't right."

"You tended to my injuries," he pointed out. "Was that not gratitude?"

"That was me being a doctor," she said. "That's different."

He wasn't entirely sure where she was going with this, and had no idea how to request that she get to the point already without sounding peevish. That absolutely wouldn't do.

However, the silence between them stretched, a yawning void that he could not bear to leave empty. He turned his head to look at her again, and that was when she kissed him on the mouth.

Chapter
THIRTEEN

Holy shit, said the reasonable voice.

Holy shit, said the rat voice.

Holy shit, the rest of her thought.

She'd been aiming for his cheek, in a more platonic sort of reward for all he'd done for her—and he had to go and turn his head at the wrong moment, and their lips sort of… crashed together.

She pulled away an instant later, her heart pounding, as he stared at her in shock, one eye wide and the other dilated until the leaves of the mechanical iris were nearly invisible.

What the hell am I doing? she thought, and then dove back in, tentatively at first. A few seconds later he relaxed into it, making a low, hungry noise in the back of his throat like a man who has subsisted on bland food his entire life and is now savoring a succulent meal. His metal hand gently cupped the back of her head, while its biological counterpart came to rest on her hip. She cradled his mismatched face between her hands as she savored the taste of his mouth, that unique combination of salt and metal that was so specifically Alistair Mechanus. The way his mouth responded, eagerly reciprocating what she had thought was an accident, lit a fire inside her that she hadn't felt in years.

Ten years of solitude or not, it appeared that Alistair Mechanus was a *fantastic* kisser. What he lacked in experience it appeared he made up for in raw enthusiasm.

Easy there, the sensible voice said, once it had caught its breath. *Slow down. Think this through.*

She did, and after what felt like a wonderful eternity, she finally tore herself away. Below her, Alistair lay there for a few moments with his eyes closed, breathing hard as though he'd just been chased all over Shark Reef Isle by a failed experiment. Which, honestly, he probably had. Finally he opened his eye, and for a few seconds he just stared at her, looking flushed and a bit poleaxed, before breaking into a broad, unashamed, and slightly dorky grin.

"Wow," he gasped. "That was. I mean. You. That. Wow. I. That was. I mean. Wow." He closed his eyes and swallowed hard, and then cleared his throat before trying again. "I… was not expecting that much gratitude."

"Neither was I," Julia said, a bit breathlessly.

"Not that I'm complaining."

"Neither am I." She studied him at length. "Where'd you learn to kiss like that?"

"I… I'm afraid I've forgotten." He bit his lip, just looking up at her for several seconds. Finally he spoke again. "Is this… what it feels like to be human?" he asked quietly.

"How do you mean?" Julia asked in return.

"Limited perceptions. Flooded with emotions. Vulnerable. In pain."

She chewed her lip. "Most of us go through that every day." She thought about how much pain she saw in the Emergency Room most days, the relief when she was able to fix what was wrong, and the anguish when she lost a patient.

"That's what I'm hoping to prevent one day," he said, his expression distant. "Starvation. Sickness. Poverty. War. All of those, a thing of the past once I…" He trailed off, and then winced. "But I have more urgent things to take care of here first." He closed his eye and shook his head. "Too many things to do."

"I know exactly how that feels," Julia said. "But you're not going to be good for anything until you get some rest."

He nodded slightly, and then opened his eye. "Stay with me," he said.

As she studied his face, she thought she caught a glimpse of the man that Alistair might once have been ten years ago—intelligent, level-headed, and utterly in love with a woman who might have been named Lauren. Now, all of that had been torn away, leaving behind someone who feared the silence in his own mind.

She wanted to ask him about Lauren, but now was not the time; he needed to sleep.

She nodded slowly. "I'll stay. At least until you fall asleep," she said.

"Until then," he agreed.

She straightened up from her position at the edge of his cot without encountering any resistance from Alistair, and started to move over to her own cot, when she noticed that he was holding tightly to her hand. She glanced down at their joined hands, and then at his face; he was watching her quietly.

"Close your eyes," she said.

He closed his eye; the mechanical lens kept staring.

"*Both* of them," she admonished.

With a soft whirr, the mechanical lens closed.

After maybe five minutes, his grip loosened, and a few seconds after that he let out a soft snore. Julia relaxed a bit, relieved to see Alistair achieve some state of peace, if only for a couple of hours. She gently worked her hand out of his, moving carefully to ensure that he didn't wake up. Once she'd released her hand from his, his fingers folded into a loose fist, his arm still dangling off the edge of the cot. She instinctively glanced around for a blanket to cover him, uncertain if he was subject to catching a chill in his sleep, and ultimately settled for grasping a free end of the disheveled blanket he was lying on and wrapping it around him to the best of her ability, focusing on his injured, sleeveless arm in particular.

She sat back, regarding her work—so much like what she often had to do back at the hospital—and as the last of her adrenaline drained away, exhaustion started to curl its aching fingers around her muscles, so she lay down on her own cot next to his and attempted to get some rest as well. While her feet cheered at the prospect of Julia not being on them for a while, her body still ached and her mind spun in circles, eventually leaving her unable to sleep.

Dammit.

She'd usually been able to catch a bit of sleep during the rare slow times at the hospital, even if it was a ten-minute power nap. Now, though, when all she had to occupy her time for two hours was waiting for Arthur to finish compiling so that she and Alistair could handle Jim once and for all, sleep eluded her entirely.

The irony was almost painful.

After an hour of trying to find a comfortable position, Julia finally fell asleep, and—

—she finds herself standing in one of the hallways of the Emergency Wing of St. Luke's Hospital in Los Angeles, a patient file in her hand. The only thing she can read on the file is the date— everything else is gibberish—and as she looks at the date her blood runs cold.

She has been here before, hundreds of times. She knows that date as surely as if it was burned into her brain, and she knows what's going to happen.

She tries to run, but her feet only move in that steady pace she had always used for making the patient rounds, making sure that everyone under her care is comfortable and generally okay. She passes by one of the very few nighttime security guards on duty at this hour, and she tries to call a warning to him, but no sound comes out, and he just offers her that same familiar wave that he always does.

Inwardly, she is nearly choking on her own helplessness as she is forced through her role like a video game character, controlled by some unknown outside force.

*No. No. No. Not again. No. I can't. No. Please wake up. Wake up. Wake up wake up **wake up**—*

She is grabbed from behind with strong, merciless arms. The smell of body odor and vomit fills her nostrils, and she chokes, even as he presses the blade of a scalpel against her throat.

Listen close, *he snarls into her ear,* *Do what I say or I'll slit your fucking throat.*

Even now she can't scream, and her limbs feel as heavy as lead.

I know you have morphine around here, *he continues,* *And you're going to get me some, understood?*

I d... don't have the key, *she hears herself say. He presses the scalpel harder into her throat and she feels a light tickling sensation run down her neck; she is bleeding. Her throat closes, her heart pounds, and she is certain that she is going to die, her throat slit by some drug-addicted whackjob on the graveyard shift.*

That's what you get for trying to help people, *the addict whispers in her ear, but his voice is the rat voice.* *That's what you get for putting others before your own needs. And this is all the gratitude you're going to get.*

She hears a tremendous impact behind her, and her attacker falls to the floor, releasing her. She staggers away from the fallen man, instinctively putting a hand to her bleeding throat. The cut isn't too deep, but she puts pressure on it anyway to stop the bleeding.

Thank you, *she says, trying to catch her breath, and then turns around to see who her rescuer is.*

It is Jim.

Well, mostly Jim.

It is Cyborg Jim, legs and arm replaced by mechanical limbs, and he has the twitching druggie's

head clasped in the three-fingered utility claw that
now serves as his left hand. The digits flex, and the
man's head explodes like a smashed watermelon with
a wet splut.

She screams—

Julia jolted awake, the tail end of her scream
escaping as a shrill yelp as she folded herself into a
protective huddle out of sheer reflex, trying to ward
off her own subconscious. For a few minutes she
stayed like that, her heart hammering, her limbs
shaking, and her breath coming in short gasps.

Shit.

Shit shit shit shit *shit*.

The nightmares had been tapering off by the time
she and Jim had left for Hawaii. This wasn't a new
one, exactly, but it was only the second one that had
not ended with her getting her throat cut. In its own
way, this one was even scarier.

She reached up and touched the thin scar on her
throat. She didn't even need to feel the slight raised
area to know where the blade had been pressed to her
skin—things like that tend to burn themselves into
one's psyche just fine without physical landmarks.
She didn't *want* to remember—but for the longest
time her brain had refused to let it go, leaving her
jumpy and sleep-deprived. It was the reason she was
on leave from the hospital, and subsequently the
reason why she and Jim had gone to Hawaii.

A hand touched her shoulder, and she jumped,
biting back another scream.

It was Alistair, awake and propped up on one
elbow, a concerned expression on his face.

"What is it?" he asked.

She shook her head, uncurling herself and sitting
up. "It's… it was nothing, just a… a nightmare, is

all." She pushed her hair back away from her face, trying to slip into the 'no really, I'm fine, don't worry about me' mode that had become so familiar to her after the attack. After all, he needed the rest more than she did right now.

It's your own fault for waking him, said the rat voice. *He'd still be asleep if not for you.*

Her stomach twisted, and she tried to screw a reassuring smile on her face.

He tilted his head skeptically. "You woke up screaming, Julia," he pointed out. "And you look like I feel after one of my flashbacks."

Her smile cracked a bit. "Look, just go back to sleep," she said, trying to keep her voice steady. "I'll be—"

He sat up, pulling free of the blankets and swinging his feet over to rest on the floor between them with a soft *clank*. He reached forward, grasping her hands in between his own, and she found the contact comforting.

"What was your dream about?" he asked.

She bit her lip; how much should she tell him?

What do you have to lose? asked the sensible voice. *It will help to discuss this with someone.*

She'd already discussed the incident with a therapist at the hospital, but she was warned that this wasn't the sort of thing one just 'got over'.

And he already knows you're damaged goods, the rat voice put in. *Might as well hammer it home.*

Her hands started to get that crawly, dirty feeling again. She rubbed them together within his gentle grip, hoping it was just an itch but knowing it wasn't. It was better than seeing them shaking, in any case.

"Okay," she whispered. "I can do this." She took a deep breath, and told him.

***

Mechanus listened. Julia spoke quietly at first, as though what had happened was a deep dark secret that had the potential to ruin her forever, as a doctor, as a woman, as the object of anyone's affection. Her hands continuously made those compulsive washing motions, slowly at first but getting faster and more vigorous as she reached the climax of her tale.

"It happened about six months ago," she said. "I was working the graveyard shift, making the rounds and checking on one of the patients. There'd been a bad car accident, and I was seeing if this one little girl who'd been involved was due for her next round of pain medication." She chewed her lip for a few seconds. "I put her chart back, and I'd only gone maybe five steps when someone grabbed me from behind and put a scalpel against my neck."

Mechanus's blood went cold at the thought, and his gaze instinctively flicked to the thin scar he'd seen on her neck. She clearly saw the change in his gaze, because she nodded.

"Yeah," she confirmed, reaching up to touch the scar. "That's where that came from. I was kind of surprised that you hadn't asked about it before—everyone does."

He shrugged; he had plenty of his own scars, after all. "So what happened?" he urged.

She grimaced. "I don't know who he was. Maybe he was a patient there. Either way, he was tweaked out of his mind and looking for drugs. I tried to stay calm, but he was so twitchy I didn't know if he might kill me anyway." She shook her head, disgusted. "I froze. I'd faced down horrible injuries for a couple of years by then, and I always knew what to do—but this time I froze. He asked me again, and pushed the scalpel harder against me. I felt myself bleeding, and I panicked. I told him I didn't have the key to the medication locker. I... begged him not to kill me. I was sure I was going to die right there no matter what I did." She took a deep breath. "That's when Jim saved me."

Mechanus's metal hand twitched. "What did he do?" he asked.

"He... brained the guy with a fire extinguisher." She shook her head, her lip trembling. "I found out later that he'd caved in the guy's skull. Killed him." She swallowed hard. "At the time, though, I was so grateful to see him and to be out of danger that... I decided to stay with him a while longer."

Mechanus watched the expressions on her face shift between horror, sadness, frustration, and exhaustion. He wanted desperately to comfort her, to say or do *something* that would assure her that everything was going to be all right, but under the circumstances such an assurance would ring dreadfully hollow. His detailed files offered him no advice on this matter whatsoever, forcing him to improvise.

"You'd been thinking of breaking up with him?" Mechanus asked.

She nodded. "For about six months by then."

A bone-deep chill ran through Mechanus then. He could not call it intuition or instinct because by habit he dealt in facts and logic, but a part of him that still called itself human told him with absolute certainty that Jim had known that Julia wanted to break up with him. It wasn't anything he could even come close to proving—not right now and maybe not ever—but it coiled itself around his cardiac pump like a venomous snake.

Julia was an intelligent woman—why could she not see even this possibility?

The answer came to him instantly: Because she was a kind-hearted woman. Because she was the sort of person to give someone like Mechanus a chance, even if she was afraid of him. Because she cared for strangers, no matter what they might have done.

Because she didn't know what obsession could do to a man.

The snake coiled tighter as Mechanus remembered what Jim had said to him after disabling Arthur.

I will kill her and I'll make sure you're watching, you freak.

Mechanus didn't exactly consider himself the paragon of sanity, but anyone who made a statement like that just wasn't right in the head. There was one question, though, that suddenly itched on his tongue, demanding to be asked.

"Did you ever tell him you wanted to break up?"

She was silent for a long time, and then shrugged. "It never seemed to be the right time. I don't know. I was planning on telling him when we got back from Hawaii." She made a face. "I feel like such a coward now."

He gave her hands a gentle squeeze. "You're not. You weren't afraid when I got injured, or when I have flashbacks."

She shook her head, more frustrated now. "I just kept waiting and waiting for the right time, and I've only just figured out that there would be no right time. He would be mad no matter what. And now…"

Between his hands, she started making the hand-washing gesture again. "Now he's gone off the deep end anyway and it's too late. It's just like…" She shut her eyes and fell silent.

He cradled her hands, gently stopping the hand-washing motions. "Just like what?" he asked, tilting his head curiously.

She sighed heavily. "It's just like… I was meaning to ask you about something you said during your last flashback, after you fought Jim."

He sat forward attentively. "What… what did I say?"

She shrugged. "It wasn't a whole lot, just a name. You called it over and over, like…" She looked up from their conjoined hands and met his gaze. "It sounded really important to you, and I wanted to ask, but you were so exhausted and I wanted to make sure you got your rest and—"

He released her hands and gently cupped her face. She stopped talking instantly, looking at him.

"What was the name?" he asked quietly.

"All you said was a first name," she said. "Lauren."

He froze at the name. The sound of it sent shockwaves through his damaged mind, coursing along neural pathways that he hadn't used in… well, it had to have been ten years now.

Lauren.

Lauren.

Lauren.

LaurenLaurenLaurenLaurenLauren.

He felt his chest grow tight, and realized that the chain reaction made him temporarily forget how to breathe.

"Alistair?" he heard Julia ask, as though from hundreds of miles away, but for the time being she seemed irrelevant.

He had a face.

He had a first name.

And in the cascading domino effect, memories spilled open upon memories, unlocking hidden, forgotten secret chambers in his brain.

Lauren Ellen Mackenzie. The love of his life.

No. Not his life.

The life he had before.

The life he had forgotten.

The life of another man, the man he used to be.

His mind was flooded with uncountable new/old memories, and he clutched at the sides of his head, trying to scream, trying to make it stop, but only a thin, strangled noise escaped his constricted throat as the past crashed into his consciousness.

It was the past of a virtual stranger, but by instinct his mind and cybernetic augmentations started sorting out and filing the uncountable little snapshots into the appropriate categories.

Seconds later, another name and face came forward, that of a tall young man, a bit on the lean side, with a slightly shaggy mop of dark hair. The name of this young man, barely out of college, floated into view soon after.

Michael James Conroy.

"I…" he managed to whisper. "I… remember who I was now."

His cardiac pump swelled with joy and delight and triumph, but then the rest of the memories came, as inexorable as the tide, and he started shaking.

"Oh… God…" he choked, and for the first time in ten years, his eye stung with tears.

Chapter
FOURTEEN

Julia could only watch as the mental dominoes fell. It was amazing what sort of stimulus could break a patient out of traumatic amnesia—especially after so long. Most people might have thought the blow to the head would suffice, but in truth any number of things could have done the trick.

In this case, it was a name from his past.

Then, as the last domino dropped, he looked like his mind was about to shatter all over again.

"Oh… God…" he choked, and his eye brimmed with tears for the first time since she'd met him. His mechanical eye was contracted down to a pinprick, backlit in blue.

"Breathe, Alistair," she urged, resting her palm against the right side of his face. "Stay with me. Just breathe."

He focused on her and took deep, gulping breaths, like a man who has nearly drowned.

"I... remember..." he choked out. "I remember... everything."

"Tell me," she said softly. "Talking about it might help you sort things out."

He shook his head. "That's not the problem. I..." His face was a rictus of remembered agony now; all she could do now was wait for him to either be ready, or not.

Finally his features smoothed, and he took a deep breath as he finally lowered his hands from his head.

"My name was... Michael Conroy," he said quietly, with almost no metallic reverberation in his voice. "I went to college at MIT. Even then I was a genius... taking a double major in Biology and Robotics." His face twitched in a snapshot-quick smile. "I met her in my first Robotics class. Lauren MacKenzie—one of two women in that class and the only one who stayed on for the rest of the courses." He glanced away with a smile, lost in the happy memories for now. "I... asked her out the second week of the course. I was... kind of shy back then, just an awkward nerd, but we'd hit it off so well in class." He snorted softly. "She thought I was cute." He looked back up at Julia. "Maybe I can find a picture of what I looked like then." He shrugged. "Anyway, it turned out that we had so much in common—it was like we were soul mates or something." He sighed. "Soul mates," he said again, sounding bitter.

"What happened?" Julia asked.

"We dated all through college," he said. "I loved her so much it hurt. I couldn't imagine life without her. I dreamed of engineering bionic prosthetics for amputees, so that my work would help people who had suffered horrible injuries to be able to walk and have a normal life. I just... wanted to make the world a better place." He paused, glancing down at his metal hand. "I think that was why she loved me so much. And Lauren... she was... smart, and funny, and gentle, and kind, and beautiful, and..." He smiled again. "And at times she could be just a big of a dork as I was. We had debates over the usual things... Kirk vs. Picard, Borg cube vs. a Star Destroyer, that sort of thing. Not arguments, really, but bystanders learned not to get in the middle of things really quickly." He chuckled quietly.

"Soon enough," he continued, "we were in our senior year and making plans for the future. Planning what we would do after we graduated." He sighed. "We each wanted the other to be our first. To make it special, once we were married. When I asked her to marry me I couldn't afford to get a ring, so I made her a pendant out of wire, in the shape of a caffeine molecule." He gave a shy grin. "She loved it. We started making plans, even before our graduation." His grin faded, to be replaced by a haunted expression. "And that's when things started to go horribly wrong."

She leaned forward and took his hand. "Go on," she said quietly.

He blinked several times, as though trying to get his thoughts in order once and for all, and then shivered. "We were on our way home from our graduation party," he rasped. "It was raining so hard that the wipers could barely keep up, but we were both excited and talking about the wedding and what we would do after. I was... distracted a bit, maybe." His expression turned pained. "Something ran into the road. I think it might have been a dog. I just reacted. There was no time to brake. I jerked the wheel to try to swerve, and we spun out."

His voice fell silent then, his face a mask of anguish, before licking his lips and continuing, in the tones of a man compelled to speak or else go insane. "I don't know how many times the car spun. It felt like we were spinning forever. We came to a stop sitting across the road. I don't think either of us was injured, just shaken." He took a deep breath. "Then the truck came."

Julia's chest tightened, and she squeezed his hand. He squeezed back, a helpless expression forming on his face.

"I..." he choked, and then tried again. "The truck hit my side of the car. I don't know how I survived, or even stayed awake. Lauren was knocked out cold. I was pinned in the car, and I smelled gasoline. I... I couldn't move, but I figured at least I could make sure she got out. I... I tried and tried to wake her up so she could get out. The car caught on fire and I was just screaming for her to... to wake up, to get out, just... doing anything I could, but..." He took a long, shuddering breath.

Julia remained silent; all she could think about was the flashback he'd had just after lunch, the one that had him screaming for Lauren to wake up. A chill ran through her at the thought of what that must have been like.

"I don't remember when the paramedics came. I don't remember when they cut me out of the car. I just remember waking up in the hospital, missing three limbs and half my face, my vocal cords ruined from smoke inhalation and screaming. I was pretty much gone from the hips down. They told me it was a miracle I was still alive. When I was able to ask about Lauren, they told me she was alive, but in a coma."

He fell silent for a few seconds, staring off into space. Julia squeezed his hand gently, and he came back to the present with a shiver, focusing on her.

He set his jaw. "It was then that I resolved to recover from my injuries, so that when she woke up she would see me up and about and walking and we could go on with our plans. There was an insurance settlement from the trucking company, so I used that to get started. I... wasn't impressed by the prosthetic options I was offered, so I started to make my own. They said that there was damage to my heart from the car accident, so I started to make my own. They told me that I would be blind on the left side of my face even if I got a facial prosthetic to look normal, so I started to make my own cybernetic eye. They told me my vocal cords were ruined and that I would need a voice box to talk, so I started to make my own. I... worked hard, using the knowledge I'd gained from school to rebuild myself. I built robots to aid me, and I think I developed what would eventually become Arthur to help me design and produce what I needed.

"The first device I put in was my artificial heart," he said, tapping the center of his chest, just over the cardiac scar. "I knew I wouldn't be able to do it myself, and no surgeon would agree to install an untested device of this kind in any patient, so I designed and programmed the robots who would perform the surgery, and I put my life in their hands." His eyes gleamed. "When I woke, I was so excited by my success that I leapt into the process of rebuilding myself, replacing every limb and organ that had been lost or damaged in the car accident.

"It took five years. Five long, busy years of designing, building, improving, replacing, engineering, grafting, and implanting, but at last I was up and about, more functional than the surgeons and prostheticians tried to tell me I would ever be. My new arm and legs were stronger than my own had been. I kept tinkering right up to the day I went to visit her, eager to show her how well I'd recovered. I'd dreamed of that moment for five years, sure that even if she was still in a coma, she'd know I was there, and maybe wake up."

He stopped, the memory of tentative excitement reflected in his mismatched features as he regarded his current metal hand, flexing its fingers slowly and turning it over as though seeing it for the first time. The fingers of his other hand tightened around her own.

"I got to the hospital where she'd been staying, all ready to visit her, but... they said she wasn't there anymore. I... I asked what had happened to her, to check again, that there had to be some sort of a mistake—but the receiving nurse said she was very sorry, there was no mistake." He swallowed, and Julia heard a small click in his throat. "They'd taken her off life support the previous week. Her family couldn't afford to pay for it anymore, even with insurance and the settlement. I... I was too late. I didn't even know she'd died. Nobody told me. I never g-got to say g... g... goodbye."

He looked up at her then, and the single tear that had been threatening to fall during his tale finally did. He inhaled once, a great wet ragged sob, and then broke down in tears, not even bothering to cover his face, which was contorted in a mask of pure anguish. Julia's own throat closed in sympathy, and she shifted herself over to sit next to him, gathering him into a gentle hug, and he leaned against her. All that work, all those dreams, all that hope, smashed on the floor like a glass plate in a single instant.

What was worse—this was ten-year-old grief, still raw because it hadn't been properly processed in all this time. He'd regained his memories, his past, his humanity—but at the risk of his sanity.

She didn't think it was pity that she felt for him—her experiences in the ER had put her beyond pity—but rather a sort of sympathetic resonance, two broken souls leaning on each other for support.

After several long minutes, he finally fell still, his tears exhausted, though he still had his right arm firmly wrapped around her waist and every part of him that was still organic still shook.

"Alistair?" she whispered.

At first, his only answer was a thick, shuddering breath.

"Alistair, I'm... so sorry," she said. It felt woefully inadequate—the English language simply didn't possess the nuance she felt was needed to even start to make things better.

"I..." he choked out, "I think that was when I broke. I went into an empty room and just... smashed everything I could find. I remember I was screaming, though I couldn't tell you what I was saying, even now. It took five people to wrestle me out of there, but I didn't care. I was... I didn't have anything left, not with her gone. I was nothing. All my plans, all my dreams, obliterated. I... I didn't think it was fair, that she died because someone ran out of *money*." He spat the word like a curse. "That her parents had to make that kind of decision because it was *too expensive* to keep her alive. In time I could have found a way to wake her, but—" He shook his head, his grip on Julia easing slightly. "Even… after I lost my mind, I remember thinking that nobody should have to suffer like that. People shouldn't be forced to make that sort of choice. With Lauren gone, I turned my back on the world and resolved to make it a better place… by force, if need be."

His voice had cleared and leveled again, and now it resonated with metallic anger, a sort of globally-directed outrage that would drive other men to, say, volunteer as a missionary in a third-world country, or join the military to fight warlords in distant countries.

"I left the United States and went searching for a new place to work—someplace far away from anyone else. I didn't want to be interrupted before I was done. I soon found Shark Reef Isle… and started working."

For someone like Alistair, though, his shattered mind had reformed into that of a mad scientist—but now it had broken again.

She had no way of knowing how it would reassemble itself this time around. All she could do now was hold him, and stroke his hairless, scarred scalp, and wait for him to recover himself.

After several long minutes, he finally stopped shaking, and simply leaned against Julia, staring blankly into space.

"Alistair?" she asked quietly.

He moved his head slightly, looking sideways at her.

"Are you okay?" she ventured cautiously. These next few moments would be critical.

He took a deep breath, held it for a few seconds, and then slowly let it out. He still looked pale and shell-shocked, but this was entirely understandable, as far as Julia was concerned.

"I don't know," he finally admitted. "I'll need to think about all this for a bit." He unwound his arm from around her waist. "This is all quite a lot to absorb. I… think I need to be alone for a bit."

She nodded, and then a biological need made itself known. "Is there a bathroom near here?"

He nodded absently. "Down the hall to your right, seventh door on the right."

"Okay," she said, and stood up carefully, watching him. "I'll be back in a few minutes."

She eased her way past him, paused, and kissed him softly on the metal plates that covered his left temple. He didn't react. After watching him for a few more moments, she picked up the Ionizer, slung its strap over her shoulder, turned, and left.

***

Alistair Mechanus felt utterly hollow. He'd reclaimed his memories, only to find despair and tragedy there. He'd been dreaming of this blonde woman—his soul mate from so long ago—for almost a week, only to find out that she was dead, and he'd been so absorbed in his work that he hadn't even said goodbye. His past was in tatters. His psyche—and if it could be said that he had a soul, that, too—was in shards on the floor.

He ran his hand over his mouth, acutely aware of the metal plates in his face for what seemed to be the first time.

It was almost like he'd been chasing some distant phantom the whole time he thought he was pursuing

Julia, with the result that he'd kept Julia in a gilded cage, trying to hold her up to the standard that Lauren had set.

A distant metallic slam reverberated up through the floor. He barely noticed.

Was his affection for Julia the result of love, or some twisted delusion spawned by the memory of Lauren? That was a question with no clear answer right now. It was true that Julia had helped him unlock the past and remind him of what it was like to be human—but at what cost? Was humanity worth the pain, the uncertainty, and the horrible memories of his past?

Yes, a voice inside him answered immediately. *Humanity is worth everything. The pain makes the victories all the sweeter by comparison.*

Another metallic slam came, somewhat closer. This one caught Mechanus's attention, and he glanced up, instinctively trying to quest out to locate its source before remembering his limited range. The skin on the back of his neck prickled warily.

He heard a soft *beep* in the back of his mind, the cheerful 'done' tone of the compiler. Mechanus nodded in satisfaction. He should be able to profligate Arthur by the time Julia came back from her bathroom break, and once he had his network connection back—and the island-wide omniscience that came with it—he would take care of Jim once and for all.

He stood, pushing aside the remainder of his worries for the time being, and returned to the server room. As he took position in front of the terminal, the words 'Compilation Completed' vanished, to be replaced with:

```
> You seem troubled, sir.
```

Mechanus sighed, wiping his eye before typing his response:

```
>  I   have   my   memories   back,
Arthur.
```

The cursor blinked thoughtfully a few times.

```
> But that's good, isn't it?
```

Mechanus shook his head slowly.

```
>   That   remains   to   be   seen,
Arthur. I remember why I broke. You
will see when we join again.
```

The cursor blinked at him for another diplomatic interval.

```
> Very well, sir.
> Upload? (Y/N)
```

Mechanus picked up the loose end of a network cable and plugged it into a port on the left side of his head. After making sure the connection was secure, he hit the Y key.

The response was immediate.

Data flooded Mechanus's mind in a merciless deluge. He flung his head back and groaned as information from countless servers, connections, and processes rammed their way into his awareness. After several hours of mental silence, the fresh cacophony was almost overwhelming. His lips peeled back from his teeth in a rictus of sensory overload, and his back arched in something that could not properly be called pain. A thin wheezing noise escaped his gritted teeth, something that might have tried to be a scream had the flood been even slightly less.

As the data flooded in, Mechanus's awareness flooded out, filling Shark Reef Isle afresh with his will, his command, his mind, until he was once again the god in the machine. He let out a strangled cry as his whole body spasmed in what, to the casual observer, may have looked like a particularly intense orgasm. He stood like that, quivering, for several seconds before he finally slumped against the computer desk, breathing hard, relieved to have his lungs back under his control.

That was when he heard Arthur's voice once again, to his immense relief, though the words were not exactly what he'd expected.

<Oh. Oh, I see.> He felt Arthur sifting through the new information, analyzing it, contextualizing it. <I… didn't know. I wasn't with you when you found out.>

Mechanus nodded. <By the time I returned, everything had gone to hell.>

<Will… you be okay?> Arthur ventured.

<I think so. I've been through quite a lot in your absence.>

<So I noticed,> Arthur observed. Mechanus felt him continuing to sift, a familiar, comforting sensation, but just then the A.I. stopped dead at one particular memory, a more recent one. There was a very long pause.

Mechanus glanced at the memory in question—Julia kissing him—and blushed. <Yes, well, it appears you misjudged her, Arthur.>

<It appears I did, sir.>

<So there's absolutely no need for disassembly.>

<It appears not, sir.>

<And you can *also* stop staring at that memory like it's the secret to cold fusion.>

<Sorry, sir.>

It wasn't that Mechanus was *embarrassed* by the memory, exactly—but it just seemed quite personal, like a precious jewel that he wanted to keep safe from prying eyes. The need for privacy was also new to him, but he would adapt—and so would Arthur, if he knew what was good for him.

On the heels of this, he realized that Julia should have been back by now, regardless of whatever arcane processes typically accompanied a woman's lavatory activities. His reintegration with Arthur had taken a few minutes at least, to judge by his network clock, but his senses had been overwhelmed during the process, so it was entirely possible he'd missed something crucial. He quested out into the surveillance cameras that lined the corridor, and peered through the one nearest the toilet.

The door hung open on one broken hinge. The hall to the left of the door bore a small splatter of red that looked like blood. On the floor in the hallway he saw the Ionizer—which apparently she'd taken with her—and saw a scar in the wall opposite the bathroom that looked like plasma damage.

Mechanus's cardiac pump froze in his chest as he worked out what happened while he was otherwise occupied.

Julia goes to the toilet, bringing the Ionizer. Smart woman.

She comes out, and finds that Jim has tracked her down.

He tries to grab her, and she resists—as well she should.

He hits her in response, knocking her against the wall and from there to the floor, and...

"He took her," Mechanus whispered in horror. "I couldn't stop him because I was getting the network back up. He took her, and I didn't stop him."

He was already searching the complex when the familiar signal came.

<Hello, asshole,> Jim transmitted.

<You bastard,> Mechanus returned, his mechanical eye blazing red. <I will find you, and I will kill you. You won't be able to hide from me anymore.>

<Come get some.>

Jim was daring him. After all this, even knowing that Mechanus had his full faculties back, Jim was daring him.

Of course, Mechanus wouldn't risk Julia getting hurt, but...

<Arthur,> he transmitted, picking up the Ionizer and settling the strap over his shoulder.

<Sir?>

<I will need a few supplies.>

<Name them.>

<Reinforced titanium arm plates. I don't want something to break while I'm tangling with him again.>

<Very good, sir.>

<Those shoes that I promised Julia.>

<Already fabricated, sir.>

<I'm going to need reinforcements for this.>

<What sort of reinforcements?>

<As many flying combat drones as we can spare. I will need eyes and ears when we find them, and I want to keep my chimeras safe from this maniac.>

<Yes, sir. Anything else?>

Mechanus turned and headed for the door. <Call the wolves.>

<Which pack, sir?>

Mechanus's eye narrowed. *<All of them.>*

Chapter

FIFTEEN

Julia's head hurt. In particular, her mouth hurt, and she tasted blood. She thought two of her teeth might be loose. Her left eye and cheek felt swollen, and a probe with her tongue revealed a cut lip. She was slung on her stomach across something that swayed and bobbed slowly as it moved forward.

Okay, Jules, said the sensible voice. *Take stock of yourself. Anything broken?*

She wiggled her fingers and toes experimentally. They responded readily, and without any additional pain.

Good, said the sensible voice. *Now, let's find out where you are and how you got here.*

Julia took a discreet breath to steady herself; the more time that passed, the more she suspected she was slung over someone's shoulder, and the worse that possibility sounded.

Not long after Alistair's breakthrough, Julia had discovered that she had to pee. Since he indicated that he wanted some time to think about his discovery, she didn't feel too guilty about asking to use the bathroom. She'd taken the Ionizer with her just in case, located the bathroom, attended to her call of nature, washed her hands, and opened the door to see—

Her blood ran cold.

Jim. It was Jim. He'd been right outside the bathroom, and then—

A hand tightened on her calf, and she nearly screamed.

"I see you're awake." The voice came from a nearby speaker, but it wasn't Alistair's voice like before; this time, Jim spoke from the walls. He sounded utterly, unnaturally calm, as though the process of being rebuilt had scoured away any emotions. She almost would have been less afraid if he'd sounded angry, or even upset. As it was, she felt like she was about to be assimilated by the Borg.

"I'm disappointed, Julia," the speakers continued, each one activating in turn as he approached and falling silent in his wake. "Really, I am. See, I was under the impression that you were my girlfriend. Good girls don't cheat on their boyfriends, you see, especially not when their boyfriends go to all the trouble and expense to give them a nice vacation, and especially not with some guy who kidnapped you. Have you ever heard of Stockholm Syndrome?"

It wasn't like that, she wanted to say. *I thought you were brain-dead, and then you tried to kill us.* She couldn't force herself to say the words, though.

"I get it, though," the speakers continued. "I guess I never thought you'd be the sort of selfish bitch who'd abandon me in my time of need."

Her stomach twisted. She knew this technique well by now, especially now that she'd had the chance to recognize it. However, arguing the point just sounded like a really *bad* idea right now.

"Fortunately, I'm the forgiving type," the speakers continued in Jim's emotionless drone. "As a matter of fact, I've got some really special plans for you and your new boy toy."

"Look," she slurred through her swollen lip. "It's not like that."

"Really?" he demanded, and she found herself dragged off his shoulder by the back of her shirt. "How is it, then?"

He was even more of a mess now than before, covered in lacerations and bruises and scrapes from what must have been one hell of a fight with Scarface. In addition to his broken jaw, which still sat at that grotesque angle, his right cheek and lower lip were torn open, leaving his teeth largely exposed in a horrifying leer surrounded by raw, corrugated flesh. A deep gash over his right eye had bled heavily, leaving a matted clot obscuring his vision on that side. A deep, blackened furrow etched a diagonal line across his chest and left shoulder. This last detail, she vaguely remembered, she had caused with the Ionizer. The rest must have been Scarface's doing.

She clapped her hands over her mouth to stifle a scream of horror; he looked less human now than Alistair ever had, and to her dismay none of it seemed to have slowed him down for long, let alone stopped him.

"Problem?" the nearest speaker mocked her.

Panicking will do you no good, the reasonable voice told her. *Maybe you can delay him. Certainly Alistair will be looking for you by now.*

"Look," she said, and her voice cracked with suppressed fear. She cleared her throat. "Look… Jim, I've wanted to talk to you for a while now."

His remaining visible eye narrowed and Lauren considered that she had just discovered the absolute worst timing in the long, tragic history of difficult discussions.

"Talk to me about what?" he demanded.

She tried to step back, but his hand was still firmly clamped onto her shirt. "I… I haven't been happy in our relationship," she choked out. "I've wanted to break up for a while now, but the timing never seemed right. I… I…" Any further words died on her lips, because she saw that he didn't look the least bit surprised. For a few moments all she could do was stare at the disjointed wreck that used to be her boyfriend. "You… you knew?" she squeaked.

"Of course I did," Jim snarled, and the harsh, metallic rasp that came through the speakers was even more chilling than the emotionless voice he'd been using before. It reminded her of grinding metal.

"How long have you known?" she whispered, and considered it a minor miracle that she was able to make even that much noise.

"Long enough," he said, and with a rough jerk he hefted her back over his shoulder and continued walking in that slow, lurching gait that his metal legs gave him. She struggled, hoping to slip free, but he squeezed her leg again, this time on the back of her thigh, painfully enough to bring tears to her eyes. "I thought you'd learned your lesson six months ago, but apparently not."

"What do you mean by my lesson?" she demanded. "What sort of lesson did I…?" she trailed off and fell silent. She'd been attacked six months ago. She'd been attacked, and Jim had saved her, and she'd given him a second chance. She hadn't even told him yet that she wanted to break up, but—

No. It was impossible that he'd known. Not then. He couldn't have.

"I bet you thought you were clever," the speakers around Jim said. "I knew, though. I could see you with your wandering eye every time we went out. Always looking for the next guy, just itching to dump me for someone else."

"No—that's not—" She was in placating mode again, and she hated herself for it. Old habits died hard, she supposed, especially in times of stress.

"Don't give me that," he growled. "I know your type. Of course the second I'm out of the way *here* you go and hook up with the freak that runs the place."

Well, that wasn't *quite* true, but she supposed it might seem true *enough* to the casual observer.

"He's… he's nice," she protested, and even in her own ears it sounded lame. Alistair *was* nice, though—a little weird, but nicer than Jim had been to her of late. And Jim made it sound like she'd fallen for Alistair right off the bat.

Her mind circled back to the attack. Every instinct screamed at her to avoid the memory, as always, but she forced herself to study it, willing her mind into the clinical mode that had always served her so well in the ER. The back of her neck prickled and a cold sweat broke out on her brow, but she made herself keep breathing.

In for four, hold for four, out for four, hold for four. You can get through this.

"What... what do you know about the attack?"

He didn't answer, but just kept walking. She became aware that the air was growing warmer.

"Jim," she pled. "Please, answer me."

Finally he answered. "I know that you don't always know what you really want, most of the time," he said. "You think you do, but I know better."

A cold hand started to slowly squeeze her heart.

"I mean, you talked about dropping out of medicine a couple of times," he said. "I showed you how medicine was always your dream, and you got through it."

That was true, as far as that went. The E.R. was tough, but she was proud of herself once she'd finished her residency.

"You said you didn't want to go out with me," he continued. "Weren't you happier and more relaxed when you got out and about sometimes?"

That was also true, at first, until it became clear that they were doing only what he'd wanted on these excursions.

"So that's how I knew that even though you might have thought that you wanted to break up with me, all you needed was a little push in the right direction to show you how wrong you were."

A push, she thought. What sort of a push could he—?

"And weren't we so much closer after that druggie nearly killed you? If I hadn't been there, who knows what would have happened?"

And that was the odd part, really—it had been two in the morning when the *incident* had happened. Somehow, Jim had just *happened* to be there at that obscure hour, when rational people typically weren't out and about. The more she thought about it, the less of a coincidence it seemed to be—and the tighter the icy hand closed around her heart.

"What *were* you doing there?" she asked. By now, the air was baking hot, like a dry California in the teeth of an August afternoon. Distantly, she heard the rhythmic chugging of heavy machinery, and decided that right now was not a good time to crane her head to see where Jim was taking her. She would rather deal with one crisis at a time at the moment.

"I was just checking up on you," a speaker nearby said.

"At… two in the morning?"

"I'm not allowed to visit my girlfriend at work, is that what you're saying?" He squeezed the back of her thigh again.

"It's just odd, is all." Her pulse was racing.

Stay calm, Jules, said the reasonable voice. *This is no time to panic.*

Bullshit, said the rat voice. *This is the perfect time to panic.*

"Odd?" The rasping metallic tone was back. "My girlfriend is fucking some mad scientist and you think my nighttime errands are *odd*?"

Her heart skipped a beat. The accusation was entirely ludicrous—she wasn't the sort of woman to sleep around. Jim knew that, or she thought he did. For several seconds she couldn't even formulate a reply.

Now can I panic? she asked the sensible voice.

Under the circumstances, the sensible voice responded, *I think you may.*

"Nothing to say to that, huh?" Jim continued on.

"I… I… I would never…" she stammered, trying to find some way out of this. "How could you possibly think—?"

"Oh, I know your type," he said offhandedly. "And I'll be very clear with this." He squeezed her leg again, and she bit back a cry of pain. "I am not about to lose you. I will not let you run off to some other guy you've only known a few days. See, our five years together actually *mean* something to me. You will not throw that away." He squeezed harder, digging his fingers into the muscle of her thigh, and she let out a strangled whimper, tears running down her face. When he next spoke, the metallic snarl was almost inhuman. "*I will kill you before that happens.*"

Something happened to Julia then, something that she couldn't exactly explain. Perhaps she simply reached a state whereby she passed clear through fear and despair and found serenity on the other side. Perhaps it was the moment when, behind Jim, she saw one of the many security cameras turn to point at her, its indicator light glowing friendly green.

Hello, it seemed to say. *I've found you.*

She smiled, for what felt like the first time in a very long time, and she barely felt the pain in her bruised face.

"Jim," she said quietly, and with more than a little satisfaction to her voice. "I think you're about to have a really bad day."

***

Alistair Mechanus had nearly gotten used to emotions by now, especially anger. As he regarded the scene framed in the surveillance camera, though, he found that he had passed clear through anger like an armor-piercing round and found a strange tranquility on the other side.

Jim had entered the central chamber of the main geothermal processing plant with Julia slung over his shoulder. It was a huge octagonal room stretching up hundreds of feet, surrounded by a maze of pipes and machinery devoted to harnessing the energy generated by Shark Reef Isle's central volcano and converting it to the huge amounts of electricity that the network and fabrication machines required to function. Jim's feet clanked heavily on the metal grid of the floor, and the orange glow of lava radiated up from hundreds more feet below, bathing the whole room in a hellish light that shone off the polished metal, making the place appear to be on fire. Mechanus could see sweat glistening on Julia's brow; this was the lowest level of this chamber at which it was completely safe for his biological employees to work for any great length of time without protective clothing.

Mechanus wasn't sure what Jim had in mind, but clearly it was nothing good.

Now that Mechanus had Arthur back, it had been simplicity itself to start regaining control of the various systems that Jim had hijacked. He moved carefully, though, to avoid drawing too much attention to his activities—for all Jim knew, Mechanus was still crippled. He would have to make sure Jim kept thinking that until the net closed, or else Julia could be in some serious danger.

For the time being, Julia appeared to be largely uninjured, but the blood left at the abduction site and the developing bruise on the side of her face told him that Jim didn't care about being gentle with her. Then there was the way he was carrying her—slung over one shoulder like she was a sack of potatoes. Did Jim ever care about her as anything other than a social ornament for his arm or, heaven forbid, a verbal punching bag?

He heard a metallic creak by his left hand and glanced down to find his metal hand gripping the metal safety rail hard enough to bend the latter several degrees. He gingerly dislodged his fingertips from the dents they'd left. Yes, he was pissed, but he would have to be calmly pissed in order to make this work. Even if Julia was not the woman he'd loved ten years ago—and who he still loved in a way, even after the revelation of her death—Mechanus still considered himself responsible for her safety. After all, she was his guest, and she had shown him kindness in his time of need.

And, he had concluded, he loved Julia—not the light-headed giddiness of infatuation that he had experienced upon first seeing her, but true affection. She'd done so much to unlock his disused humanity, and he would do anything to repay her for this. He would defend her to the death against the mistake he'd created out of Jim, and even—most surprisingly to him—offer her transport back to the United States if that was what she truly wanted.

And if Jim ever hurt her, Mechanus was prepared to break his fucking neck.

So it was that Mechanus had spent the last hour and a half closing in on their position and, with the careful precision of a spider checking its web, taking back control of the surveillance and security systems, closing in on them with what he hoped was enough subtlety to keep her safe. Keeping part of his attention on these processes, he approached a metal blast door that opened obediently for him with a soft hiss. The orange glow was not as intense here, but the heat at the top of the geothermal processing plant was stifling. He stepped out on the catwalk, marking Jim's position with his precious cargo through the latest of the reclaimed security cameras.

Presently she caught the change and glanced up at the camera in question. The bruises on her face were even more evident now, and he saw the streaks of tearstains on her cheeks, but he forced himself to remain cold and logical. She seemed to focus on the camera, an analytic expression on her face as she worked something out, and then she smiled. It was really quite a beautiful smile, and even considering the bruises and swelling it made her face light up like a sunrise. Mechanus took a deep breath.

Yes, he thought, *I'm here. I'm coming for you.*

"Jim," he heard her say, "I think you're about to have a really bad day."

"Let him come," Jim replied.

Mechanus knew a dramatic cue when he heard one.

With a thought, he closed all the doors to the geothermal processing plant. The BOOM of metal against metal was deafening. Jim glanced around warily, and Mechanus was satisfied to feel a transmission of fear from the other man, this brute who had dared to hurt Julia.

"You called?" Mechanus asked through all the plant's speakers at once.

"Show yourself!" Jim demanded, pulling Julia off his shoulder and holding her up by the back of her shirt. His pincer, damaged from its impact with the wall earlier, could no longer spin in that drill of death, but two of the digits still flexed as he held it close to her throat. It was a clear message: play by my rules, or something bad happens to her.

<Send in the wolves,> Mechanus instructed. <Distract him.> As the dire wolves leapt to follow his command, Mechanus navigated the maze of catwalks, positioning himself carefully. He was about a hundred feet above where Jim held Julia hostage, but it was unlikely that Jim would start anything serious until Mechanus got there. After all, he wanted Mechanus to watch him kill Julia.

Well, *that* wasn't going to happen on Mechanus's watch.

"Patience, Jim," Mechanus said through the speakers. "We both know you don't want to do anything prematurely."

"You're hardly in a position to make demands, asshole," Jim retorted.

Mechanus could not suppress a grin that was nearly a snarl.

He tracked the coordinated paths of the wolf packs as they navigated their way down to the plant, their claws clicking against the metal floors as they went. Within minutes the first of them had reached one of the doors leading in. Mechanus opened it for them, and the pack of giant wolves surged in, howling a challenge.

After that, several things happened in rapid succession. Jim turned in the direction of the howling, reflexively pulling the utility pincer away from Julia's throat. Julia took advantage of his distraction to slip out of her shirt entirely, running off in her bra to lose herself amid the heavy machinery, ducking and dodging and stepping gingerly on the hot floor. Mechanus let in a wolf pack at the other side of the room, and they encircled a very surprised-looking

Julia with their huge, furry bulk. Another pack streamed in and charged at Jim, forcing his attention away from her.

He swiped at the nearest ones with his utility claw, knocking one of the smaller ones aside. It hit a tank with a yelp and the crunch of breaking bones, and lay still. The others circled just outside his reach, occasionally darting in to snap at him to keep his attention as far away from Julia as possible.

Mechanus positioned himself on a walkway above the circling dire wolves. He glanced at the fallen wolf, zooming in and scanning it.

<He is alive, sir,> Arthur informed him. <He has a broken back, however.>

Mechanus gritted his teeth. <That can be repaired,> he said. <Watch over him.>

Five of the battle-drones moved to a position above the wolf, ready to blast anything that wished him harm.

He marked Julia's position—safely away from the impending fray. She was surrounded by the other pack of dire wolves, who would act as a barrier should things spill in that direction. At the very least they would keep her safe from Jim.

His priority targets thus secured, Mechanus measured the distance to the level below. One hundred feet. Had he been fully human the fall might break both his legs. He smiled grimly. It was time to end this.

He vaulted over the safety rail.

Mechanus landed in a three-point crouch in front of Jim; the impact strained the shock-absorbers in his legs, buckled the metal floor slightly, and rattled his teeth together. Fortunately, Arthur's balance-correction assistance kept him on his feet, and he straightened up before his foe, staring him down.

"Asshole," Jim said, his voice emerging from a speaker in tones close to those of a polite, if chilly, greeting.

"Deranged cur," Mechanus responded, likewise. "I'm afraid I've made a dire mistake with you, Jim—one that I intend to rectify very shortly."

"What mistake is that?" Jim demanded.

"Two, actually." Mechanus began circling Jim, who turned to keep him within view. Two pairs of metal feet clanged against the metal floor. "One of them was underestimating your willpower. I admit I'm a bit out of practice in dealing with other human minds, but your determination to break free was quite unexpected. You caught me by surprise. This will not happen again. The other, of course, was in resurrecting you in the first place. You were intended as a gift for Julia, not as the source of her terror—and I intend to rectify this mistake. I know all about the nature of obsession and mental fixation, but *really,* Jim—enough is quite enough. If you can't come to terms with the changing social dynamic, I'm afraid I'll have to put you down."

What remained of Jim's face contorted into a snarl like that of a rabid dog, and he started to advance on Mechanus—away from Julia, Mechanus noted with satisfaction.

Mechanus watched the entire unfolding scene from every angle at once, through countless surveillance cameras and drones surrounding the two of them—and also watched Jim's neural signals for flickers of intent.

Jim lunged for him, swinging his utility claw like a club. Mechanus twisted and blocked the blow with his own metal arm, the impact sending a shockwave up the titanium carapace even as he deflected it up and past him. In return, Mechanus swung at Jim's face with his metal fist. Jim was ready this time, though, and dodged backwards, out of reach.

"Forget it, asshole," Jim said through the speakers. "You made me too well. Whatever you did to revive me is going to make me nearly impossible to kill. You said as much to Julia. And you lost your control over me. I don't have to follow your commands like everything else here."

He swung the utility claw again, aiming for the unarmored side of Mechanus's head. Mechanus dodged aside, feeling the wind of the claw's passage.

"That may be true," Mechanus said, "But you forget whose lair this is. *And* you forget what I can do."

"You can get your ass kicked," Jim retorted, and aimed a vicious kick between Mechanus's legs.

There was a loud *clang* of metal against metal. Mechanus was jolted briefly off his feet, staggering back, but the crippling burst of masculine pain he'd half-expected did not come. For the first time in recent memory, Mechanus fully appreciated the advantage of not having external genitals.

Jim froze, momentarily startled by the lack of effect his unsportsmanlike low blow had on Mechanus. In response, Mechanus casually popped his neck.

"Did that make you feel better?" he asked.

In response, Jim assaulted Mechanus mentally through the network connection. Mechanus rocked back on his heels.

<Not so fast,> Arthur chided, and returned fire. Jim howled in agony, clutching at his head.

<You have forgotten something very fundamental, Jim,> Mechanus informed him through the haze of distortion that now fogged Jim's mind. <I have been doing this a lot longer than you have. I am better versed in this network than you are. I have Arthur back. What I have made, I can and will unmake.>

<You and what army?> Jim demanded, defiant to the last.

In response, Mechanus closed his eyes and mentally reached out in several directions at once. First, he seized Jim's mind in a vice-like grip, paralyzing him where he stood as completely as if he'd been turned to stone. Second, he cut off Jim's access to the speakers; there was no need for Julia to hear what would come next. Third, he summoned every battle drone in the area—all three hundred fifty of them—to a swarm behind him.

<This army,> Mechanus said simply. He tapped into the speakers then. "Julia, don't look."

He flung his arms out to the sides—unnecessary, he conceded, but theatrical all the same—and gave a mental command. The battle drones converged on Jim like Japanese honeybees and started to methodically disassemble him. Mechanus did not watch the process, but was assailed by Jim's frantic, panic-laced transmissions through their mutual link to the network, ranging from threats to bargaining to frantic screaming. Flashes of inner thoughts, memories, and mental images flooded across Mechanus's mind as Jim tried to find something—*anything*—he could do to save himself.

The barrage continued for a few minutes, though to Mechanus's perceptions it felt a lot longer. Jim was not dead, however, when Mechanus gave the command to cease. The robots withdrew, hovering a short distance above Jim's paralyzed remains. All that remained of him was a dismembered, blood-spattered torso; all his cybernetic limbs had been removed and reclaimed, and the arm he'd had left was taken as well. All his amputated stumps had been diligently cauterized, but he wasn't going to be going anywhere. Jim's mind was a shattered mess, but he still responded to Mechanus's light query.

<Jim, there is one more thing I require of you before I will release you.>

<?>

<What do you know of the attack on Julia six months ago?>

The response was immediate; no words came, but rather a memory, subconsciously summoned by the question.

<Arthur, record this,> Mechanus said as soon as he recognized the context.

<As you wish, sir.>

Jim stands outside the hospital, in low conversation with an agitated, unshaven man who wears a sickly stench like a jacket. He needs his next hit, and doesn't much care where it comes from. He's perfect.

I know where you can get some, but you have to do exactly what I say, *Jim says,* ***I know who can get you what you need, okay?***

The addict is only too happy to agree, and Jim leads him into the hospital by one of the side entrances he used before to meet with Julia, back before she started cooling off towards him. He isn't about to lose her—he isn't the sort of guy that women break up with, after all—and he's going to make sure she understands how important it is that they stay together. She isn't allowed to break up with him.

He isn't worried about the addict, really—these assholes are a dime a dozen, and he won't be missed.

Jim grabs a fire extinguisher as he follows the addict through the hospital corridors. He doesn't know the man's name—never cared to learn it, really. Jim points out Julia, keeping the extinguisher out of sight, and then sits back and enjoys the show, just waiting for his cue...

Mechanus watched the memory play out, attempting to remain dispassionate but only partially succeeding as the events unfolded to their brutal conclusion. He wasn't even sure if he should show this to Julia, even though it directly concerned her. It was a cowardly thought, though—she would need to see it, but on her own time.

The memory finished, and Mechanus regarded the broken remnants of Jim. The limbless torso twitched, just once.

<You don't deserve her,> Mechanus pronounced finally. <Nobody who would do such a thing deserves a woman as special as Julia is. You are a monster.>

And without waiting for any sort of a reply, he stopped Jim's heart with a thought.

Chapter
SIXTEEN

When the dire wolves showed up, Julia had been expecting wolves the size of bears, not *full-sized vans*. They flooded towards her in a tidal wave of fur and fangs and rippling muscle, surrounding her before she could get it into her head to run rather than freeze up.

The biggest of the group headed for her, his golden eyes gleaming with predatory intelligence, but to her relief it didn't seem inclined to tear her apart or whatever it was wolves did with prey. Instead, it lowered its head, tail wagging, and nudged her with its nose.

"Hello," she said hopefully, but it came out as a whisper. It seemed friendly enough, but it was still a giant wolf.

The wolf glanced in the direction of combat and let out a low growl. Julia followed its gaze, craning her neck to see past the machinery, and caught a glimpse of Alistair and Jim facing off. She bit her lip anxiously. She didn't want Alistair getting killed, but she didn't know what she could do to help. The wolf nudged her again, and when she turned it let out a low *whuff* and crouched down.

If she didn't know better, Julia might think the giant wolf wanted her to climb on its back. It *would* be more comfortable than doing the hot-sand dance on the metal grating.

"Okay," she said to the wolf. "I haven't been horseback riding in a while, so bear with me."

It licked her hand encouragingly, and she grabbed a double handful of thick fur on the ruff on its neck and heaved herself onto its back. The muscles under its pelt rippled smoothly as it stood up and padded away from the fight, surrounded by its pack.

It came to a halt at the far end of the cluster of tanks. The sounds of combat had ceased by now, replaced by a tense, watchful silence. Julia bit her lip, both curious to see who won and desperately afraid that she would see Alistair broken and dying with Jim standing over him.

"Julia, don't look," Mechanus said from a nearby speaker. Julia didn't think she had a line of sight on the battle anyway, but she resolutely looked away from where she'd heard combat. Whatever was about to happen was going to be gruesome, even by the standards of a mad scientist. Her stomach twisted.

Please, please let Alistair be okay, she thought.

That silence was the eeriest part. During the previous fight between Alistair and Jim she'd heard at least sounds of violence—the lightning gun going off, meaty impacts, and the like—right up until she'd opened the door. Now, aside from the insectile whirr of the drones' rotors and the odd meaty slice, she didn't hear much of anything over the steady bass hum of the refinery equipment. Now there was only the low hum, and the horrible anticipation. She was sure that one of them was going to come and find her. She earnestly hoped it would be Alistair. She lay down along the dire wolf's back, hugging its flanks like it was the biggest, meanest teddy bear in the world. Its breath came in huge, heavy pants, and while it seemed relaxed, its ears were forward and alert.

CLANK.

The sound of metal on metal made her jump and the dire wolves tense. Sure she was surrounded by dire wolves that seemed determined to protect her... but if Jim came out on top, how much help would they be?

CLANK.

CLANK.

CLANK.

She realized that she was hearing the steps of metal feet approaching. They were slow, deliberate, and purposeful. She had no weapons, no protection if it was Jim—hell, she had to wiggle out of her shirt to get away from him—and so all she could do was wait and see. And hope.

Suddenly, the dire wolf raised his head, ears forward, and gave a happy bark.

"Julia?" she heard a familiar metallic baritone call, not far ahead of her. Her heart skipped a beat.

"Alistair?" she called back, sliding off the dire wolf's back and hurrying forward, limping slightly from the bruises Jim had left on her leg.

In seconds she saw him emerge from around one of the huge metal tanks—tired, haggard, and splattered with blood, but overall triumphant. He saw her at about the same time, and she rushed forward, flinging her arms around his neck as he folded her into an embrace.

Their lips collided like protons in a particle accelerator, and for a while the rest of the world just faded into the background. He held her close, his sleeveless right arm warm against her mostly-bare back, while he twined metal fingers through her hair. She cradled the mismatched sides of his face between her hands, feeling the seams and rivets and access plugs under the fingers of her right hand—though by now the metal didn't even matter to her—as she savored the salty taste of his mouth against hers.

As the chemical reaction eased in intensity, so too did the intensity of their embrace. Even as time seemed to stop, he took his time with her, exploring her mouth with the careful thoroughness of a scientist. He brushed his lips gently across hers, savoring her like a fine wine, in sips rather than swallows.

She brushed the pad of her thumb down the scar at the front of his throat, and he shivered, letting out a slow, shaking breath against her lips.

"Be careful what you start," he murmured, brushing his fingertips lightly over her bruised cheek. "Certain chemical reactions are difficult to stop once triggered, and I think we have a bit of an audience."

She froze and opened her eyes, to find that, indeed, a dozen flying drones the size of hummingbirds seemed to be watching the proceedings with great interest.

She giggled helplessly at the whole situation, but she didn't pull away just yet, leaning her forehead against his chest.

"Are you okay?" he asked at length.

She nodded. "I think so, yeah," she said. "Nothing broken, anyway. He just…" She reached up to touch her face where she was sure Jim had punched her and winced. Sure enough, her lip and cheek were swollen.

"You won't have to worry about him anymore," Alistair informed her grimly.

"He's… is he dead?"

"Yes." He pronounced the word with a profound certain finality.

"Thank God. I'm… I know I shouldn't be this happy about that but… I'm just so relieved he's finally gone." She pulled away slightly and looked him over. "You're covered in blood—are you okay?"

"It's not mine," he informed her, and offered her a weary smile.

She felt a slight chill as she imagined what could have caused the blood spatter, but decided she didn't want to know. Instead of asking about it, she just hugged him, leaning her head against his chest and listening to the *thrum-thrum-thrum* that he had in place of a heartbeat as he cradled her close. It was over—almost.

"And now," he said after maybe fifteen seconds had passed, "I believe I still owe you dinner."

She looked up at him, surprised. "Dinner?"

He grimaced. "Yes. Well. I did tell you I'd made plans for this evening." He gestured vaguely. "But then everything happened, and…" He trailed off.

She reached up and touched his cheek. "I'd love to have dinner with you… just not tonight. I'm beat."

He digested this, and then nodded. "Yes, of course—after what happened and all… you'll want to relax tonight, I expect." He sighed. "And I need to attend to a bit of cleanup." His gaze grew distant as he checked an internal map. "I have a room near here where you may sleep. I will take you there directly."

With that, he swept her up into his arms in a bridal carry, startling a squeak of surprise from her. She reflexively clasped her hands around his neck as he settled her comfortably in his grasp—or as comfortably as could be managed with a metal arm digging into her back.

"What are you doing?" she asked, a bit breathlessly.

"I know your feet hurt," he replied. "Just relax for a bit."

This was true—her feet hurt, her face hurt, her bruised thigh hurt—everything hurt. She was tired and achy and wanted to sleep. She was sure that he was tired as well, but he was clearly determined to attend to her first. Even after being here for almost a week, the idea of letting someone take care of her was still strange to her. She tried to make herself relax, all the same, and rested her head against his shoulder. He smelled of sweat, metal, and disinfectant—a strangely comforting combination.

She closed her eyes and dozed off.

***

Mechanus was exhausted from the day's events, but he was not going to neglect Julia, who had been through so much more than he had, and deserved her rest. He flagged down a passing flying drone for assistance, and it followed him to the spare room and pulled back the blankets and sheet. Its mechanical whirring made a sort of mechanical lullaby as Mechanus carefully placed Julia in bed. He hesitated, uncertain how comfortable she would be sleeping in a bra and pants.

He could always remove them, so she would be more comfortable—

...No. That would not do at all. He remembered all too well how upset she'd been the last time she unexpectedly woke up nude, and he wasn't going to do that to her again.

Instead, he reached down and smoothed down her tangled hair with one hand, and pulled the blankets up over her. She shifted, moving from a supine position to half-curled on her side, and let out a soft sigh as she snuggled into the pillow. He watched her sleep for several long minutes, and then tore himself away at last, turning and leaving the room.

He had so much to do, after all.

<Arthur,> he said.

<Sir?>

<Compile a casualty report for this incident.>

<Of course, sir. How is Julia?>

Mechanus's gait slowed. <Sleeping quite soundly.>

<Not surprising, sir,> Arthur replied. <You both had quite a harrowing afternoon.>

Mechanus sighed. <And now all that's left is the cleanup.>

<Yes, sir. And now, for the requested casualty report...>

He listened as Arthur listed off how many assets had been lost in Jim's rampage. To Arthur, they were numbers, creations to be rebuilt or replaced, but Mechanus had become familiar with each and every one of them—and when Julia started naming his robots… well, it reminded him of how precious they were as well.

In total, a dozen chimeras had died, despite Mechanus's instructions—though he was sure many of them had been in the wrong place at the wrong time before the briefing—and three dozen robots of various shapes and functions had been destroyed, but the crucial functions had been largely preserved. Jim hadn't gotten to the items specifically earmarked for his global conquest project. It could have been a lot worse.

He sighed. <Injuries and repairs?> he asked.

<In progress, sir. The fallen dire wolf is on his way to surgery as we speak, and should be able to walk again. And you need to have your arm properly mended.>

<Good. I shall.> He rubbed his eye, and he got another flash of Lauren, as vivid as though he'd just seen her the previous day. His throat closed, and he leaned against the wall.

<Sir?> Arthur queried. <Are you okay?>

Mechanus took a deep breath. <I'm not sure,> he admitted. <In time I might be, but… right now I'm so confused.> He straightened up from the wall and continued walking, aiming for the nearest infirmary.

<Perhaps I can help, sir.>

<I hope so. I did program you to fulfill all aspects of social companionship.>

Arthur hesitated. <Except for providing emotional support, sir.>

Mechanus reached the infirmary and walked in, settling himself in a chair. Several surgical appendages started peeling away the bandage on his upper arm. Julia's sutures were tidy and regular, and did the job just fine... but his own methods would seal the gash more efficiently and leave no scar.

<I can, however, provide a sounding board,> Arthur added helpfully.

Mechanus sighed, idly watching the sutures being removed. <Very well. Here are the facts as I understand them.> Bullet points appeared on a nearby monitor with each item. <First, I love Julia. I did from the moment I saw her. It may have been infatuation at first due to loneliness but I think it's developed into something more.> Blood welled up and was delicately dabbed away.

<Yes, sir.>

<Second, I love Lauren. I... I know she's dead, but I still love her. She was my first love, and... I know it's been ten years, but it feels like it only happened yesterday. Everything is still raw.> He felt the pain cancellation function activate as the gash was cleaned and trimmed of ragged flesh.

<Yes, sir.> Arthur's voice was patient and, in its own way, comforting.

<I can't imagine life without Julia. There would be a big empty hole in my life without her... but it seems somehow disloyal to Lauren... like I was courting Julia immediately after her death.>

<Not necessarily so, sir,> Arthur pointed out.

Another cluster of delicate arms began busily knitting the gash together, layer by layer. <How do you mean?> Mechanus asked.

<The fact that you still love Lauren means that you haven't forgotten her, and the fact that you love Julia means that you are still capable of forming such emotional bonds.>

Mechanus turned this over in his mind. <Go on.>

<Additionally, Julia can offer you the support you need in order to properly mourn Lauren, because it is quite clear that you have likewise won her over.>

Mechanus smiled to himself. <Yes, it appears that I have.>

<Thus, in embracing this new stage in your life—literally or figuratively, as the case may be—you can honor Lauren's memory.>

The tissue-sealing process reached the top layers, and the last of the appendages busily knitted together the edges of skin, leaving behind a hair-thin white line that would disappear in a day or two.

<I still crave closure,> he said. <And there is still the matter of that memory of Jim's that you recorded.>

<Yes, sir. There is a 99.57% chance that showing her the memory will upset her, a 73.2% chance that it will offer her the beginnings of emotional closure regarding Jim, and—> Arthur was silent for several seconds. <And a 98.62% chance that she suspects the truth regardless of our intervention.>

Mechanus grimaced. <It seems logical then, that I should let her choose whether or not she wants to view it.> He flexed his newly mended arm, satisfied by the handiwork. <Record the file onto a data disc and send it to her when she wakes.>

<Very good, sir. Now that the crucial items are taken care of, would you like to begin preparations for dinner?>

Mechanus sighed, grateful that they were moving off of potentially dicey topics.

<Do you recall the first meal Julia ate here?> he asked Arthur.

<Sir?>

<It was striped sea bass. I want our special dinner to be built around that.>

<How elaborate, sir?>

Mechanus interlaced his fingers behind his head, leaning back. <Five courses, I think. And wine.>

<I believe white wine pairs best with fish. A nice Chardonnay, perhaps?>

<Yes. See what I have in my stores.>

<Of course, sir. Initiating analysis of five-course fish dinner—and while that is running we can talk about your wardrobe for the event. Surely you're not planning on wearing that?>

Mechanus frowned and looked down at himself, only to grimace when he saw the tattered condition of his clothing. <Observant as always, Arthur. I'll need fresh clothing for the event.>

<Something special, in fact,> Arthur put in. <A lab coat simply will not do for this event, even a clean one. You will need something more formal for dinner.>

Mechanus sighed; clothing was clothing, as far as he was concerned—to cover or to protect oneself from the environment. He would be sending Julia a fresh dress, of course, and all the appropriate accessories. He even had an idea for an item that would honor Lauren's memory while making a lovely gift for Julia. As for himself, though…

<What did you have in mind?> he asked Arthur.

Chapter
SEVENTEEN

Julia woke up snuggled warmly between crisp linen sheets. It took her a few moments to remember how she'd gotten there—as this was not the bed where she'd been sleeping the past several nights—but when she remembered Alistair carrying her, she smiled and curled further into the warmth, savoring the opportunity to rest. Then she started thinking again.

You should give him something, the reasonable voice informed her tartly. *He's done so much for you. He saved your life.*

Okay, but what? What do you buy the man who could make anything he could possibly need?

You get him the one thing he hasn't had in ten years—closure.

She sat up suddenly at this thought. Closure. Of *course*. She glanced around at the door, looking for the speaker that would be just above it. To judge by how quickly Alistair ended the fight with Jim, it was a fair bet that Arthur was back. And if he was, he would be able to help her with this.

"Arthur?" she asked.

"Yes, Miss Julia?" Arthur's polite tenor responded promptly. She smiled.

"It's good to have you back, strange as that might sound," she said with a smile.

"It is good to be back, in light of everything," Arthur replied brightly. "Was there something you required?"

She rubbed her eyes, still feeling sleep clinging to her. "How long was I asleep?"

"Fourteen hours, Miss Julia. You and Dr. Mechanus were both quite tired from your respective ordeals."

"No kidding." She stretched; the aches and pains had receded during her rest, but her face and mouth were still sore and probably would be for a while. As her body woke up, her stomach growled. She looked down at it reproachfully, and then back at the speaker. She opened her mouth to speak.

"A meal will be brought to you directly, Miss Julia," Arthur preempted her.

"Thanks," she sighed, swinging her feet over the edge of her bed. She glanced around and saw only one door. No adjoining bathroom, then. "A hot shower and some fresh clothes would be nice, too."

"I will send someone to show you to the appropriate facilities."

"And I need to know where Lauren MacKenzie was buried."

There was a long, slightly scratchy silence from the speaker.

"Arthur?" Julia called.

"I am still here," Arthur said finally. "I presume you speak of Dr. Mechanus's previous love?"

"That's right," she replied. "I want to know the address of the cemetery and the plot number, if there is one."

"Any specific reason?"

She sighed. "I don't think he ever got the chance to say goodbye. Not really."

Arthur processed this for several seconds.

"As you wish. I cannot say for certain if he will be willing to leave Shark Reef Isle for such a journey, though."

"All I can do is offer," Julia replied.

"Of course."

"How has he been?" She glanced down at herself, frowning in momentary confusion at her current state of dress before remembering having to ditch her shirt to get away from Jim. Clearly, Alistair was too much of a gentleman to undress her further, even for comfort's sake.

"Well enough, all things considered. He eagerly awaits dinner with you."

Julia smiled. "I imagine he does. What has he been up to? How is his arm feeling?" She got up and started taking stock of the room. It was simpler than her guest room, with just a bed and a few cabinets with drawers for storage. Upon further investigation, she found some medical apparatus that she recognized, alongside more esoteric tools that she didn't. Her imagination supplied a number of colorful suggestions for the possible uses of the latter, though.

"His arm is doing much better, now that he has properly repaired the laceration. He wishes to pass on his gratitude for your sutures all the same."

She sighed; the unspoken remark that her sutures weren't a 'proper' repair was annoying—but then again, Alistair had performed a fully functional limb transplant in a day without blinking an eye. "I did what needed to be done at the time," she said.

"You may be pleased to know that he has resources available to minimize your own injuries as well," Arthur continued.

She reached up and touched her swollen face with a grimace. Her eye wasn't swollen shut, but she probably had a decent shiner, and the cut on her lip still stung and tasted of copper when she probed it with her tongue. "What sort of resources?" she asked.

"Agents to reduce the bruising and speed up the healing process. He used similar agents when he gave you your new leg."

She glanced down at the limb in question. That would explain why it hadn't *looked* post-surgical when she first saw it.

"After all," Arthur continued, "He wishes for you to look your best at dinner this evening."

Ah. Yes. Dinner. And dancing. With Alistair. Who'd saved her life. She tried not to imagine what he'd done with Jim afterwards, telling herself instead that it didn't matter, that Jim had gone psycho, that it was like having a rabid dog put down...

She still would have expected some sort of noise from the process, though...

Her thoughts were interrupted when the door chimed in that familiar manner.

"Come in," Julia called.

The door opened to admit Scarface, who had somehow stopped being frightening sometime during the last twenty-four hours. The wounds he'd earned in his fight with Jim were now bandaged; whether or not they'd also been stitched was anyone's guess, as was the question of whether sutures were even viable on a shark-man. He had not yet mastered the fine art of smiling without exposing a lot of jagged teeth, but he seemed to be trying his best. He bore a tray with a cover on it, which he offered to Julia. No hot food smells issued from the tray, and when she lifted the lid she found tuna salad sandwiches—plain but palatable.

"Good boy, Scarface," she said, and snatched up one of the sandwiches and began devouring it. She usually didn't like tuna salad, but fourteen hours of hunger can season the blandest meal to perfection. After licking tuna and mayonnaise off her fingers, she glanced up at the shark-man, who still stood there patiently.

"I guess you're here to take me to the bathing facilities?" she asked.

He nodded his torpedo-shaped head, the chainsaw smile mercifully back under wraps.

"Give me a minute," she said, and wolfed down the other sandwich. He waited patiently until it was gone, and all that was left was licking her fingers clean. She might have to think about eating tuna salad more often in the future.

"Good?" he asked, tilting his head.

She paused in licking her fingers and sighed. "Not usually my favorite, but I was hungry. Now, about that shower?"

"Dr. Mechanus has one more thing to offer to you, Miss Julia," Arthur said.

Scarface looked up at the speaker.

"What sort of thing?" Julia asked.

"It is a digital recording of Jim's last thoughts—his memory of the night you were attacked."

Julia's stomach turned over. "It... are you sure?"

"As sure as such things can be. I have no reason to believe he would be in a position to deceive at the time the memory was recorded. Do you wish a copy?"

Julia felt queasy at the thought and closed her eyes, swallowing hard. On the one hand, it would help to know for certain whether or not her suspicions were accurate. On the other hand, if he was involved in the way she feared he was, what did that mean for her, that she'd dated a man who was capable of that?

It doesn't reflect on you, dear, said the sensible voice, which Julia only now realized sounded a lot like her therapist. *You couldn't have known.*

"Yes," Julia said, and in her own ears her voice sounded strangled.

"Very well. We have facilities to allow you to view it at your convenience."

"Thank you, Arthur." Now she *really* needed that shower.

The shower in question, located in a room down one of the longer corridors she'd seen so far, was an elaborate device that seemed to have an octopus as part of its inspiration, with an art-deco arrangement of pipes and showerheads arranged around a central space easily big enough to accommodate three or four adults. Out of habit, she glanced around for any surveillance cameras; finding none, she closed the door, undressed, and, after a bit of puzzling over the controls, took a hot shower. She scrubbed away the grime of the previous afternoon's ordeal, feeling the nearly-scalding spray prickling against her skin and relaxing her aching muscles. Luxury was luxury, after all, even if it came from a plumbing octopus. Once again, the shampoo smelled of lavender—she was starting to suspect that it was his favorite scent—and she allowed herself to savor the relaxing aroma as she washed her hair.

When she emerged from the shower she saw that, as expected, her dirty clothing had been taken away, but instead of the plain clothing he'd been giving her, the replacement came in the form of a sleek red dress on a hanger carried, of course, by Stickman. She stepped forward, securing the fluffy bath towel around herself, and carefully reached out to touch the red dress. It was one of the most beautiful garments she'd seen in some time—medicine didn't offer many opportunities to dress up—and it felt like satin. She bit back the instinct to ask if it was really for her—of *course* it was for her. Alistair wanted her to look nice, didn't he?

"It's… beautiful," she said instead, lightly pinching a fold of the glossy red fabric and rubbing it between her fingers.

"Dr. Mechanus would be honored if you wore this dress to dinner," Stickman buzzed in his electric-shaver voice. "He is also providing a number of utility drones to aid you in your grooming."

"And shoes?" she asked, feeling overwhelmed.

Stickman raised a limb to show her a pair of soft, flat-soled shoes, apparently made of a similarly satiny material matching the red dress.

"Flats," she sighed. "Thank God."

Stickman tilted his head, as though confused by her thanking someone other than Alistair for the items, but said nothing.

"Never mind," she said. "Tell him yes. I will absolutely wear this to dinner. The shoes, too. Now bring on the grooming robots. I want to see what they can do with my face."

A small swarm of kitten-sized robots flew in, so promptly that they might very well have been waiting just outside the door.

***

Mechanus anxiously paced in the greenhouse he'd set aside for dinner. He wasn't used to waiting, but he'd wanted everything to be just right, which of course necessitated her preparation time. He wouldn't begrudge her this. In his pocket he had a final gift for her, one that he hoped she would wear for a number of overlapping reasons.

<Sir?> Arthur said. <She's here.>

<Thank you.> Mechanus's cardiac pump was whirring madly in his chest, but he steeled himself and turned to face her.

His jaw dropped open and just hung there when he saw her, thinking to himself that his life would never be the same from this point forward, now that she was part of it.

She was a goddess in the slinky red dress he'd offered her, with the plunging neckline and the sexy slit up one thigh. Her golden hair was swept up in an elegant updo that probably necessitated an unholy number of pins, leaving her neck bared in a way that made him break into a cold sweat. Arthur—that genius!—had managed to minimize the swelling in her face with the anti-inflammatory agents that Mechanus had originally developed to streamline the chimera-building process, leaving behind only the slightest yellow discoloration, and the cut on her lip had been cunningly concealed.

<Close your mouth, sir. You're attracting flies,> Arthur scolded him gently, his artificial voice tinged with amusement.

Mechanus shut his mouth with a snap, and then swallowed hard.

"Julia," he managed to choke out. "You look… wonderful." As adjectives went, it was woefully inadequate, but he didn't think she'd respond well to *pulchritudinous*.

"Thank you," she said with a smile. Her glaze flickered briefly over him, and she raised an approving eyebrow. "You look very dapper yourself."

He glanced down at the suit he was wearing. While ordinarily he wore only the single layer of lab coat, this evening he wore a crisp white shirt with a wingtip collar, black silk cravat, burgundy waistcoat with a watch chain, formal tailcoat, pinstriped pants, and top hat. "Yes, well, I wanted to wear something nice for dinner," he said, grinning giddily.

She stepped forward and adjusted his lapels, and then brushed an invisible speck of lint from his shoulder. "Fortunately," she said, "I've found it's just about impossible for a man not to look good in Victorian costume."

He decided not to tell her that this was the only suit he currently owned, manufactured that day for this exact event.

"I have one more item to give you," he said, "Something I made special while you were asleep." He fished in his jacket pocket and pulled out a small box about the size of his palm. He offered it to her, and watched closely as she took it and opened it.

Inside, on a bed of velvet, was a silver pendant crafted of wire, in the shape of several interlocking hexagons.

"What's this?" she asked, pulling the pendant out on its delicate silver chain.

"It's a caffeine molecule," he said, and held his breath as recognition blossomed.

"This is…" she started, and then bit her lip. "Is this like the one you gave to Lauren?"

He nodded slowly. "It's… a bit complicated. It was an in-joke between us, but… I would like very much for you to wear this tonight."

"But… why?" She didn't sound angry or upset, he was gratified to note, just confused.

"You know that I loved Lauren more than life itself, right? That I would have done anything for her?"

She nodded slowly.

"You mean… every bit as much to me. You helped me uncover my past, my humanity. This pendant… that's what this represents." He closed his eye. "I'm not skilled with poetry, or flowery language, but… you make me feel whole again. Like I was *before*. Being around you reminds me of burning magnesium, like putting potassium metal in water, like—"

She smiled gently and put two fingers over his mouth, silencing him.

"As far as I can tell, you're comparing your feelings to explosive chemical reactions, am I right?" she asked.

He nodded.

"I feel the same way. And… under the circumstances, I think it's sweet that you want me to wear this. It's beautiful." She stretched up to kiss him on the cheek, and he reflexively bent a bit to meet her. "Help me put it on, will you?"

She held out the pendant to him. He took it by its delicate chain, unclasping it as she turned her back to him. He settled the pendant above her cleavage and clasped the necklace in place. She touched the silver molecular diagram and smiled over her shoulder at him.

"Shall we head to dinner, then?" she asked.

He took her hand, lightly kissed her knuckles, and led her deeper into the greenhouse, along a path lined with red roses. This was another arrangement that Arthur had suggested, but Mechanus didn't need to ask what the red roses meant.

"Wow," she breathed. "This is all so beautiful! You really didn't have to—"

"But I did," he replied, finally back in his element. "I don't like to take half-measures with anything I do. It wouldn't be fair to either of us."

In the center of an arrangement of planter boxes, they came to a large dining table designed to look like carved mahogany. At its center sat a carefully chosen and arranged floral centerpiece, and off to the side were a bottle of Chardonnay, two glasses, and two place settings.

He led her to one of the chairs and pushed her in, giving a mental command to his servitor drones to bring in the first course. Her face lit up anew with each course that was brought in: smoked oysters, hot-and-sour seafood soup, roasted striped bass, a Caesar salad, and finally tiramisu. She savored each dish with low noises of appreciation that, he thought, sounded a *lot* like the sounds she'd made during their last kiss, which lent the whole meal a fresh degree of sensuality that he'd never exactly associated with food. Food was for nourishment, after all—but then, he'd made this meal to impress her, and clearly he'd succeeded. The meal was savory and delicious and a treat for all the senses, a far cry from the utilitarian meals he'd consumed before Julia entered his life.

"You've really outdone yourself, Alistair," she said as she spooned up the last remnants of her tiramisu.

He smiled, basking in the praise. "I have more planned for this evening, remember?"

She let out a satiated groan, sitting back. "No more food, please," she begged, laughing. "I'm so stuffed I can't possibly eat another bite."

"Not quite—we've finished with dinner, actually."

She sat forward again. "What, then?"

"Well, I promised you drinks and dancing as well, you may recall."

She looked him over speculatively, her expression thoughtful. "That was something else I meant to ask you—when did you learn to dance?"

He coughed modestly. "About five minutes before you arrived." He smiled and tapped his cranial implants with a fingertip. "I have detailed files."

She raised her eyebrows at this. "In that case," she said, "I'd like to see how well the installation went."

He took her hand and drew her to her feet. At his mental command, a squadron of servitor drones converged on the table, bussing away the dirty dishes but leaving behind the Chardonnay and glasses. As he led her away from the table, more utility robots came forward and smoothly shifted away the planter boxes of roses, making room for a spacious dance floor. Overhead, flying hummingbird drones trained a trio of searchlights on them, but then dialed back the intensity to a soft glow. She looked around, grinning like a schoolgirl at the arrangement.

"Oh my God," she breathed, putting her free hand over her eyes. "This is… I don't know. This is beyond anything I'd ever dreamed of. I mean, I knew you had dinner and dancing in mind, but I've never..." She laughed, a quiet, breathy sound that would have prickled the hair on the back of his neck delightfully if he had any. "You've really pulled out all the stops on this."

"Always," he said, pulling her into a dancer's embrace: his hand intentionally placed on the small of her back, her hand resting on his shoulder, free hands clasped easily. With another thought, he started the music playing, and as the drones tracked them with their spotlights, the two of them danced that romantic dance that lovers do.

He saw a delicate pink blush color her cheeks, and his cardiac pump skipped a cycle. He could hardly believe after everything that they'd been through, that he'd succeeded at this venture—that he'd finally managed to charm her and, by all accounts that she'd fallen in love with him.

Not that he was looking a gift horse in the mouth, he considered as he twirled her through a dance step. Gracious, no. He would no more look for reasons why he should not have such a beautiful, gentle woman as Julia than he would try to talk himself out of world conquest. He had succeeded. He was triumphant. He had his memories back, he had Julia, and soon enough he would have the world… but still something seemed to be missing. He had not yet completely closed the door on his previous life. Lauren's phantom remained, and the part of him that she had occupied felt utterly hollow. He wasn't sure how he could fill this space.

"Miss Julia?" Arthur said from the vicinity of the ceiling.

She glanced up, but Mechanus spoke first.

"What is it, Arthur?" he demanded. "As you can see, I am a bit busy."

"I have information that Miss Julia requested earlier today," Arthur said, unruffled by the irritation in Mechanus's voice.

Mechanus blinked and looked down at Julia. She was closer to him than when the dance had started—almost brushing against him, in fact—but she did not appear to be surprised by this interruption. She met his gaze.

"Yes, Arthur?" she asked.

"Mount Hope Cemetery, Norfolk, Massachusetts. Section 5—"

"What's this about?" Mechanus demanded, though he had a strange, foreboding feeling that he already knew.

"Miss Julia requested the location of Lauren MacKenzie's burial site."

For a few moments, Mechanus couldn't quite comprehend what Arthur had just said. Then the full significance crashed into him like a derailing train.

"I…" he choked out, but then just stared at Julia. She continued to meet his gaze, her expression gentle and sympathetic.

"You said you'd never had the chance to say goodbye," she said quietly. "I figured this might help. I can go with you if you want."

Mechanus's right hand started to tremble against the small of her back. The offer was simple enough, but once again her charity had caught him by surprise, and the implications of such a journey were profound. He'd snapped immediately upon learning of Lauren's death, and events had progressed too quickly from there to have allowed the possibility of finding out where her grave was, let alone visiting it. It might be good for him—and if not, then Julia would be there.

"Arthur," he said, keeping his voice as level as he could manage.

"Yes, sir?"

"Where did you say her grave was again?"

Julia smiled and gave his shoulder a reassuring squeeze.

Epilogue

A few days later, Mount Hope Cemetery found itself host to a strange spectacle. A small flying craft like a helicopter slowly swooped low over the treetops, its twin rotors buzzing like the world's largest hornet, while the body of the craft bore glowing green tracery that pulsed like the beat of a mechanical heart. It landed delicately within the cemetery itself, agitating the tidily-mown grass into overlapping crop circles that centered around one particular grave marker.

Once the ornithopter came to rest, two gull-wing doors opened in the sides, and its passengers stepped out. Dr. Alistair Mechanus, clad in another black suit, a simple sack coat and grey waistcoat combination that was in high fashion a hundred or so years ago stepped down onto the grass, instinctively raising a gloved hand to shield his mismatched eyes from the brilliant sunlight, while the other clutched a bouquet of white lilies wrapped in green tissue paper. From the opposite side, Julia Parker likewise stepped down, clad in a navy blue dress.

Mechanus glanced around; some distance away, another funeral service was taking place. Its participants seemed to be paying no attention to the newcomers. Finally his eye fell on the granite headstone. It bore a carved angel on top that seemed to be watching over the grave itself, and on the front were the words 'LAUREN ELLEN MACKENZIE— Beloved Daughter' and, below this, '1974-2002'. Mechanus took a tentative step towards the gravestone, looking like a man in a dream from which he fully expects to wake.

Julia gently touched his elbow. He glanced over at her briefly, then back at the gravestone, as though mesmerized.

"Are you going to be okay?" she asked quietly.

He considered this, and then nodded. He stepped forward, slowly and reverently, and sank to one metal knee before the gravestone, resting his free hand against the rough granite and laying the bouquet of lilies before it. Julia stayed back, giving him the privacy he needed. Ten-year-old grief closed a vise around his chest, squeezing the breath from him for several seconds until it returned all at once in a hitching sob. This time was not as severe as when he'd first recovered his memories; it appears that repetition and time dulled the pain, just a little with each iteration.

Julia walked softly over next to him; he became aware of her presence when she squeezed his right shoulder. He glanced over just as she knelt next to him. She said nothing, but her warm presence comforted him beyond words. Julia was right. Coming here did help, if only to bring closure. Fortunately, he now had all the good memories to offset the loss of Lauren, and with them permanently archived on the network, he could revisit them as he wished.

<Sir?> Arthur said in his ear. <I don't mean to interrupt, but your army and all related resources are now at 100% readiness.>

<Thank you, Arthur.>

What did one give the woman who had given him back his past?

He looked up from his meditation and over at Julia.

He would give her the only gift that would possibly convey the amount of gratitude he felt towards her.

He would give her the world as her dreams would want it to be, whatever she desired. Would she want to stay in the real world or go back to his world on Shark Reef Isle? She gave him a sweet glance and pointed upward as if to say, *Let's go back to your world.*

Mechanus placed his arm lovingly around Julia's waist.

<Prepare to launch,> he instructed Arthur.

ABOUT THE AUTHOR

Elizabeth Einspanier is the author of the Weird Western novella *Sheep's Clothing*, as well as a number of short stories and poems published in magazines like *Dark Fire Fiction*, *Down in the Dirt*, and *Abandoned Towers.* She is a member of the St. Louis Writer's Guild. While she lives in St. Louis, MO, she frequently spends time in worlds of her own creation.

Heart of Steel is her first romance novel.

Connect with Elizabeth online!

Website: http://elizabetheinspanier.com
Facebook: https://www.facebook.com/elizabeth.
einspanier.author
Google+:https://plus.google.com/u/0/+Elizabeth
Einspanier/about
Twitter: @GeekGirlWriter

If you enjoyed *Heart of Steel*, please show your support by writing a review! Independent authors love hearing from their fans!

Made in the USA
Middletown, DE
12 January 2016